We Are All Legends

DARRELL SCHWEITZER

"Sir Julian, a knight in medieval Europe, falls into the clutches of a witch. Faced with overwhelming force, physical and magical, his knightly code tells him he ought to die fighting, but his instinct of self-preservation prevails. Afterwards he is tormented by guilt. In hopes of escaping damnation for his sins he embarks on a crusade, but strange and bizarre adventures befall him. Like Sinbad, he is wrecked on a fantastic island; he meets centaurs and lamias, sorcerers and lamas, and a passionate vampire; loses one hand to a demon; ventures to the Far East; encounters other worlds, other gods, other dimensions. The reader ends with the feeling that he has undergone a strange and haunting experience. The brightest of today's rising generation of fantasists."

L. Sprague de Camp

We Are All Legends

DARRELL SCHWEITZER

ACKNOWLEDGEMENTS

Chapters of this novel have appeared as the following:

"The Hag" in *Swords Against Darkness #3* © 1978 by Andrew Offutt

"The Lady of the Fountain" in *Void #5* © 1977 by Paul Collins

"The Veiled Pool of Mistorak" in *Void #3* © 1976 by Paul Collins

"The One Who Spoke with the Owls" in *Void #4* © 1976 by Paul Collins

"The Castle of Kites and Crows" in somewhat different form in *Swords Against Darkness #5* © 1979 by Andrew Offutt

"The Riddle of the Horn" in *Heroic Fantasy* © 1979 by Gerald W. Page and Hank Reinhardt

"Divers Hands" in *The Year's Best Horror Stories #7* © 1979 by Gerald W. Page

"The Unknown God Cried Out," "Island of Faces," and "Midnight, Moonlight and the Secret of the Sea" in a somewhat different form under the title "The Faces of Midnight" in *Distant Worlds* © 1981 by Paul Collins

"Into the Dark Land" in *Alien Worlds* © 1979 by Paul Collins

"A Fabulous, Formless Darkness" in *Other Worlds* © 1970 by Paul Collins

"L'envoi" in somewhat different form in *Nightflights (Myrddin #5)* © 1981 by Lawson W. Hill

WILDSIDE PRESS
PO BOX 45
GILLETTE, NJ 07933-0045
www.wildsidepress.com

For the keepers of the Faith:
Paul Collins
Andrew J. Offutt
Gerald W. Page
Mark Mansell
Dorothy Amelin
Jason Keehn

Contents

Introduction *by L. Sprague de Camp*

The Hag 7

The Lady of the Fountain 21

Island of Faces 29

The Veiled Pool of Mistorak 45

The One Who Spoke with the Owls 55

The Castle of Kites and Crows 69

The Riddle of the Horn 83

Divers Hands 99

The Unknown God Cried Out 123

Into the Dark Land 139

A Fabulous Formless Darkness 157

Midnight, Moonlight and the Secret of the Sea 171

L'envoi 187

Introduction

In this duodecade of weird tales, Sir Julian, a newly-made knight in medieval Europe, gets separated from his hunting party and falls into the clutches of a witch. The hag coerces him into taking her place in servitude to Satan. The Dark Angel appears as a beautiful, dead-black giant with the wings of a gigantic black swan. The Devil kindly dismisses Julian, telling him to wander the world and enjoy life; he will belong to Satan when his time comes.

Losing his castle and estate to covetous neighbors, Sir Julian, miserable with the thought of the everlasting torment in Hell awaiting him, embarks on a Crusade. Soon, like Sindbad, he is wrecked on a fantastic island.

Young Julian was brought up in the certainties of medieval Christendom. The old knight who taught him as a boy never wearied of insisting: "It's order, young Julian, that is the principle of all things. God in his heaven, man on Earth, and the Devil below." But in his wanderings, Julian finds that, as he had suspected, things are not so orderly in the universe after all; that in other parts of the world the writ of the Christian God does not run.

Strange and bizarre adventures befall Julian. He meets centaurs and lamias, sorcerers and lamas. Sometimes, when he is faced with overwhelming force, either physical or magical, his knightly code tells him he ought to die fighting; but his instinct of self-preservation prevails. Then, afterwards, he is tormented by guilt. He is not conscientious enough to avoid sin but too scrupulous not to suffer pangs of regret afterwards. He cannot, like a true adventurer, simply do what the expediency of the moment demands and never trouble his head with the morality of his deeds.

For instance, Julian passionately loves a beautiful vampire, who preys upon him. Julian's squire saves Julian's life by killing the vampire; but then Julian, in a fit of rage, kills the squire. In hope of escaping damnation for his sins, Julian sacrifices his left hand to a demon; but the demon's answer to his question, while candid, gives no comfort. Both God and the Devil, Julian comes to realize, are mad. Venturing to the Far East, he learns that there are other gods, other worlds, and other dimensions; but that there is no salvation or lasting security anywhere.

This collection of twelve short fantasies by Darrell Schweitzer, one of the brightest of the rising generation of fantasists, reminds the fantasy reader of Lord Dunsany, James Branch Cabell, Michael Moorcock, and perhaps George MacDonald, author of the Victorian adult fantasies *Phantastes* and *Lilith*. But Schweitzer is his own man not an obvious imitator of anyone. MacDonald, although in his dream-narratives he explored many worlds of fantasy, remained basically a devout nineteenth-century British Christian; he had in fact been a Congregational minister before retiring from his post to devote himself to writing. Schweitzer, on the other hand, belongs to the skeptical, uncertain, pessimistic, polydogmatic twentieth, wherein people believe six impossible things before breakfast and nothing at all in the afternoon. Schweitzer himself says that, although he has read many of the stories of the writers mentioned, the actual inspiration for the tales of Sir Julian consisted mainly of medieval romances and ballads and Ingmar Bergman's motion picture *The Seventh Seal*.

A flawed and tragic hero, Julian struggles through this cosmos of incertitude, brilliantly depicted in Schweitzer's smoothly unobtrusive style. These dreamy—often nightmarish—narratives are mood pieces, the mood of which the author achieves with deceptive ease. The reader ends with the feeling that he has undergone a strange and haunting experience. He might not wish to undergo it every day as a regular thing, but he is glad to have had to remember.

L. Sprague de Camp
Villanova, Pennsylvania
May 1980

3

"Order," the old knight who lived at my father's castle used to say to me. "It's order, young Julian, that is the principle of all things. God in his heaven, man on Earth, and the Devil below. That's the beginning of it. The days proceed from that first morning in the Garden, all the way to the Judgment, marching in rigid rows, bright and dark, smiling or scowling within but all alike on the outside. Days, like the Emperor of Byzantium's guards on parade. Order. That's the middle of it. Everything has its place in the sequence of our journey through this life. And above, the stars and planets move in their spheres, each orb spaced in order, equally apart from all the others, suspended by the golden chains the angels wrought—"

"But they don't look evenly spaced. They're all scattered," I said. I was a small child then. The two of us sat in a garden on a summer evening beneath a clear sky. The old knight's beard glistened silver as the moon rose.

"That," said he, "is due to the imperfection of the human eye, which cannot perceive true order, and hasn't been able to since our first parents fell from grace. But, as the learned Ptolemy says—"

"Wasn't he a pagan?"

"Do not interrupt! Are you already too wise for your own good? What shall it profit a man to learn all things, if he loses his soul? You ask too many questins. But, to answer briefly, so we can get on with the matter: yes, he was a pagan, but can not the Creator use even the most corrupted of his creations to his own incomprehensible ends? Can not the pure hand wear a tarnished gauntlet and still remain pure?"

"I suppose so."

That was the beginning of it. When I slept that night I had my first premonition of death, although I did not understand it for many years. I saw myself buried at a crossroads—like a heretic or felon—and my unhappy ghost hovering over the spot, telling woeful tales until the listeners fled away, or the dawn banished me back into my grave.

That was the beginning of it. When I was grown taller, my father sent me to another castle, there to serve as a page and a squire and learn the arts a gentleman of the sword must learn. And one winter my master sent me to a great city, to study God's ways at the cathedral school, "so you'll stop your infernal questioning," as he put it.

1

The Hag...

Long, long ago, when I was a young man and newly made a knight, my cousin the Duke Orlando was to be married, and on the day before the wedding a great hunt was held to procure fresh meat for the feast. I was there. I sat up with the others the night before that, drinking and boasting about the great beasts we would slay, and when the hour grew late I retired with them. On the morrow a trumpet blast awoke us and we breakfasted, and while the party was being made ready, the Duke took me out a few steps beyond the gate of his castle and pointed over the fields, which rolled green and crop-filled over hill after hill, to the place where they stopped and a deep forest began.

"Those woods," said my host, "are entirely uninhabited. Once you leave the open ground and enter into them you are as far gone from civilization as if you walk the bottom of the sea. The trees swallow you up."

"Why does no one live there? Can the land not be cleared?"

At this my uncle laughed. "Most generous, courteous, brave, and noble Sir Julian, if we stand here talking all day we shall not be back from the hunt before sundown!"

"If no one lives there, why do you fear the woods after dark?" I called after him, but he did not hear me. He was already shouting orders to the keepers of his hounds.

It was a wild ride that day. The dogs caught a scent early and let out a collective yelp of delighted blood-lust, then were released from their leashes and let run. We followed them with a thunder of hooves down dusty roads, over fences and hedges. We brushed through fields of ripened grain. We scattered the peasants before us and laughed to see them scramble. Then we came to the edge of all human domains that my uncle had shown me, and plunged beyond that edge into the unknown, into the forest of dubious repute, led by the howling pack. At once two careless riders, two overplumed dandies whose names I had never taken care to learn, were swept from their mounts by overhanging branches. We left them behind. The horns of the huntsmen echoed through the leafy abyss like the cries of Neptune and his giants beneath the green sea, both to let men know where their fellows were and to frighten the quarry ahead of us, whatever it was.

I glimpsed a shape once, during that glorious, reckless, and seemingly unending run. It was little more than a patch darker than the surrounding brush, and moving, before my eyes for an instant and then gone. All the rest of the day we galloped, horns blasting, the prey unseen, running, running, running before us. No one saw more than I had.

Horses fell behind in exhaustion. Mine was covered with foamy white lather. Gradually the hoofbeats and the sounds of the horns diminished and remained always at my rear, until I realized that I was in the lead. My steed that had carried me to my first battles and back was hardier than all the rest, and the killing would be mine. I looked over my shoulder and saw only one rider near me, the Duke.

"Ho!" he cried. "You and I shall have the quarry!"

But at that instant, as if to belie him, his horse stumbled—over a root I think—and sent him catapulting over the pommel of his saddle and onto the ground. I heard the shriek of the animal and the Duke's trailing curse, and I looked back again and saw them thus. I reined and turned about to see if he was injured, but he got to his feet and waved me on.

"Keep going you fool! Keep going! The prize is yours now if you don't let it get away!"

So I continued after the hounds, my horse laboring. I knew the animal could not go much farther before it dropped. The chase would soon be over, one way or the other. All I could hope was that the beast I would be facing alone would be tired also. It would have to be, if it were an earthly creature at all.

Then the cries of the dogs changed, becoming snarls of anger and howls of pain. They were fighting with something. The underbrush ahead of me rattled, as if Titans were wrestling in it.

I passed one of Duke Orlando's best bloodhounds, disemboweled on the ground, yet still alive and snapping. And another, and a third this way, and a fourth. The shape, the patch I had seen, showed in the greenery again and crashed away. Finally in a clearing, the thing I pursued turned to face me and fight, and I saw what had driven the canines to such frenzy. It was a huge wild boar, the biggest I had ever seen, as large as a pony and more massive, with blood-smeared tusks like curving swords, and red eyes all aflame.

I lowered by spear, shouted with all the strength left in me, and charged. The boar remained frozen almost to the last minute, glaring at me, until my lance tip was no more than a hand's breadth from it. Then it darted off to one side and disappeared again into the forest. I went on a ways before I could stop, turn, and follow, and in the process my lance caught among branches and snapped. The force was almost enough to unseat me. When I had recovered myself I saw that I was alone and out of the clearing, the trees towering over me again, their ancient trunks like rows of Olympian legs. Darkness was already gathering where the leaves were the thickest to mark the beginnings of the end of the day.

The shadows deepened. I bent low against the overhanging boughs and vines, galloping still in the direction the beast had

fled, maintaining a pretense of pursuit. I wondered how I would conquer my enemy with only my sword left to me. Yes, I thought of the boar as my foe—it had defeated all the others and I alone was left to give it battle and snatch the victory. I had not seen another hunter for hours. If I failed this day's effort would be wasted, and the Duke's wedding the following morning would be without new-slain meat.

But my efforts, too, came to naught. There were no more hounds to lead the way. Either all had been slain, or they too had given up the chase. Once or twice I heard the boar itself trampling ahead of me, receding, the sounds of the trampled underbrush growing fainter and fainter, until I could hear nothing and unavoidably came to realize that defeat was mine. When there could no longer be any doubt of this, I reined my already staggering steed. The poor creature could not have gone more than a few more steps anyway.

I dismounted and sat on the trunk of a fallen tree, only then feeling the full weight of my weariness. I could hardly bring myself to stand again to relieve myself. I had been in the saddle from dawn till dusk, riding hard. The excitement of the hunt had given me extra strength, but now it had deserted me. I sat down again, soaked in already stinking sweat. I took off my helmet and wiped the grime from my brow. My hair was plastered down. I felt just then that the unfortunate Orlando would not only have to do without a roast boar for his wedding, but he would have to find someone else to fill my seat. I was in no condition to go anywhere.

A brook rippled nearby. Stiffly I rose once more, and the blood rushed from my head and I felt faint, but when I had recovered my balance I led my horse by the bridle to the water's edge. We both drank deeply. I sat still in the cool of the evening and watched the night birds circle above me as the stars came out.

It was while I sat there by the edge of the stream, the twilight giving way to a night that yielded to another twilight when the swollen harvest moon rose, that I noticed something not part of the natural forest. It lay on the opposite shore and downstream a ways. It was too low and too wide, too square-shaped to have grown where it stood. I rose wearily and waded a distance for a better look. It was a building, a hunting hall long abandoned and fallen into ruin. No light came from its empty windows. There were no sounds from within.

I brought my horse over to the place and tethered it to a half-grown oak. I would spend the night here. I could never find my way back to my cousin's castle in the darkness, and I knew it. I didn't even know how far into the forest I had gone, and the path of the hunt had turned several times. I wasn't even sure of the direction.

The front door hung ajar, but would not move. For generations now vines had grown over it, making it theirs, holding it in place where hinges no doubt would have failed. Sideways I slipped into the hall, rustling the leaves of the vines, and I looked upon the place where long ago some lord, perhaps even a pagan chieftain swearing mighty oaths to his strangely named gods, had feasted with his huntsmen. Still there were overturned benches strewn about. The dirt floor beneath my feet was soft and damp. In the center of the room, in what had once been a firepit, straggling weeds grew beneath an opening in the roof. Off to the sides, hidden from direct light, pale toadstools flourished.

I went back outside and gathered up some dry twigs and leaves, then returned, set them down in a heap at the edge of the pit, and striking flint to steel lit a fire to keep cold and the wolves away for the rest of the night.

Then I lay down on the spongy ground and tried to sleep.

I did not rest long. Perhaps an hour passed, perhaps a few minutes, while mosquitoes whined in my ears and I tried to ignore them. Then I heard my horse outside stirring uneasily. I sat up, hand on sword hilt. Moonlight streamed through the opening in the roof, and through the half overgrown windows, illuminating patches and bands on the floor, including the spot where I was sitting. I kicked out the fire, retreated into darkness, slid my sword out of my scabbard, and waited.

My horse neighed, then stamped, then shrieked with terror. Suddenly all the forest was alive with the cries of night-owls and goblins, and then, as if the sounds had been to announce something that had just arrived, all was silent once more, save for the frantic horse that tugged at the tether rope, then broke loose and galloped off. All this took place in the space of a few seconds. By the time I could run to the window to see what the matter was, my mount was gone and I knew what had frightened it.

Thousands of serpents had surrounded the house like a coiling, living sea.

They oozed in over the windowsills, through the vine-held door like a liquid mass, yet with intelligence and a single purpose. I crossed myself helplessly in holy terror. Instinctively I drew back from them. It was all I could do to keep myself from screaming, from moving quickly and insanely, from doing anything that would draw their attention to me. I returned to my corner in the shadows and stood with my back to the wall, as far away from the windows as I could be. I was rigid as a stone man. If they came over to me, a single motion would betray me. I stared

12

wide-eyed as they amassed in the center of the room where I had been lying. They circled the ashes of my fire and passed under and through them heedless of any remaining heat, looking for something that wasn't there. I had not been noticed. It was impossible, but none had ventured within three cubits of my feet. Once satisfied, or disappointed in their search, these creatures left the hall, again at once, as if a single mind directed them, and they slipped out the way they had come. They drained away like water over the doorstep, and through unseen cracks and holes at the bases of the walls.

When all were gone I had only one thought—to quit this haunted place. I had no horse now, but I knew my feet would carry me far and fast.

But again the branches of the trees echoed with screeching, and again something was announced and something arrived. This time rats came, an army of them storming the unmanned defenses of the hall, their eyes glowing in the moonlight like the pinpricks of a billion tiny torches. They too poured over the windowsill. They scratched down the walls and rattled the vines as they flowed over the door. They came to the center of the room as their predecessors had, circled, probed my dead fire, and left, never noticing me where I stood.

And again before I could escape a third invasion was heralded. This time it was of wolves, strangely silent; a sea of their eyes, muzzles, and tails filling the entire room. They crowded against me but still, incredibly, showed no awareness of me. They pawed the ashes, sniffed, and departed. Next came hawks, bursting through the chimney hole and the windows until the air was filled with their voices and whirring wings. Then they were gone, leaving only a few drifting feathers to assure me of their reality, and it was then that I thought I understood. These things were preludes, coming as rain and hail come before a cyclone.

The cyclone came immediately thereafter, in this form: the front door of the hall exploded into splinters, the vines rent aside, and in burst a battering ram of flesh, the very same titanic beast I had pursued all the day, the boar with its teeth like swords. It too ran into the center of the room as if expectant, stopped, and prodded the ashes with its hooves, but unlike the others it did not go away. It turned directly, knowingly, to where I stood. Digging its feet into the ground and snorting as a bull does, it made ready to charge.

I had some fantastic idea of killing the thing for Duke Orlando's feast. Some spirit of madness whispered to me that this was possible, that the hunt would not be fruitless after all, but my rational mind knew that the animal before me was not mortal. It was a thing beyond nature, sent by God or the Devil for a purpose, and that purpose was more profound than filling the stomachs of a hundred lords and ladies.

I lowered my sword, knowing it useless. Then I addressed the beast, saying, "What are you truly and why are you sent?"

The boar backed away, grunted, and began to change. Its form collapsed like a punctured waterbag. I felt at that instant as if mighty forces were contending all around me, tides pushing against supernatural tides, crushing me between them. I was a puppet as I approached the melting mass. I watched as it grew darker, as its hide became shiny, and hairless, as it flowed and sank down into a pool of shapeless muck, and I jumped back in amazement when it expanded and rose again in a new form.

It was now a unicorn with a deadly, lance-long horn, with a pale body and ugly red eyes.

And again a falling, a shifting, a change yielding a small dragon, golden scaled and hissing blue flames. And again—a black, two-headed bird taller than a man, called by the pagans a roc; this melting into a scarlet cat the size of an elephant, with claws like long razors.

At last it settled and became an old woman with bent back, shoulders twisted out of shape, and a head that rested oddly on a short neck. The face was hideous, pockmarked with scars, covered with boils, and wrinkled like badly tanned hide.

She laughed with a voice that wasn't even remotely human. It was—what?—the creaking of rusty hinges, the chatterings of all the rats in the billion sewers of the universe, the snapping of dry bones.

"Well, well, a noble knight is to be my guest."

"Your—your guest?"

She twitched her mouth from side to side, picked her nose and sneezed, then pointed a shrunken finger at me and laughed again.

"Yes, to pay for my hospitality with favors. To wait on me and mine—"

With that a wave of revulsion and unthinking terror. "No!" I cried, and I raised my sword to strike.

For a third time she laughed.

"You cannot harm me. I who have lived so long will not be put to rest so easily. Sheathe your weapon, Sir Knight. Know that I I can snatch your soul out of you before the blow falls."

I put my blade away, pretending I was planning, waiting for a better opportunity.

"Listen to me," she said. "I brought you here for a reason. All you have gone through this day has been my doing. I beguiled the hunters and separated you from them. I brought you here to do the deed I have in mind. I shall ask a great favor—"

"A favor? How can you—?"

"Quiet! Listen! Many years ago, many centuries past, my fathers built this hall and lived in it. Here they boasted and made merry and planned their feuds, and some of them died. Others were born here and the gods smiled on them, for they were a proud, fierce, mighty race, pleasing to the ones above. But then the new god came and drove out the old, and the priests came. Most of the folk listened to the new word and abandoned this place, but my parents did not. They stayed and clung to the old ways and worship, until a curse was put on them by the priests of the new god, and they died. And the curse continued even to me. Look on my face and you are sick. You turn from me in disgust. This is my true face, and this the body into which I was born. Such are the gifts of the savior Christ. Such are the products of his mercy. This was the burden he sent me to bear, and to finish the fine picture he threw the paint pot in my face. No man would ever touch me; *no man*, no matter how desperate, would have me."

"Lady, this is a tale filled with woe, but what can I—?"

"*Listen and you shall learn!* Can it be any wonder that in the end I called on the Dark One and took him into my bed? He gave me powers and many forms, but he bound me to him."

"Why are you telling me this? Am I a priest that you have called me all this way for a confession?"

"Not a priest," she answered, "but a servant even while you are a guest. Many knights have I met here, and all have prepared a meal for me. You shall do the same."

"A meal? But there is no food here. I have nothing."

"Your horse. Go outside and bring it here, then slay it. It fled but I have recalled it. Do not try to mount and escape. The shapes you have seen can bring down any prey, and man most easily. I will be satisfied, by courtesy or by force."

Many courteous knights had she met in this hall. What had become of them? I doubted very much that they all walked away, minus their mounts. There was something more than that. Every minute the trap into which I had stepped closed tighter and tighter.

I did as I was commanded. Outside, my steed was waiting untethered, as the hag had foretold, and I led the weary, trusting animal into the hall. It was easy now that the door had been smashed. And when I was again before her, treacherously, I carried out the rest of my mission. I slew my mount with my sword. Killing a horse is a messy business even when done with a single stroke to the heart. The dying creature fell, thrashed about, whinnied, and spat blood and foam from its mouth. I stood back from the flying hooves and waited until it expired, then drew back even more in horror and revulsion when the old lady, the witch-thing whose "guest" I was, threw herself onto the corpse, put her mouth to the wound, and began to suck.

Her eyes were wide with delight. She choked once, spitting blood down her chin and neck, and then continued, clinging to the animal like an obscene leech, impossibly draining all the substance from it. As I watched, the ribs began to protrude and the skin stretched tight over legs, shoulders, neck, and skull. At a glance it would have seemed that famine took the horse's life, not the sword. It was an empty husk.

I wanted dearly to pass my sword through the heart of the crone, but there was no chance to surprise her. Even as she crawled over her feast she remained aware of my every motion. If I even shifted weight from one leg to the other she would glance up, her face communicating a wordless warning, as if she could anticipate my thoughts.

At last when she was done she stood up and smiled, slobbering flesh and gore. She was the same as she had been before, her form not changed at all. It was not as I had expected. I'd assumed she was drawing some special power from the life of my poor steed which would enable her to make a special transformation.

As it turned out I was halfway right.

"Now take your clothes off," she said, "and spread them on the ground here that we may lie on them."

I knew right then what I should have done, what my vows of chivalry demanded of me. I should have charged with my sword aloft, in the faint hope that the witch could be killed by the downstroke of my dead arm. I should have died then a martyr to my God and to all mankind and cast my soul into the arms of some angel who would bear it softly heavenward. I should have, but I didn't, for I knew deep within me that my death would be for nothing. The monster could not be slain, and whether I died or lived she would remain as she was. The only matter at stake was my life and then more than ever before I wanted to live. I told myself that the blue of a clear sky, the flowers of a sun-blest field, the laughter of children, the love of a beautiful maiden, all could wash away the stain of what I was about to do. I weighed these in one hand against the boar, the dragon, the wolves, and the darkness of the unknown forest in the other, and need I say which I found more desirable? All my oaths, all my vows of knighthood fled from me and were gone, impossible, unworkable, ridiculous.

Beneath her garments the hag was fouler still, blue like a week-old corpse with huge vivid veins like clotted rivers spread over her. Her flesh was soft, too soft, and sticky. The stench was unbearable. I gave myself up to her and all my senses deserted me.

After an eternity of terrible dreams I awoke, naked on the floor of the ruined hall, atop a heap of my own garments. It was still night. The moon was low but its light was still bright, the almost horizontal beams filtering through the forest beyond the western windows.

Beside me lay another, and when I saw her I thought I still dreamed. It was not the putrid hag at all, not the Devil's whore, but a lovely, perfectly formed child. Her flesh was pale and utterly flawless, her features beyond the power of the most skilled artists to portray. Her soft yellow hair flowed down over her tiny breasts like a river of silk.

She awoke and saw me, and seemed disoriented for a time. Then she spoke directly, clearly. Her voice was musical. She was almost singing. She hugged her own naked shoulders and smiled rapturously at the feeling.

"I think you understand many things about me now," she said.

"About you? I have never seen you before. How did you come to this terrible place?"

"I am the same who was here before. Behold, I am in the form I have wished for always. It is part of the curse upon me that I can tell no one of my plight unless I am in this shape. I have been in it many times before, but always in the presence of the Dark One who gave me the power to change. This is the rest of my tale: When I called him to me in the agony of my desperation he told me that he could make me fair, but only by his touch. So he touched me and took my body to his and I was fair, and all that night I gratefully praised the name of Satan. But then, on the morrow, when I went into the village and said to the men there, 'Am I not beautiful?' they mocked me. They spat on me and with a hail of stones drove me back into the wood. I was not beautiful at all. The spell had worn off. The next night when my winged lover came I cursed him and he laughed, 'If you can get another to take you as I have done, as you are without knowing what you shall be, then you shall have this beauty unfading forever, even when you come into the flames of my kingdom. But after you have accomplished this I will try once more to take you, and if I succeed you shall be then as you always were, and our tryst will continue each night until I tire of it. Thus the one who transforms you must meet me that same night. He must be your champion.'"

I jumped up, grabbing my clothes, dressing as I stood.

"Nay! Am I mad? I'll not do it!"

She wept and pleaded with me, and overwhelmed my reason. I knew that this could easily be just another guise she was in, that the story could be a fabrication, and underneath the lovely face lurked the hag. It seemed likely that she could change into this form as the occasion demanded, the same way she would become a dragon or a boar. She called me now as a siren calls—no, as a beetle does when it hides in the depths of a flower and springs out to devour the bees that come to suck the honey. But, as I said, she overwhelmed me and I could not turn away. Her beauty, her seemingly renewed innocence, which I could not bear to see spoiled, defeated me more surely than any foe.

"Are you a knight?" she sobbed. "Is this chivalrous game you play a lie?"

"Lady, I confess that it probably is. At times I have been certain. I want to live as much as anyone else. I'm not willing to lay down myself for another."

"But you have had something of a life already, and I haven't. I was cheated at birth. Let me live my first life now. Make all the noble things you swore mean something, as they never have before. *Help me...."*

In the end I consented.

"What must I do?"

"When he comes either fight him or do all he asks. Nothing more can I tell you. I must go now, before he arrives."

She pulled on the soiled rags the crone had worn—still I could think of them only as two, never one and the same—and they seemed no longer ugly, but comical, as the famed Helen would be wearing a potato sack. I wanted to laugh.

As she started toward the door I said, "Wait." I fell to my knees, outwardly in jest, but inwardly in all earnest. "Fair lady, I pray you give me your hand once before you depart."

And startled, she did, and I kissed it as one kisses the hand of a queen. Then she knelt down and kissed me on the mouth and embraced me, and the horror of all that had gone before was forgotten.

I waited the rest of the night through, alone, ready for another battle with no hope of victory, yet with a purpose in my defeat. It was a beautiful, tranquil thing, infrequently lanced through with worries. *How far has she gone now? Can she find the path out of the forest?* I would guard the hall for her and keep her adversary at bay as long as I could, granting her more seconds of precious time. I felt triumphant, as a father feels when word is brought to him that his child has been brought safely into the world. I was more the father of this girl than anyone else, I had created her, given her shape and flesh. Now I would be her champion, as brave as any in romance, so that she might live and be fulfilled.

So I waited, and just before dawn the enemy came. I heard first the flapping of heavy wings, then a thump, then clattering like a stallion running across the roof, and I drew my sword and waited for him to appear in the ruined doorway.

His feet were cloven hooves, but above the ankles he was a man, naked and splendidly muscled, with skin not dark brown like an African's but shiny black, the color of hard coal. From his shoulders stretched graceful feathered wings, the wings of a huge black swan.

The most beautiful of the fallen angels stood before me and smiled, understanding all that had happened.

"She has done well," he said, "and I am pleased. Her purpose is served and I release her. Now you, Sir Julian, are mine, but I shall not take you now. You will come to me in your own way and at your own time, but still you will come. For now I command you, live, wander, and see all the strange world in my name."

Then the sun came up and he was gone, and the world was revealed to me by the light, a world that was for me new, strange, and terribly different from the one I had known the day before.

Order. Everything in its place, as a part of the great design. My father died and his castle and lands proceeded, like the days, into my hands. There was a brief time of outward peace, troubled only by visions in the night. But then, while I journeyed far, enemies came together and stormed the castle, burning it and slaying or carrying off all within, partitioning the lands among them.

Mene...mene...tekel...peres.... I had been weighed and found wanting.

"And I alone survived to tell thee," said the one who brought the news.

No one rallied to my cause. I rallied to another, then, and sailed east. Later, I learned from quite a different source that the old knight who had instructed me had fallen in that fight, and when the crows came to peck out his eyes, they stood in a neat line, each taking their turn, in order.

2

The Lady
of the Fountain...

It was in an old land that the battle had taken place; a country of empty halls and deserted castles where ruined walls stood protecting nothing from nothing, and roadways faded into the earth and led nowhere. For three days in this place the swords of the two armies sang their terrible song on shields and armour, and when the fighting was done and all was still, a deep fog covered the sodden ground.

I rode away from the field of slaughter, at the edge of a wood where the land sloped upward into the mountains, and I heard still the whimperings and curses of the dying behind me. I shuddered with cold and revulsion, and wrapped my cloak more tightly around me. I pressed on.

I reminded myself that I was on a quest. Thus far I had journeyed over lands unknown to geographers, braved marauders and wolves, seen wonders and met hardships, and still I sought my perilous goal. I knew that mine was indeed a goodly and forthright mission, and that once it was ended I would become a hero and perhaps a saint, and all Christendom would sing my praises. At the moment, though, this was all very far off and it meant little, for I was exceedingly weary. Yet I would not lie down and rest among the dead, so I forced my horse on a little further.

At length the land began to rise about me, the path twisted between hills and grew steep, and I knew then that I could not stop, lest in my weakness I lie down and freeze, or fall prey to whatever wild beasts might be roaming about. It was in the fall of the year, and winter already lurked in the highlands.

The way grew harder and harder, and I felt my horse struggling beneath me. The creature's every breath was laboured; foam poured from its mouth, and I could see that the animal was as near to exhaustion as I was. So it seemed like a miracle, a boon from God in answer to my unspoken prayers, when in the midst of all those cliffs and steep ways I found a low and sheltered valley, where fair blossoms bloomed and tall trees stood all about. The sun was almost down, but as I entered the valley the chill of the mountain night seemed to leave me.

It was not long before I came to the fountain. It stood in the very centre of the valley, nestled among shrubs, its splashing waters breaking the silence of the velvet evening. Above me the clouds broke, and the hunter Orion peered down out of a darkened sky.

I dismounted and drank, and washed the grime from my face. My horse drank also. After I was refreshed I sat and strove to forget all the things I had done that day, how many I had slain, how many I had crippled. My sword was a wreck in my scabbard and it troubled me not. I cared little that Count Mordantas of Grey Mountain lay slain in the mud with all his thanes, or that his hireling host was scattered. I too had fled the battle when all was clearly lost, for I had no wish to perish. I chose life over chivalry even though the Count had been good to me and given me bread and shelter during the Holy Days. Somehow my breach of honour seemed like the only sensible thing and it meant nothing that the army of the red banners now held all the land from Thandaroum to the sea, or that the army of the blue banners would charge no more. And it did not strike me as wrong that I failed to mourn for my squire Jon, my faithful companion in all my wanderings who was now lost to me, and was now doubtless the object of ravens' feasting. These things passed through my mind like a masque, something distant and strange, and I had no strength left for sorrow.

After a time I came to notice the engravings on the marble base of the fountain and ran my fingers over them. Old and worn they were, only half legible, in a script like some rare and ancient Latin carved by the noble Romans of centuries past, or perhaps something even more ancient, something unspeakably timeless and without age.

I could not think more on it. I rose, stumbled a few paces until I found a comfortable spot, dropped to the ground and slept.

That night I dreamed I saw all the kings of the past before me, all the empires rising and falling before my gaze, crumbling as the years fell aside. Rome I saw, Carthage, Nineveh and Thebes. I saw the handwriting on the wall of Babylon, the last days of Ur of the Chaldees, and then I was carried back more quickly through the ages to the years when strange gods trod upon the earth and there were lands where there are now seas, and seas where now stand mountains. I saw towns other than those of history, and in my dream I knew their names, strange to my ear: Belhimra, Gldathrion, Sithuil, and Kosh-Ni-Hye. All these did I glimpse before they faded. Great men and small walked the world, and in their ships they rowed to the very edge where all oceans plunge downward into the abyss. To the farthest North they went, to the lands of endless snow and ice where the Elf Kingdoms still stand, and to the West where jungles creep into ancient holdings where in legend King Aznaroth quested forever after the golden sunset city.

Still onward I was swept on the river of dreams, until at last I came to a timeless span before the coming of years; when gods unknown to Christ had freshly hewed the world out of primal Chaos, and Garil the Builder raised up in the morning of the Earth the blest Throramna, the Father of Cities. It was here that I came to rest, and I found myself before the golden gate of that city. I climbed a low hillock and read the inscription above me. It was written in an ancient tongue, but the voice of my dreams whispered to me its meaning: *HERE STANDS THRORAMNA, MEMORIAL TO THE FORTY-NINE GODS THAT WERE.*

I pondered on this a minute before entering. I found the gate unlocked and unguarded, and I was drawn by the sound of laughter from within.

Five maidens met me in the courtyard, which I was told was called The Place of Coming Sun, and they danced about me and caressed me, saying: "Put away your weapons, you who are tired and weary of battle. Lay down your sword and your shield and your helm, for the gods are good and there is no war in this land. Come, for we have wine and soft music, and there is feasting."

In a daze I was, and half bewitched, and I left my armaments in a heap on the cobblestones, and went with the five. We passed down streets wide and narrow, lined with houses of coloured marble, each exquisitely and uniquely carved. At last we came to a great hall made of wood and bright stones, and inside there were men and women gathered around a vast table. Much laughing and joking and singing filled the room as wine flowed freely and a great feast was laid out before them. He who sat at the head of the host rose and bade me come and sit by his right hand, that I might join in the merrymaking. This I did and we drank a toast to his gods, whose names I did not know. Now always had I been taught that there is but one God, namely the Christ, but the world I knew was far from me then, and in the joy of the moment my sin passed by me unnoticed. I accepted the good drink offered me and toasted with the rest, and after the toasting was finished the meal began. Fine meats and rare fruits were served, while birds sang the songs of the Beginning, poets recited lines from the Epic of The Lost Gods, and maidens danced before the assembled company. Soon all was warm and hazy, and a drowsiness overtook me.

I vaguely remembered being carried away by many hands and laid on a soft bed, and all the while I heard somewhere not far from me a light and beautiful voice which said, "Be gentle with the stranger, for his world knows not the peace of ours, and he has suffered much."

It was a bright and peaceful morn when I awoke after what seemed many days, and I sat up in bed and stretched myself, glad to find my strength renewed and my muscles no longer sore. Soon I saw that my wounds were healed, and I felt restless and eager, like a youth who has been kept inside all winter. I rose, and without thinking sought my armour. Then I heard the voice again.

"There is no need for your things of metal. What would you

do with them here?"

"Aye, there is truth in that," I said, and in turning I beheld for the first time Llania the Fair, Princess of this city, whose name means Flower of The Morning Sun. At the sight of her my eyes were bedazzled, my heart sounded to the very core. I knew then the sweet wound of love, and I was hopelessly ensnared in a silver web. More wondrous of form and face was she than any other maiden; like a goddess she was with her long golden hair, yet at the same time earthly and warm. I knew at once that whatever gods ruled this place were good, and that it had been fated for the two of us to meet like this and to remain together always.

We wandered through the city that day, and she spoke of things great and little, and whenever I worried that these things might not be true, she rendered them so with a kiss. Soon I forgot all about my Christian God and my quest and my world. Indeed, I forgot even the name by which I had been known during my former existence. She gave me a new one, Arandil Re' Neth, meaning in her own tongue, He Who Is Reborn. No longer was I the knight Julian, born of a mad duke and baptised by a bishop. Now I was Arandil Re' Neth, the lover of Llania, and nothing else mattered. I had started my life anew.

Summer came and went, and autumn was mild. Not once did we toil or know sorrow in all those months. Often we rode the hunt with the lords and ladies of Throramna and stormed through bushes after the hart. Aye, that was goodly sport. And again there were times when the two of us would go off into the forest alone without fear, and speak with the friendly sprites that dwelt there. We heard them tell things clever and marvellous, and we both laughed merrily when a water nymph told the story of Why The Centaur Comes Not Into The Daylight.

Always I was with my Flower of The Morning Sun, and like the orb of her name, her radiance shone upon me always, soothing me, driving away my little fears. I knew a peace not granted to ordinary men. Time did not seem to pass, and I did not age. I dwelt in a golden pocket of the universe, where pain and strife were always excluded. I loved my Llania deeply, so much that my heart would flutter like that of an unbearded boy when I was with her, but again her kisses would remove all anxieties. Kings, wars, monsters, and other matters seemed trivial and meaningless, like a bad dream nearly forgotten.

One night we climbed a tall mountain beyond the city, so that we might gaze at the stars and speak to the spirits of the upper airs. And as we sat there breathing the deep freshness of the heights, I drew Llania close to me and whispered into her ear: "On the morrow we shall be wed, and dwell always within the city. We shall raise ten tall sons and many daughters. Never shall we leave this place."

And she replied. "It is good!"

We kissed then, but as we did there was a rushing of winds, and a darkness fell over the stars. The moon in its brightness was blotted out, and I felt the ground crumble away beneath me. Suddenly, I was falling through space, and far away from me I could hear the fading voice of my Llania, screaming and calling out my name.

"I shall never leave you!" I cried.

She screamed all the louder, and there was agony in her voice.

Then all was still.

I awoke on a wet lawn, cold and still, dressed in my damp and battered armour. For a moment I knew not where I was, but then I saw Jon my loyal squire standing over me, he whom I had thought dead.

"Oh Jon! I have had a wondrous dream! I wish I had never awakened!"

"It was not a dream, Lord," he said, "but a terrible reality."

"Terrible? Nay! It was beautiful! I loved a damsel. Her name Llania."

"Not Llania, Sir, but Lamia, the Vampire. I thank God that I could save you from her in time. Hear now my tale: When I was separated from you in the battle I lost all heart, thinking you slain. I hid in a glen until the fighting was over and the victors had departed. I searched among the corpses for you and had a reborn hope when I did not find you. After that I followed this road, knowing that you had to come this way, for all other roads are held by the enemy. This night I came into the valley and found you here in the arms of the vampire, which through the grace of Our Lord Jesus I destroyed."

I was too dazed to say anything to this. I tried to stand, but was suddenly overwhelmed by nausea. My legs collapsed beneath me, and Jon caught me before I fell. My head throbbed as if it were a gong and a giant was beating on it, and the landscape, which seemed far more barren than it had been before, danced about me. When it grew steady Jon took me by the arm and led me, speaking as we went.

"She was lying on the ground beside you, her lips red with your life's blood. Already she had stolen much, and you had begun to grey, as you have now. With my cross I drove her back to her tomb behind yonder fountain, and with my sword I cut her head off."

"This is madness," I was able to mutter.

We passed by the fountain which was filled with rainwater and scum, not flowing, and came to the wreck of a house, or perhaps a palace. Great chunks of broken stone lay about, and fallen columns sank into the mossy ground. Indeed there was a tomb there, half covered with weeds and stained green with age, so old that its very marble was beginning to crumble. There was an inscription at the base, long since worn to illegibility.

The lid of the tomb had been pushed aside, and in the blood splattered tomb lay the body of a maiden, her head cut off and lying with her. I knew her face in an instant. It was my Llania.

"Murderer!" I screamed. I pulled away from Jon, then turned to face him, my strength renewed by grief and rage. "She loved me! She loved me as no other woman has! For once I was not a pauper knight, but one who was to wed the fairest lady in all creation. Now you have murdered her!"

I drew my sword. It was battered but it could still slay.

Jon drew back from me in horror. "No, my Lord! She is a fiend out of Hell! Look at the fangs in her mouth! Behold the tomb she resides in!"

My blade rose and fell, and there was silence in the valley. All around me even as I watched the trees faded like smoke and were gone. The blossoms were no more; the land was bare of grass as the last illusions passed from it. I turned once more to the sepulchre and beheld not my beloved, but only dust.

I looked down at my hands, and at my beard, and saw the hands and beard of one older than myself. Truly years had passed—or been stolen—and after a single night I was young no longer. Only the body of Jon remained as it was. His red blood poured forth onto the ground, and I knew by it that I was thrice damned. I had loved a vampire out of the darkest Pit, and a great sin this was. I had toasted her pagan gods, which is something the Lord forbade in his first commandment to Moses—this too was a great offence. And I had slain my pious servant, who had done no wrong. For this there could be no forgiveness.

I mounted my horse and rode away from the tomb and the fountain as the new day dawned. I descended the far side of the mountain range and continued on my journey, heading away from all the lands I knew. By noon the last wisps of fog were gone and the day was bright and clear.

Occasionally, I would come across a fallen warrior with flies on his face, and bucklers and spears discarded in hasty flight. The battle had reached even this far. I spurred my horse to a rapid trot, and all this time I thought of nothing but the beautiful Llania, of my sins, and the paradise that could never be. I paid no attention to where I was going, and it was only for the intelligence of my mount that I did not stray from the path and become lost.

That afternoon I passed through a squalid village, and filthy little peasant brats ran after me and tried to seize my horse's tail, but ceased when the beast kicked one of them. I glared at the bent and ugly hags that laboured over churns, ran their petty errands, or gossipped on street corners. Here and there a man with a low brow and a face like a monkey crossed my path, and with a wave of my sword and an angry shout I would send him scurrying. A maid in the window sang a happy song and I spat on the doorstep of that house, and she was silent. I departed that place and was glad to be again on the road, alone with my thoughts and my sorrow.

And so I continued on my quest of a goal whose worth escaped me.

3

Island of Faces...

I

I sought the Lady Catherine upon the sea. I had loved her long ago. She had been my first beloved, but had married another, and I saw her no more. I had thought her forgotten, cast out from memory, but when I returned from the East and heard that she had vanished, my passion rose anew and my grief knew no bounds. She had sailed to a far land where her sister was to be wed to a great king, and the feast was held, but no ship ever returned. So, when messengers brought no word save that she had departed homewards long since, and searching fleets availed nothing, I went after her myself, and this tale is the result of it.

I pulled a mandrake to find my course. I was already damned then; I had conversed with the Adversary; and my prayers went into the night like invisible moths to die in the cold and the dark. So finally, in the desperate fever of love renewed, I stole by moonlight to a deep forest grove and there seized the stalk of the May-apple and plucked the forbidden root out of the ground. It was like a gnarly little man beneath the leaves, and the thing screamed as I killed it and the scream echoed through the wood. I went mad with the sound, and in that madness between the crashing of black oblivion and the trembling of hot delirium I heard a voice telling me in a whisper to make my way where no man had ever gone before of his own will, to places indicated on maps as lands unknown and on sea charts with scattered monsters. Then the spirit of the mandrake passed wailing into the night and echoed beyond the distant hills, and I fainted, sleeping a long sleep and dreaming dreams filled with terror.

When at last I awoke, cold, stiff, covered with three days' dampness, I returned to my castle where, with monies I still had in those days, I sent my servants scurrying to hire me a ship and crew.

We set sail on a fog-filled morn, attending mass first to maintain appearances. The sermon warned against vain striving. From the start it was a strange, ill-omened voyage. On the first night the clouds broke overhead and we beheld the haggard old moon, with the new moon drowned in her glowing hair. And from beneath the sea, echoing weirdly through the hull as we lay in our bunks, came the long and mournful songs of the sea-elves, wailing, so the sailors told me, of ships wrecked and skulls turned to coral. For ten days and nights we went on thus, and on the morning of the eleventh day, when the sky was black as any midnight, the rough sea gave way to a gale which blew us far, until the captain had no more idea of where we were than would one who never sailed before.

Night came and the storm did not abate. The helmsman struggled with all his strength to keep the vessel turned into the wind, and a wave swept him away. Another man took the tiller. Then suddenly it was calm, the sea as placid as if oil had been poured over it, and the sailors all looked about with amazement and fear, knowing this to be no natural abating of the tempest. A heavy fog descended and all peered helplessly through it, unable to see an arm's length beyond the bowsprit.

Finally something was seen and a cry went up, and the cry changed into a frenzied prayer when it was clear that a shape like a man walked on the water toward us. I saw the thing too and leaned over the railing to have a better look. I called the captain to my side asking him if I was mad. Was this a dream, or a miracle? And he said it was neither, and I saw as the others did an old, bent man dressed in black tatters hobbling slowly over the shimmering surface of the ocean. The fog seemed to part before him.

The stranger came up to the side of the ship, not six cubits away from me, and spoke:

"Sir Knight, I have travelled a long way. I beg you, give me shelter aboard your vessel."

"Don't do it!" whispered the captain. "If he touches this deck all our souls are lost for sure!"

"I shall not," I said to the spirit. "Leave us, and find your rest elsewhere."

At this the black clad one only laughed and turned away, vanishing almost at once into the mist. At the very second he did the wind rose once more, and the storm was renewed in its violence. The ship pitched and rolled wildly beneath me and I was nearly tossed head first over the side.

The captain shouted orders to the mariners, who were already rushing to furl the sails, to make this and that fast, to lighten ship, and as he yelled he stepped on a black cat which snarled, swiped at his leg with a claw, and darted away.

"The Devil!"

"That's not a ship's cat!" someone cried.

"Indeed! The Devil! Look!" As I pointed the sea was no more of water, but of cats, thousands and thousands of them rising and falling in waves of glittering eyes and dark fur. They swarmed over the gunwhales irresistibly; they covered the masts and rigging like locusts; more and more of them came until by the very weight of those countless bodies the deck tilted more and more, and the yardarms stopped to touch the sea.

Next came a torrent of crashes, screams, curses, prayers, the sound of splintering wood, a shower of debris, and a headlong plunge into the frigid brine with something heavy and unseen above me, pushing me down, down. I struggled furiously to free myself from entangling wreckage and to reach the surface. When I did I saw the looming black shape of the capsized roundship above me. The sea was normal again, white-foamed, roaring, deadly. I heard the shouts of the others around me. I saw a swimmer far off, and another, and in an instant waves hid them. I tried to reach the still floating hull but was borne away from it. After a time it disappeared, and there were no more voices around me. I was alone with the sea, riding up and down the waves from crest to trough to crest, swallowing half of God's ocean and spitting it out again. All I knew was that I was lost, that my strength was failing, that I could swim no longer.

I could not move my arms and legs. My head seemed like a leaden weight I could no longer hold above water. I felt myself sinking slowly, gently to rest, into numbness, and as the life fled from me I had a vision of whole armies of fish beneath me, all gathered together to bear me up with their bodies, and there was a white marble ship, so bright against the clouds and rain that it burned like brilliant fire, and I neared it, and afterwards there was nothing at all.

II

When next I opened my eyes, I gazed up at a still grey sky. It was twilight, presaging either morning or eve. I knew not which. I found that I lay on sand by the high tide mark on a wide, featureless beach. I had no idea what land I had come to. The waves which had deposited me lapped a short distance beyond my feet. My clothing was soaked and the air seemed bitterly cold. I trembled with the damp; my teeth chattered uncontrollably. I rose and walked inland, hoping to find some wood with which to build a fire. To me only warmth mattered. I had sailed with an enchanted sword by my side, with the sign of the Endless Knot on my shield, which could not be unravelled till my quest was done. I had had a brave squire to aid me. Now all these were lost, sword, shield, squire, plus my ship and crew, but I hardly thought of them. I wanted only relief from the cold and to be dry.

I had not taken more than a dozen steps when I came to a great marvel. A face peered up at me out of the sand, buried save for the eyes, nose, mouth, forehead and cheeks, and it spoke to me.

"So, so, so, one has come yet living. Surely a great portent of something."

I stood astonished for an instant, then dropped to my knees and began to dig away at the sand, thinking to rescue some poor fellow who had been so cruelly placed there. But as soon as my hand touched the face it vanished, and there was only a heap of sand. I started—this was some illusion of the Fiend.

Even then the voice called out once more, "I thank you, friend, but no hand may free me thus."

I whirled about and saw the face again as it formed like something blown into shape by an impossible wind. I studied the features more closely. It was an old, old man, who bore the lines of long years of toil and pain, whose eyes and expression lacked any lustre of hope.

"You wonder much," he said, "and I shall enlighten you as best I can. My name is Andreas. Men called me a philosopher once, but as the years burdened me further I cared less and less for the pressing questions of astronomy and geomancy and metaphysics and the like. They had been pressing since long before I was born, and I knew they would continue to be so as long as there were two students left to argue over the difference between the real and the ideal. I wanted only to rest, and I found much peace sitting at the end of a wharf with a piece of string in my hand, fishing like a simple man. But one day as I sat there the sea swelled up—it was not during a storm—and reached out as if it were a hand guided by an eye, and snatched me away. There followed only a drifting greyness until I found myself as you see me, here in this place."

"I too came here by strange means. But tell me, if you can, what is the name of this land?"

"The Island of Faces. That is the only name I have known it by. When you travel a little more over it you'll know how it got its name."

I wanted to ask many things, but his eyes closed and he seemed to go to sleep. His features dimmed, became more like sand again. I could just barely make him out.

"Farewell Andreas," said I. "Perchance this is the purgatory God has willed for you, and someday you will find rest by the waters of Paradise." I left him, and I knew I did not believe my words. This place was not divine. It was enchanted, which was a different thing altogether.

I met other prisoners in the sand as I went along, taking care not to step on any of them. They could tell me little. Many spoke languages unknown to me. Some repeated tales of woe. A few babbled mindlessly. Those had been here longer than the others.

The beach gave way to boulders like the debris at the base of a cliff, and tufts of grass grew between them, along with

occasional scrubby, dwarfed trees. And among the stones were three men's heads, all of them dark-faced and black-bearded, people from some eastern land, each with a golden ring in one ear. I touched them to see if they were real, and as Andreas had, they vanished, and behind me three stones that were not stones took on faces. One mouth drooled and gibbered; one stayed silent; and the other repeated over and over a single line:

"The questing knight comes to the castle black, and sorrow, sorrow, sorrow."

"Friend," I implored him, "tell me your name and what you know of this place." But there was no acknowledgement of my presence in his look, and he went on with his sing-song. His wit was entirely gone, like the others. Surely, I thought, these three had received far more mercy from the maker of this place than many, who were aware of their captivity and the years crawling heedlessly by.

The sky darkened. It was night coming over all. Had I been in the water a day, two days, more? I had lost count of time. In any case I was still wet, and shivering all the more as the wind rose. After a time the clouds overhead rolled back, and a nearly full moon was revealed. It was by the light of this that I came to a field of high grasses bounded on the far side by a forest, and all the island seemed to come alive with trapped souls. No more were there only a few faces in the sand, or three gibbering Moors among the stones. Now every tuft, every shadow, every boulder, fallen log, ditch or streambed had a visage, one, two, a dozen, folk of every land and time, speaking to me in a whisper and a windy wail in tongues I knew and tongues strange to me, all relating their individual dooms, how they had come to this place and been imprisoned.

As I entered the wood I found even more of them, hanging above me in the darkness like dimly seen fruit, sometimes brilliantly illuminated for an instant, framed in moonlight as the wind waved a leafy branch aside. From these I learned of a black castle in the center of the isle, but of the one who dwelt there and was lord over it they knew nothing. They were denied movement. They had never seen him. If he moved among them he was a creature invisible, for they never slept.

I was not sure—perhaps I imagined once, but then I was beginning to trust imagination in the absence of reason—but I thought I saw a tall, thin figure in a flowing robe with a staff in one hand and a lantern in the other walking away from me in long strides, but in the blinking of an eye he had vanished among the trees. This, real or not, I took to be a sign; I knew I had not come to this place unbidden or without purpose; and I went in that direction.

The forest ended at the sheer face of a mountain. Atop it was the castle I had expected, dim, unlighted, darker than the clear parts of the sky, looming when ragged clouds passed behind it. Before me, at the base of the cliff, was a wall without a gate, made entirely of human hands and forearms. As I attempted to climb over it they came alive and forced me back. Angrily I stabbed at them with my dagger, which of all my armament I still had, but it was no use. They were made of stone.

Then three cats of the army which had overwhelmed the ship appeared, stood still, and grew into two woman-headed leopards and a lion with the face of a man, all crouched ready to pounce. I clutched tightly at the useless dagger and backed away, fearful that a sudden motion would provoke them to leap. The sounds from the forest rose in a wild crescendo of words and moans and song, and suddenly, as if the net of a spell had dropped over me, my limbs grew heavy and I was weary beyond all control. It was hard to stand, harder still to keep my eyes open. I fought against this, desperately aware of my peril, but I could not triumph; and in the end the weapon slipped form my limp fingers and I felt the earth rise up to catch me.

Waking and dream had become confused. In one state or the other a huge serpent took me in its coils. I felt them wrap around my body, cold, dry, and implacable, firm but not crushing. I was carried up the mountain to a level place, there put in the arms of a horned centaur whose flesh was shiny coal-black as night, and brought into the castle through a secret door. There was no sound. The voices of the woodland were silent. Above, clouds covered the moon.

III

He was a wizard as all men have imagined wizards, not young, not old, but ageless, with a thick, greying beard, hard-lined face, and intense eyes.

He stood over me.

And he was mad—

"Have you ever thought yourself trapped inside a ritual and struggling to get out?"

All senses returned. I was lying on a frigid stone floor. I raised myself on my elbows and said, "Who are you?"

"I have had many names from time to time," said the mad wizard. "Among them, Apollonius and Simon."

I made to speak again, but he foresaw, and answered.

"I have brought you here to witness and bring about the birth of a new heaven and a new earth. For this task one such as you is needed, whose spirit is uncommitted, given neither to the one who calls himself savior or to his enemy. I can detect such a void in a man by means of my art. In you I have recognized it, and so have caused you to be brought here."

"I seek a lady—"

"A lady is here. Behold! Come! Rise up and let all be revealed!"

He helped me to my feet. His manner was friendly, inviting, and for a few brief seconds I knew purest joy in my anticipation, but then it was snatched away, like the fruits in the Greek underworld which vanish whenever you reach for them. His lady was an earthen lady, an iron lady, a massive image a full head taller than any man, constructed with extreme cunning out of brick and mud and metal, with thighs like Babylonian pillars and breasts like warriors' helmets. Her face was exquisitely fashioned, a beautiful, ancient, polished deathmask.

I did not think for an instant that the magician had built this woman out of madness, as a prisoner will fashion himself a mud and straw lover when he has been locked up for too long. No, his was not that sort of madness, but something beyond order and knowing, a madness with a power behind it.

Then said I, "A great wonder in heaven; a woman clothed with the sun, and the moon under her feet, and upon her head a crown of twelve stars."

And the maker smiled and nodded and replied, "Not that exactly, but you have the substance. She is with child, and her womb shall give forth new gods to remake all things, and all that now is shall pass away. Think about it—all the sins of men forgotten, all the damned released from their abolished infernos."

These were mighty things, and he had the power to convince me that he could actually do them. His manner was that of a sky filled with storm-laden clouds, just before the first lightning bolt leaps forth to make the earth tremble.

"Are you a god yourself, that can perform this?"

"Not a god, or even one who can explain. Understand only that what I say shall come to pass, and the souls of those who make up the flesh of this island shall be melted down and poured like new metal into the mold of the Mother, and out of her shall come marvels unending, a new era of magic and darkness. Look! Look! Even now she moves!"

And the figure did move, stir, open eyelids to reveal twin caverns within, and stand upon its feet, a monster prepared to tear down the firmament. Then I saw that the wizard Simon-

Apollonius-of-many-names had a wand in his hand, and with it he directed his creation, causing it to walk stiffly like one in a trance. As it moved the creature seemed to gain increasing control over its limbs, to become more alive with each step, more independent. Muscles rippled under the now flexible skin, the joints growing more lithe.

"She shall dance the dance of life as the world turns, to the music of unseen spheres with you in her arms, for in the end a man of earth and mortality must consummate her."

As he spoke the centaur separated itself from the shadows—either it had entered silently by a secret way, or it had been in the room all along—and began to play a strange tune on a long, thin flute. The notes spoke of distances, like the wailing of the sea-elves beneath the ship at night, like the wind in a far mountain pass, and to the movements of the music the automaton stepped, dancing about the room, clumsily at first, upsetting tables and stands of alchemical bottles, brushing books from shelves with flailing arms. But after a while she grew more graceful, until finally she whirled and swayed and leapt with astounding agility.

And she—indeed now a she, the Great Mother, and no longer a sexless thing—came toward me with arms outstretched.

"Take her," said the magus, "and make her living an unending glory. Take her and her flesh shall be yours and yours shall be hers—"

Her eyes were now furnaces, no longer blank but wild with feeling, desiring me more fiercely than the damned desire their freedom. My flesh would be hers. Yes, that was evident. She would crush me against her body until I was part of her, gone, no longer aware of being myself, like the others melted down and poured molten and new and dead into the soul of this creature.

I would not do it. I, who hated God as much as any and was hated by him, could not offer myself up. I could not even think of others, of those who bore His eternal curse. I thought of myself. If I could have lived on to see the new creation, yes, but if I could not, then I would escape. In the end it was painfully clear that I had not the stuff of martyrs, saviors, or heroes in me.

There had to be a resurrection beyond death, and this time there wouldn't be.

I backed away from the thing. Again, as I gazed upon the goddess, it was neuter, a thing, a monster of mud and metal. I seized a stool and tried to push that body away, but the strength I met was mightier than a thousand armies. All those souls, all those lives, fused into one...I could only run, dodge, evade. In desperation I even yanked the cross I still wore from around my neck and held it out to ward off my enemy in the name of One who would never, never, come to my aid.

"No! No!" the magician screamed. "What are you doing?"

The trinket had no effect. I threw it away and ran to the only door of the chamber, and pounded on it. It would not open to me. I turned then to the only window, finding it crossed with iron bars and looking down from a great height, from the top of a tower. All this while the man-horse played its song, rapt in its own trance, unaware of the peril and fury around it. And its master shrieked at me, tried to seize me but was easily shoved aside, while the goddess-thing danced, danced, danced. I thought once to seize *him* and throw him into the deathtrap arms, but he fell to the floor and rolled, for a moment embracing the iron knees, then scurrying to safety on all fours like a maimed dog.

I had no sense of time as we went around and around and around, the wizard and I frantic, the gyrating thing caught up in thoughts no one can ever imagine, but finally, breathless and staggering, I came to the window, looked out, and saw a faint glow in the east. The stars had begun to fade. The sky was clear again.

"The night is almost over," I said.

"*What?*" Simon's voice was hoarse, his single word a pained gasp. He lunged at me, and I was sluggish to react. His shoulder slammed into mine and I tumbled to the floor. Now he hung on the bars and stared out. "The stars are gone from their stations. Never again can the thing be done," he said.

And the dancer missed a step. Its movements were clumsy again, finally lumbering, swaying, its limbs out of control, until the knees buckled and it went crashing over backwards onto the floor. Then it lay still, and all vestiges of humanity were lost from it. Once more it was only an inanimate lump of clay and iron and polished bronze.

The magician showed no sorrow. He did not weep. According to rumor they can't. I feared his wrath, but he did not curse me. He only spoke to me softly, distractedly, like a confused old man.

"It cannot be done again. Because you would not take her the God you know and the Devil you know are made eternal. You can never escape them. All other gods shall fade as quickly and as unresistingly as tonight's dark sky. I take no vengeance on you who have spoiled my great labor. No, I shall tell you only this— there is a place where one can go, apart from the universe and its wheel of Heaven, Hell, and sin, where peace is forever and there is no judgment. I go there now. Behind me the door is sealed. You cannot follow."

I believed him. I wanted so desperately to believe all he said except those last three words.

"Wait!"

He only smiled, and sighed, "I have seen too many centuries." Then he traced a rectangle in the air with his forefinger, and a doorway appeared in faint light. He stepped through, vanished, and the room echoed with a great clang, like a prison gate being slammed shut.

Stunned beyond any sense or immediate feeling I got to my feet. Slowly I approached the fallen she-thing. This? *This* was to stand all things on end? I prodded its swollen womb with my foot and it gave way, like a badly baked earthen pot. Inside was an idol of glass. I took it up and held it to the window. The shape caught the sunlight, and I saw that it was not at all human. I wondered if anyone could have been at peace in the new age.

IV

The centaur had stopped playing about the time its master had disappeared. I hadn't noticed it then, but when it moved from where it stood I said, "It is finished. He is gone."

The creature understood me at once.

"It was fated to turn out this way from the beginning, and to the ending so it is fated. He, being a man, never could understand that. You shall always be the one to drive away the gods. You are the destroyer. It is your fate and your role."

And it bade me climb on its back, and without questioning I did, for I was amazed beyond all questioning, benumbed into dullness. With a touch of an ebon hand the door that would not yield to me opened, and we went, stooping under archways, down a winding flight of stairs, across courtyards, and out of the castle. By a path I had not seen before we descended the mountain, until the cliff was behind us and at a gallop we passed through the forest of silent faces. They hung limply from the trees. They were dead.

"We must go west of the dawn," said my mount. Somewhere we made a subtle turn, for we did not emerge from the woods where I had expected. It was another beach. We fled with the night and the darkness over an impossibly long and delicate bridge, the stars still over us, away from the island and the dawn, until we came to another shore.

The centaur would not touch the sand. It stopped at the edge of the pavement and said, "Get down, and go into this land." And I did, and watched the creature turn around and race back along the bridge, which vanished like a mirage viewed from a different perspective before the creature had gotten half way to the island. And the Island of Faces itself trembled, and with a rumble and an avalance of crashing, sank. The sea which had received it was wild with foam, and huge waves pounded onto the beach. I ran back a distance, lest I be swept away.

I watched until the waves had subsided, and many objects bobbed up and down in the brightening morning light. They were corpses, thousands of them, all the drowned prisoners of the isle, returned to their deaths. Some of them I knew, the captain of my own ship, Andreas the philosopher, one of the Moors, and another, rolling gently onto her back and over again at the water's edge, with her long hair streaming out all around her like some rare and beautiful weed. I stared into the pale face for a long time.

Thus I found the Lady Catherine. The quest ended.

Once, when I was deeply ashamed of my sins, and yet afraid to confess them, I put on the garb of a common man to disguise myself, and went to hear the mass. It was in a vast cathedral in a vast city, and I mixed among the folk like a drop of water in the wide ocean, sure I would not be recognized. I dared not come dressed as one of God's holy warriors, even though none in the flesh knew of my iniquities, for by some word, some action, I would surely betray myself.

And it happened that my attention wandered and I looked over the heads of the congregation, and saw, standing by a pillar in a distant alcove, a man wearing a gleaming iron mask in the shape of a boar's head. No one else seemed to notice him. He was staring directly at me.

I trembled as I received the Sacrament, fearing that my sins would shout to the heavens with the tongues of the stones. But the stones were silent.

As I turned away from the priest I beheld another masked apparition standing in the great doorway, leering, horned, with an oak leaf on its tongue. Surely everyone could see it. It was in plain view, and all turned to face it, and yet no cry was raised.

When the crowd had departed, I lingered. First I went to the pillared alcove. There was a face carven in the wall, and it was indeed of a boar's head. I touched the damp stone. Above the entrance, where the doorway arched to a point, was another face, horned, with an oak leaf on its tongue, likewise carven and unliving.

Outside, I had not taken a dozen steps when the heavens burst asunder with rain and wind, and water came down in sheets. Lightning flashed just above twin steeples of the cathedral. I turned back, around the side of the place, and there I found a little door. Within was a narrow room. The rain roared behind me, like a waterfall over the mouth of a cave.

The room was lighted by candles. A man sat on a bench, painting a series of pictures on the walls.

"You are welcome to stay here," he said. "It's foul weather God sends all of the sudden."

I asked him what it was he painted.

"It is the tale of a knight. Here, in the first panel, he is born and as a child is instructed in the paths of righteousness by wise men. They marvel at his own precocious wisdom. But, as he moves on the pilgrimage of his life, he goes astray in the tangle of a forest, and here he lies with a maiden and speaks with the Adversary. Beyond this panel, I paint in a darker hue. All the colors have to be remixed. The mural goes on and on. I don't know where it ends."

"And what," said I as the terror rose in me like a tide, "are you painting just now?"

"Behold," he said, turning from his work to face me, "how the fool sneaks into the Lord's house as if it were a den of thieves, and thinks a simple disguise can hide him from the sight which penetrates even unto the soul—"

Screaming, I fled into the rain.

4

The Veiled Pool of Mistorak...

I no longer bore the cross on my shield. My sin was too great, and I knew that even Christ would not forgive me. Therefore I abandoned his sign. I had blasphemed and worshipped false gods. I had lain with a she-fiend from Hell. I had murdered my good squire Jon. For these things my honour and my soul were lost. My quest had ended. I could no longer hope to redeem my house from the madness that had befallen it, for only a virtuous man could do that, and I was no longer virtuous. So I painted my shield a solid black and wandered about the world. I went far to the south, where the sun has burned men's skin the colour of coal, and driven them to lie naked in riverbeds by day lest they be scorched further. I passed through a land where men have wings instead of arms, talons instead of feet, and live in trees. I came to the borders of Nubia and Ethiopia; I crossed over Althakores and Thrae, wandering on, going nowhere.

Somehow I gained a new companion in my travels, a gay knight whose sole aim was to find adventure wherever he went, and to make love to every maiden in every tavern in every town. His name was Hugh of Heron, third son of Duke Richard of Whitelake. He had won great fame in the Crusade, but had chosen not to return home. For he knew he would inherit nothing since both his brothers had survived the war, and he seemed to prefer common wenches in great numbers to the single proper wife he would find himself within his own country. He joined me, I think because we were so different. We were opposites always—he always cheerful, singing songs of marvels, and me always grim, contemplating my damnation. "You shall temper me when my gaiety grows to great" he would say, "and perhaps I shall bring some joy into your life, O melancholy sir." Perhaps I fulfilled my half of the bargain. A few times I did restrain him when local authorities would have had him for their dungeons, but he did nothing for me. I knew nothing of joy in those dark days.

Now there came a time when my existence grew unbearable, when I sought nothing but escape from this world. Yet I knew that there could be no escape, for beyond death the Judge Eternal waited patiently to proclaim my doom. Still, I did not resign myself entirely to this fate. I am a fighting man, and always I have been taught to draw my sword and plunge into the conflict, even if the numbers of the enemy are overwhelming. Always to fight, even if there is no chance of winning.

So it was that I called on the Elves. I wanted to ask them many things. I wanted to know if there might be some hope for me yet in some strange, blasphemous way. I could not rise in the universe, for the gates of Heaven were barred to me, and definitely I did not wish to descend as it seemed I inevitably must. Still I entertained one vague hope, that I might go sideways, into some forgotten pagan paradise that lingered at the edge of the cosmos, something that the Lord in all His might had never bothered to obliterate. Perhaps I might find some shadowy Elysium where no angel or theologian had ever chanced to look.

I called upon the Elves. I was no longer a Christian, and I had dabbled in the black arts since my fall, and thus I was able to summon and speak to things unhallowed by God. I went to a deserted grove one night, while Sir Hugh wenched away in a nearby town. I wore no iron and bore no rood, and I brought with me a wooden bowl filled with a mixture of milk and mead, as is pleasing to the Faerie folk. This I laid on a stone, and speaking words I had learned from witches, I called upon the Elves.

And they came to me. They came on their wind-swift steeds, three tall elfin lords in their strange armour and helms. They glittered in the moonlight as they rode out from the trees and across the forest path, but as they drew rein I heard no hoofbeat and no clatter of metal. They took my offering and drank, their leader sipping first, then passing the bowl to his companions. When all had partaken of it, the foremost of them said, "We are well pleased," and I asked my question. I asked them how I might find an ending to all things, even eternity.

All of them answered at once, intoning their words like some ancient dirge. Sometimes the voices of each were distinct; at other times they blended together like a chorus.

"Seek the Vale of Mistorak," they said. "Seek the city that is no more. Seek the land that lies in dust. Seek the man doomed ever to live....

"Find the head of Kardo Katha; King he was over all the world. Ere Babylon rose he was smitten. We dare not name the one who feared him, who rules the stars and fears but man...

"He could not rob him of his knowledge, things far older than the world. Where Adam ate of the fruit tree, Kardo Katha seized the sun...

"Kardo Katha sees into shadows. Kardo Katha knows all things. Kardo Katha hears the thoughts of men...

"Kardo Katha moves not...

"Kardo Katha has no limbs...

"Seek the head of Kardo Katha. Seek the Pool of Mistorak...

"Beware, O man, the price he will ask."

They were gone in an instant, like the fading flash of a lightning bolt. I had wanted to ask them more of Kardo Katha but could not. I had heard the name before, always in doubtful context. Witches spoke it in their secret caves. Occasionally an old man would utter it in a fit of drunkenness or delirium, only to be rapidly silenced by his fellows. I knew only that Mistorak lay far away, somewhere beyond the Eastern steppes.

To Sir Hugh the whole thing was another adventure, something to be experienced and enjoyed. He did not share my apprehension as we set out, for his cheer upheld him as ever. Thus we passed through many lands; through Calamye, where men cast themselves down before the wheels of a great idol, that they might be counted as martyrs to their god; through Ind, where husbands and wives are burnt together when one dies, even though the other is yet living. We travelled through jungles and over hills, down steep valleys and across parched deserts. We saw folk of many shapes and sizes, and always we asked them of the land of Mistorak. Sometimes they would merely stare at us, as if we spoke in something other than words, and other times that refused to answer. Perhaps the most encouraging reply was a sullen, "Mistorak lies far to the east. Go there and leave us alone."

At last, by going ways that no others went, by listening to those deemed mad by their fellows, by following roads that men dreaded even to look at, by crossing grown-over fields lorded by empty castles, we came to Mistorak. It was a desolate country, its ground sere and hard. There were only a few shrubs about, and the fruits they bore were dry and bitter. What streams there were ran black and foul, and the air was filled with fumes that assaulted the eye and nose.

All was silent. Not a deer ran before us; not a sparrow flew overhead.

"I have heard," Sir Hugh remarked, "that once this was a rich and fertile land, but like Sodom and Gomorrah it became corrupt, and God destroyed it with fire."

"I have heard another version—that its splendour rivalled his own and he was jealous."

"Who knows which is right?"

"I imagine he does, but either way the land is charred forever."

The road sloped upward, and before us stood a row of jagged peaks. Beyond them dark clouds broiled, thunder rumbled, and lightning flashed. As we drew nearer the sky darkened, and the air became unbearably warm. Sir Hugh took

off·his helmet and wiped his brow, then looked up at the
threatening clouds above us. He held his hand out.

"Methinks it shall rain," he laughed.

"If so, then not water."

We rode in silence after that, topping the rise. The way was
steep and treacherous, the ground strewn with gravel and dust.
When we finally looked down into the endless expanse of smoke
and sand that was the Vale of Mistorak, I asked Sir Hugh once
again if he desired to descend with me, for he had no cause to
share my doom.

"Nay!" cried he. "Not a doom but an adventure, and share it I
shall!"

So share it we did. All the way down the other side of the
slope, as our horses carefully and reluctantly made their way
through the sand and ash that at times came to their knees; as
we faced a blast of heat coming out of that valley as if from the
mouth of a furnace; as we peered ahead at the giant, twisted
columns of stone before us, scarcely visible in the clouds of
thick, oily soot; as we rode by chasms licked by tongues of
unquenchable flame; as we wended our way through this mad,
impossible land, the product of some demon sculptor—all this
time I felt that my end had come, as if without knowing it I had
died and come at last to my prepared place in Hell. Yet Sir
Hugh's spirits were still high, and when we reached the valley
floor and he could for a while divert some of his attention away
from the task of avoiding the thousand deaths that lay all
around us, he began to sing. It was a coarse song, bawled like
something out of a brothel, which was in all probability where
he learned it.

It went something like this:

"King John he's gone off,
And fought a war for God.
King John he's dead now,
And buried 'neath the sod.
He fought for gold and cross;
He fought for church and fame.
When pagans caught and killed him,
He left nothing but his name.
His castle's cold and empty,
And all his sons are gone.
Jerusalem they've sailed to,
And met the fate of John."

"Please, no more," I said. "What a terrible song!"

49

"I forgot the rest of the words anyway."

We pressed on. Somewhere in this endless expanse of dust and stone there was the dwelling place of Kardo Katha, or at least what remained of him. The Elves had said that he had no limbs, yet lived forever. This I could believe. Yet they had mentioned a pool, the Pool of Mistorak, and in this heat, when all the air was filled with ash, when sweat ran down our faces and under our clothing, when grime gathered on our eyebrows and hair, on helmets and mail, I found the idea of a pool of water utterly fabulous. But the Elves, I knew, did not lie to men who pleased them. So we continued on, deeper into the mouth of that vast cauldron, to the very bottom of the Valley Perilous, where great stone shapes rose up to be lost in the clouds, where arches cut by the wind towered over us, and huge boulders like pebbles flung from the hand of a giant lay scattered over a land so barren that it sheltered not even the asp and the adder. There we found the city.

At first the dust-encrusted shapes seemed like other rocks, mere natural, tormented things, but after a time they became larger and more distinct, until we came to the ruins of walls and houses and amphitheatres. Broken shells of guard towers still stood, their faces blasted smooth by the sand and heat. We found a gateway of exquisite workmanship which had somehow survived all the centuries. It stood alone in the dust, the wall it had once been part of long since gone.

And we found the inhabitants of that city. Their bones were everywhere. There were vast fields of them, houses filled to overflowing, palaces piled high in death. There was a throne, whereon sat a skeleton crowned. Others, the remains of counsellors, maidens and flatterers, lay at his feet. Servants, lying atop golden trays once bearing food, were all about. Guards were tumbled in heaps, their skulls grinning blindly from beneath their helmets. There was even a full armoured knight there, his ruined armour crushing his skeletal steed. A baker lay slumped over his bread, each loaf now transformed into a rock. In viewing all this I recalled the vision of the bones the prophet had seen. It must have been very much like this, only his bones rose up and lived, and these never would. The prophet was a friend of God, and for such people wonders can happen. For enemies, for outcasts, there is only the kind of wrath which can strike down an entire nation, killing its people before they can even know fear.

In the central section of the city there was a square, and in the middle of it a pedestal the size of a small house, on which was written: BEHOLD DURION THE GLORIOUS, HERO FOR ALL AGES.

But there was no sign of him. Only his sculpted feet

remained, easily three cubits from toe to heel, broken off at the ankles. The statue had long since fallen away and crumbled into nothing. Sic transit gloria Durion.

A short distance beyond the pedestal the earth gave way, and my horse stumbled. I was thrown from the saddle; I rolled over the pommel and down the neck in a sommersault and fell onto the ground in an ungainly sprawl. Painfully I rose to my feet, feeling around for broken bones. There were none, but the beast was less fortunate. Both its forelegs were broken, where they had been caught in the crack in the ruined pavement.

"We shall have to slay it," said Hugh.

The horse screamed as our swords pierced its throat from either side. It fell down and writhed in the dust. Its blood gushed forth and vanished, sinking into the sand. Even as the struggling stopped the entire body seemed to be drained of fluid. The skin became shrunken and tight, the bones protruding everywhere.

"The land is hungry for life," I said as I climbed up behind my companion on our remaining steed.

The pool itself was only a short way distant. It stood amid the ruin of what must have once been a fine garden—I recognised the statues and stone benches, but of course whatever had grown there was gone without a trace.

The pool was perfectly round and perhaps fifteen cubits across. It was made of a strange blue stone, so cunningly wrought that one could not tell where the pieces had been fitted together, so that at a glance it seemed to be made of one huge block. It rose to waist high, and of all the things in the city or the entire valley, besides the arch, it showed no sign of decay.

A rough slab lay over the top like a lid. This Sir Hugh and I pushed aside with some difficulty, and once we had sweated and strained enough it thudded to the ground and we saw water within.

"Ah! A drink is what I need!" cried my companion.

I too was thirsty, but I cautioned him.

"Don't. This whole land is poisoned. So must be its water."

So we stood there, looking down into the unnatural depths of the Pool of Mistorak. I say unnatural because it seemed very deep, many fathoms in fact, when of course one should have been able to wade in it. And as we gazed, there appeared a spot of light far below, as if at the bottom of a very deep well. It rose steadily toward us, growing brighter and larger as it came. Soon the placid surface of the water began to stir, then bubble like broth, and then it turned a bright, bloody red.

"Not poisoned," gasped Sir Hugh. "It's enchanted!"

Steam arose; the excitement of the pool grew greater; and the water changed colour again, this time to a dull, muddy brown, and the head of Kardo Katha appeared.

I know not what my companion saw, but whatever it was it caused him to tremble and scream with fear and repulsion. I know I screamed at what I saw, for there was something people had told us in so many words, which now proved true. Kardo Katha had no form of his own, his visage having been obliterated with his land. In its place he had only shapelessness, and when one looked on him one saw something from the past, something from out of the innermost regions of the soul, something haunting and un-forgettable. I saw my Llania, her face not as she was when she left me, but foul and dead and corrupt, as she had been in her tomb, her mouth dripping stolen blood.

"Murderer, you have disturbed my rest," a deep voice thundered.

Indeed Kardo Katha knew all.

I fought to regain my composure and spoke to the ghastly apparition as calmly as I could.

"I have come to ask something of you."

"Then you must pay my price. You must feed me."

"Feed you?"

"I desire life. Give me meat."

"Perhaps this will do," said Sir Hugh, and he reached into his saddle bag, drew out a piece of dried beef, and tossed it into the pool.

"No! I want living meat! Flesh! Give it to me or I shall take it! No man leaves this place and leaves me unsatisfied."

There were few things I feared then, save the silence of this demon oracle, and surely he would not speak if left unfed. So I gave him living meat. Of myself. I placed my left hand in the water and said, "Will this do?"

There was no answer except for an explosion of pain, and violent flashes of red and orange and black. I fell back in a swoon, and the next thing I knew I was being roused by Sir Hugh.

"By the saints! Your hand! There is no blood!"

I had no saints to swear by, but I looked at my hand, or rather the stump where it had been. The sleeve of my jerkin was blasted away, and my arm blackened to the elbow. The hand was entirely gone, yet the wound did not bleed. It had been seared shut. My whole side throbbed, and my feet seemed to melt away beneath me as I was helped to my feet, but leaning on Sir Hugh I was able to again stand before the pool.

"Ask what you will," said Kardo Katha.

So I asked. I told him of my plight, how I had come to be hated by my God, how damnation awaited me. I asked how I might

52

escape with my soul to some place where there was peace and rest and an end to suffering. Nothing more than that did I desire.

"O foolish man, you have given your hand in vain! All these things can be found within you and without you. Peace you shall have when you stop searching. Rest you shall have when you labour no more. Love you shall have when you are willing to give love. You are like Judas. You think that your crime is so great that even God will not forgive you. But he will. There is nothing so terrible about what you have done. I who was glorious, who might have been a god myself, I cannot humble myself to ask forgiveness, so I remain here. But you, you have humbled yourself in a thousand ways. Now you are a fool. Perhaps you shall find contentment when you become a holy fool."

Then the head turned to Sir Hugh and said, "And what would you have of me?"

He was taken aback. "I hadn't thought about this," he whispered to me.

"Ask for *something!*" I muttered back.

He addressed the thing before us. I think he had grown used to whatever horror he saw it as, for his tone had grown much bolder.

"I-I want gold," he said. "You who are so great can surely make a man rich. I want lots of gold."

"You too are a fool," intoned the head, "but a far greater fool than the other. You have not fed me, either with your steed or of your body, yet you ask for pretty baubles. You ask for gold when there is gold everywhere when well earned. But fool, nevertheless you shall have your gold. Look to the earth!"

As we stood there the ground beside Sir Hugh split open, revealing a vast hoard of buried gold. His jaw hung slack. "I'm rich," he mumbled. He was rich, out of the bosom of Kardo Katha. The rift was easily ten cubits long and five deep, filled to the rim with golden ingots.

"There isn't that much among all the treasures of Tartary!"

"Don't take it. Surely it is accursed."

"Nay. Metal is only lifeless metal."

Greed overcame him. He left me to fall to the ground while he stepped into the trench. I managed to attain a sitting position against the side of the pool while he wallowed in his gold.

"I shall be a king!" he cried. "I shall buy a kingdom with this gold. Hail King Hugh of Heron and to Hell with all others!" But even as he spoke the gold pieces became flaming worms which streamed over his body. The joyous shouts became screams. He screamed and screamed all the louder as they devoured him, burning and tearing the flesh from his bones while he still lived. I watched it all, helpless to aid him. I watched as he became a gory, writhing mass, stripped of all humanity. I watched as he thrashed about, as the muscles fell from his arms like old rags, and his head became such a ruin that I couldn't tell where his face had been. Still he screamed and screamed and screamed, incredibly alive.

"*Now* you have fed me," came a distant voice that seemed to grow farther and farther away in the mist as nausea overwhelmed me.

I awoke in what must have been evening. Still the dust and smoke hung overhead, but the valley was darker. I could not see to the end of the garden, and all the highest towers of the ruined city were lost in shadows.

The cleft in the ground was gone, and with it whatever might have remained of Sir Hugh. I seized the side of the pool and dragged myself to my feet, and as I did I discovered that the covering had of its own accord assumed its original position. The land was still, save for distant thunder. Sir Hugh's horse still stood where it had been tethered. Gathering all my strength I stumbled over to it and crawled into the saddle.

As I rode out of the valley by the route we had come, I contemplated the horror of that day, and the madness of the answer I had received. All was a cruel deception. How could I ever love again when the one I had loved most dearly had turned out to be a monster? How could I stop searching and then find? How could I ever go crawling to the priests and tell them of my sins and beg forgiveness? And how could forgiveness ever come? Christ the terrible, Christ the executioner awaited me with flaming sword. I envied Kardo Katha then, for he alone had managed to stay outside the eternal cycle of death and damnation.

I came to the edge of the valley at dawn. I knew it was dawn not because I saw the sun rise, but because the blackness above me lightened into a filthy grey. More than anything else I longed to see the colours blue and green again, for they were entirely lacking in this accursed place.

The peaks stood as sentinels before me, twisted and forbidding and dead. I wondered if ever I would see another clear sky, if I could ever exist in the world again, along with the evils I had once wrought out of love and horror.

5

The One who Spoke with the Owls...

Truth? I have studied the world and beheld its foundations;
all dreams, all veils, all the darkness of death; but Truth I have not
seen.

— Theodoric of Cappa

Once, in a dream, I saw myself lying still, as if sleeping or dead, in the middle of a darkened plain. Over me there stood an angel, shining in all his glorious light, and opposite him, on the other side of me, huddled three witches.

"Take this one away," the angel said. "He is one of your followers."

"No, no," said the witches. "We know him not."

And the light of the angel seemed to grow greater, and the shadows were driven back off the field. There stood others in the distances, men of all races, of all nations, and of all times. And the angel and the witches turned to them, saying, "Take this one. He is one of yours."

And the multitude answered as one, "We know him not."

Then the shadows retreated further, and behind the men there were beasts of every description, great and small, all milling about, and the angel, and the witches, and the great mass of people said to them, "Take this one. He is yours."

And the beasts replied, "We know him not."

And still the darkness fell away, and beyond the men and the beasts there stood a great forest, filled with tall trees, and the angel, the witches, the mass of men and the beasts all said to the trees, "Take this one. He is a stranger to us."

And the trees replied, "We know him not."

Then the shadows fled from the light, and flower bedecked hillsides were uncovered, and beyond them ragged mountains, and vast rivers; and the light raced to fill the world unto the horizon. And the hills and the flowers and the mountains and the rivers all said as one, "We know him not, we know him not." And the darkness fell away even from the stars, and they shone brilliantly in the heavens, and the cry continued, "We know him not. We know him not." And unto the very ends of creation, from the highest pinnacle of glory to the deepest abyss, to the edges beyond which no stars shine, all things replied to the question, "We know him not. We know him not."

I awoke and began to wander over the world again. After a time the stump of my severed left hand ceased to pain me, and I had it capped in bronze, and a small hook attached to it. The hook I used for holding my horse's reins, so that my remaining hand might be free for other things. The bronze cap was very heavy, and good for knocking on doors and men's heads.

I was a frightening figure to most, a gaunt, maimed knight who spoke with a foreign accent, with clothing ragged and helmet and mail all tarnished. My shield I had painted a solid black, with the crest of no house thereon. Always I made men uneasy in my presence, and always I would move on, never remaining in one place, never knowing the joys known to other men.

But wanderers and outcasts are men, and they need what men need. They must eat; they must find shelter from storm; they must seek the company of other men, no matter how hostile, lest they go mad. For the first of these they need money, and for the last they need the excuse of seeking those before it.

Now I shall tell what I did for money.

I entered the Valley of the Hand through the index finger. I rode over lush slopes, bursting with forests of fir and ash, until the hills rolled and folded and fell and became the index finger of the Valley of the Hand. There were five such small, narrow gorges, and they all joined together in a wide plain, forming a shape which some claimed to be the imprint made by the Creator when he rested his hand on the seventh day of creation. And indeed the valley did seem to be a place of unnatural bounty and life, for everywhere fruit trees grew, and tall flowers and grasses covered the ground. Vines hung from branches and rocks, heavy with grapes. Cool, clear streams ran bubbling down into the heart of the valley, and as far as I could see there was greenery, stretching off to cushion the horizon. Surely the sun always smiled on this land, and there were no droughts, no storms, and no famines. Surely this place provided for its people, and they knew nothing of want or strife. These things I knew as I rode across their untenanted fields, breathing the freshness of their blossom-filled air. It was such a wonderful relief to be away from the steppes and deserts which make up so much of the East.

Yet when I saw the first signs of habitation the ecstacy of the place seemed to dim. When there were wagon ruts on the road the greenery seemed slightly less green, the sun slightly tarnished. And when there were crops in the fields instead of flowers I thought I was losing hold on an ethereal vision, as if I were about to awaken from a rare dream.

After a time there were fences along the roadsides, and I spied farmhouses far off, on the slopes of the outlying hills. I passed a mill with a great waterwheel, and my steed's hooves clattered on the bridge crossing the mill stream. Still it was a fine valley and fair, more bountiful than any I had seen in a long time, yet the wonder of my first entering it had vanished.

At last, as the sun was beginning to drop low over the green horizon, I came to an inn nestled among the ancient trees on the edge of a forest. I handed my horse over to a stableboy and left my shield hanging on the saddle. I walked to the door and it was only then, as I stood on the doorstep, that my heart sank and the wonder of the valley fled altogether.

There was a metal crucifix over the door. Here, near the very edge of the world, beyond the reaches of any map, where even Prester John's realm was a half known myth to the west, even here the priests had come. Had not He commanded them to teach all nations? Had they not traveled like seeds on the wind, through every forest, over every mountain, across every sea? I was vain to suppose that they had not come here, that I could find peace in this place. Once more the facade had to be maintained.

I knocked loudly on the heavy boards and the door opened. A loutish fellow with untrimmed hair and beard eyed me suspiciously.

"I am a stranger from a far land. Seeking shelter. May I come in?" I spoke with obsequious politeness.

The knave trembled and hesitated, his gaze racing from my helmet to my mailshirt to my sword and back again. His mouth hung wide like that of a drooling idiot. Then suddenly another came and pushed the first aside, saying, "Peter! Be more gracious to our guests. Welcome under my roof, good sir." This second person, obviously the innkeeper, was a stout man of middle years. His clothing and beard were neat, and along his generous waistline there hung a leather money bag. He constantly folded and unfolded his hands. His narrow, night black eyes glanced from side to side. I knew the type, a usurer, a hypocrite hiding behind the sign on his door. He was interested only in what coins I could give him for his services. Instantly I disliked the man, but I kept this feeling well hidden, for he had offended me in no way and seemed willing to treat me well.

I was taken into a large room, where a dozen or so men in rough clothes sat on benches before a table eating and drinking. All of them ceased their conversation and looked up when I came in, and the smells of sweat and burnt meat hung in the silent air.

The room was long and narrow, and one had to descend three steps to reach its floor. The walls of bare boards, and heavy beams, some, with dried herbs hanging from them, ran parallel across the ceiling. I assumed I was to sit and eat with the rest of the folk there, but my host called again to the servant who had first opened the door, "Quick! Go fetch our best chair for this noble guest." In a short while I sat at the end of the table, apart from the other guests, in a chair of carven and polished oak, which looked like it had been stolen from a merchant of some note. It was not particularly comfortable.

I was brought a meal of some indefinable meat, potatoes, cooked greens, and a great deal of wine. It was the best I had eaten in a long while, and it made me drowsy. I slouched in the chair while the other men, who had gotten used to me huddled at the other end of the table and spoke in low tones. Occasionally one of them would glance at me quickly and look away.

I sat and thought sombre thoughts, about the meaningless vision of Mistorak, about the curse that lay upon me, and about my inevitable damnation. In despair I knew that my soul was as lost as my left hand, swallowed up in centuries of time, in leagues of space, and the unfathomable reaches of what might have been. I wanted to curse God, but I dared not. Yet more painful visions came to me at the very thought.

I must have been asleep or nearly so, for I had not seen the men gather around me. Someone placed his hand on my shoulder and shook me. I sat up with a start.

"You! What is your name?"

I looked up into blurry faces. "Julian...I am called Julian. There was another Julian once, and they called him apostate."

"I saw your shield where it hung on your saddle, the stableboy showed it to me. There was no insignia on it. What is your house?"

"The tower." I was more awake, and could see that my main questioner was a man I had not seen before, a short, thin fellow with no beard at all, who dressed in fine furs and silks.

"The tower?" he said. "I have never heard of the knights of the tower."

"Yes, the tower. When I was a child I heard about a man, a very, very old man, whose father had been a werewolf. So they took him, the son, while he was yet an infant, and shut him up in a tower. He remained there always, never knowing love, never knowing life. I, too, live in a tower, only mine is invisible and I carry it around with me. Its walls are just as strong though."

"Are you a werewolf then?"

"Only in my heart."

The richly clad one grew impatient. "Please, good sir, speak clearly. I am Bors, and I am mayor here. I would ask a service of you."

I tried to rise, but suddenly my head felt as if cloven by a war axe. The room reeled around me, and I struggled to maintain my balance. The wine had been far stronger, or I had drunk far more of it than I had thought.

"Innkeeper! "Innkeeper!" I did not see him about. "Innkeeper, I wish to retire now. How much do I owe you for the meal?"

The innkeeper materialized out of a hazy corner like a jackal drawn to carrion, eager for payment.

"Two copper pieces, sir."

I took my purse from my belt, and still swaying back and forth, remaining upright with some difficulty, I poured its contents out, and made to catch the coins with my bronze stump.

"Devils!" I had forgotten that I no longer had two hands. I looked around for the coins and saw only one, a small copper disc, so thin as to be almost worthless, on the floor at my feet. I was puzzled, but then recalled that I had heard only one drop. I bent over, my head swimming as I did, picked up the coin and gave it to the innkeeper.

"Alas, this is all I have. Now I must rest. Show me to my bed."

My host's face went slack with horror. Nothing frightens a miser more than the prospect of not getting paid.

"But—but, this can't begin to cover the expenses. I must have more."

At that moment Bors the major spoke. "Perhaps I can help."

"Perhaps you can," I mumbled. "On the morrow I shall do this deed for you, and with the money you pay me I shall settle my debt with your friend here."

That seemed to satisfy everyone. The mayor took me by one arm and the innkeeper by the other, and they half led, half carried me up the stairs and into a room. I do not recall touching a bed.

II

Dawn came bright and fresh through my window. Small songbirds sat on the windowsill of the room and sang, only to fly off when I stirred. The day was warm and the sky incredibly blue, and the very air seemed to bring strength to me. I breathed deeply and rose from the bed refreshed. The previous night was a half remembered dream at best. I knew I had been in a long dark room with other men, and it had been hot and stuffy, and there was something about a coin. I knew also that I had ridden along and hard the day before and not eaten since the day before that, but I could not believe that I had gotten so drunk. It must have been something in the wine I told myself.

I was about to go downstairs and ask about breakfast when someone knocked at my door. It was the innkeeper, and he bore a tray, whereon was some bread, dried meat, and fresh fruit.

"I hope you have slept well," he said.

"I have slept without dreams, and that is well enough."

"Here is some food for you. When you have finished the mayor wishes you to go with him and meet the people. They want to see their hero."

I took the tray and placed it on the bed, then sat down beside it and began to eat.

"And why am I suddenly the hero of the people?" I asked, chewing on the meat.

The innkeeper looked genuinely surprised.

"Why—why noble sir, *brave* sir, you are their hero because you have promised to slay the Witch of the Wood."

I choked on a mouthful of meat, then spat it up. "*I what?*"

"Last night. You promised good Bors that you would slay the witch for him in order to earn the money to pay for your board."

It came back to me. I had indeed promised to perform some unspecified task, but no one had mentioned a witch. I was sure of that, yet I said nothing. I did not wish to antagonize the people of this new land.

"Very well then, I shall slay this witch. Now take me to the mayor."

After I had finished my meal we went from the inn, through the trees a short way. Peter the doorman followed leading my horse by the reins. The beast had been groomed well, and even my shield had been cleaned and polished.

In a short while we came to a clearing. Thatched huts stood all about, blending into the forest behind them. In the centre was a bare space, with a well in the centre of that. Perhaps thirty or forty people, all as roughly clad as those I had seen at the inn on the previous night, milled about. There was also one cow present.

"Will you indeed kill the witch?"

"I will, if you tell me something about her first."

"She is evil beyond all things. She lies with the Devil by night and mocks the name of God."

I was amused. "Has anyone seen her do this?"

"She brings disease and death!"

"So do many things. There is disease and death in my own land and we have no witch."

An old woman came forward. "Three nights ago the witch came to my house and stared through the window. I screamed and my husband raised an axe against her. She vanished. The next day he was repairing the roof, when the ladder slipped from under him, and he broke his neck."

I said nothing.

A younger woman led the cow to me and pointed to its udder, which was shrivelled like a prune.

"Behold, the witch uttered a word and my cow gives milk no

more."

This went on and on, with the simpletons blaming their everyday woes on the witch. By the time they were done I had begun to doubt that there even was a witch, yet still I said nothing. At last the mayor proclaimed that I should have a guide, to show me where the witch lived. He and the men of the village conferred, and after a while a guide was chosen for me.

The guide was a boy, skinny, stoop-shouldered, and not more than fourteen years old if that. He seemed dirtier and more unkempt than even his elders. He was pushed forward from the crowd with obvious reluctance on his part.

"This one will show you the way," Bors said to me. "Be patient with him. He's a little slow in the head."

"If so," I replied, "why don't you come? Surely I can use the leadership of a wiser man."

Bors looked horrified. "I have never been to the witch's house. The boy goes there occasionally and spies on her."

"Then he is braver than all of you?"

"No, he is stupid. Do not confuse stupidity with courage."

"Or courage with stupidity."

The mayor blinked and said nothing, and without another word I lifted the boy onto my horse, and mounted also, and with him before me in the saddle I rode off to slay the Witch of the Wood in order to earn a few pieces of gold.

We traveled east and the village fell behind and was gone, and the forest pressed in upon us. Quickly the boughs met overhead, and the road became a trail and then a pathway with a thick green roof. Thousands of birds sang and raced from branch to branch, and once a doe and her fawns watched us from a short distance, as if they knew no fear of men. The earth itself seemed alive and bursting with living creatures and with flowers, and the forest was a leafy sea whose depths one could not fathom. After a time I spoke.

"Boy, what is your name?"

"Matthew, sir. I am named after the saint."

"Matthew, they told me you were slow in the head. Is that so?"

"No sir, I am very clever, but I keep my cleverness hidden, so that it and what I know may be doubly secret."

"And this one called Peter, the one who met me at the door last night, is he also secretly clever?"

"Him? No! He's an *idiot!*"

"Beware of appearances, Matthew."

We rode till the sun hung low in the sky, and the shadows began to slip out of the forest like phantom veils. The day birds hid themselves and the night birds emerged. An owl flew across the way in front of us. I could see no sky, but I knew that the stars had begun to appear. The moon, hidden by the trees, sent its light filtering down, glowing golden on the upper branches. The boy directed me, and I turned my horse from the path at a certain point, and plunged into the rapidly darkening forest. Soon all was black before me, although Matthew seemed able to see still and tell me where he was going. After an hour or so we came to a clearing filled with moonlight, and there stood the house of the witch.

It was old, very old, made of ancient boards and thatch, covered with folds of ivy from top to bottom. There were two floors, and from a window on the second light came.

"Tie your horse and creep forward on the ground," said Matthew, and we did and came to the very edge of the forest, where only saplings and underbrush hid us.

"Now we must wait until her head flies away into the night."

"What? Are you mad, boy?"

"Sir, you have been kinder to me than most and I would not lie to you. Likewise I am not mad. I have lain here many times and seen her head fly from that window. In that way she does her mischief and goes beyond the world to feast with devils. She joins herself to the bodies of monsters when she does."

So we waited, I half believing and he tense but not afraid, and crickets, birds and beasts concealed the sound of our breathing. As always the wood was alive about us.

Midnight came and passed, and the moon dropped to the treetops, its light flooding almost horizontally into the clearing. This light and that of the stars met with the glow from the witch's window. Then suddenly the window was dark. I had almost dozed off, as had the boy, but when something round and white with trailing blackness streamed out of the window, I snapped instantly alert, and elbowed the boy.

"It is her!" he gasped.

The flying shape circled the clearing once, and we pressed ourselves lower against the ground. Then it passed over the top of the house and was gone. I knew what I had to do.

"Matthew, stay here and warn me if she comes back."

I stood up, sword in hand, raising my shield as if ready to do battle, and I ran to the door of the house. I listened and all was still within. I pressed on the door and was surprised to find it unbarred. I went inside.

"Halt! I am Gorm! Who defies Gorm?" a tiny voice cried.

I whirled about and saw over the doorway a creature with the body of a rat and the face of a man. I struck at it with my sword, it dashed away with more than natural speed.

The stairs were before me and I raced up them, taking in three at a time. I found the room with the open window. In the dim light I could see ancient books lining the walls, and the instruments of the witch's art standing all about. In the centre of the room was a bed, and on it lay the body of the witch.

I approached in amazement. She was fair of form beyond words, with lithe figure and firm breasts visible beneath her silken white garments. Her head was indeed gone, but there was no bloody wound, only an ending of flesh. A cloud of mist shrouded the expectant neck.

"You! Who are you? I smell no evil in you and no good. You are not of the new god, and not of the old either."

The rat-thing crouched on one of the bedposts. I swung at it and got it this time, slicing its body in half. It hurled against the wall and fell to the floor a wreck, and even in the darkness I could see that it bled great pools, more than I would have expected for a creature so small.

I knew what I had to do. I had to destroy the body of the witch as it lay helpless before me, and I had to do it quickly, lest her head return and she rise up in all her power. It was a sickening, terrible job, that butchery. I drove my sword deep through the heart and the whole body heaved and convulsed, and blood burst forth as if from a fountain. I struck again and again, hacking and hacking until no limb remained, until the silken gown was a sticky scarlet red, until the corpse before me lay in unrecognizable ruin.

Suddenly a great gust of wind blew through the window, sending books tumbling from the shelves. Far away, on that wind, and borne by that wind, there came a scream. Then there was another scream far closer, and I stood hypnotized by the horror of what I had done until I saw Matthew running across the clearing waving his arms to fend off something round and streaming and black.

"Witch!" I cried from the window. "Witch! Leave the boy alone! I am the one you seek!"

She rose from him and came straight at me.

"Matthew! Run! Don't look back!"

Then the witch was upon me. The head flew through the open window and circled behind me. She swooped at my face, her teeth snapping like a rabid dog. Barely was I able to raise my shield and beat her away. Again she came, and again my shield stopped her. And again she flew around the room, knocking more books and candles and old skulls from the shelves, sending a jar of feathers crashing. Feathers filled the air, feathers swarmed about her,

64

feathers clouded my face. Again I saw a movement and I brought my shield around, and she smashed into it. I struck with my sword, but smote only feathers, which hung in the air like smoke.

Again I half heard, half felt her behind me, and I ducked and whirled and the teeth snapped at what would have been my neck. I swung with sword point and pressed with shield, and she eluded me. She came at me low, but I was too quick and I jumped up and she passed under, and when she circled around she met my black shield. The shape of a demon rose from the floor, as large as three men with the body of an ape and the head of a crocodile, but it was only a shape and not a body, and my blade passed through it without resistance and it was gone. Again the head came at me, and I blocked it.

At last the feathers fell to the floor, and the head hung motionless in the air. I raised my sword, but did not strike. For the first time I saw the witch's face, and even though she was battered, her hair bedraggled, she was very beautiful. There seemed to be no evil in her face.

She was crying, pleading with me.

"Why? Why have you done this? You have won. My strength is gone and you have conquered, but why?"

I found myself without words. "The men of the village told me you were a witch," I managed to say after a minute. "They paid me gold." I felt like a child explaining the inexcusable. I knew then that I had been wrong, that I had been sent on a worthless mission.

"I am not a witch. I have never sold myself to your Satan. I knew him not. I am mother to this forest. Each night I fly through its branches and speak with the owls, asking if all is well. Each night I bless the flowers that they may grow. Each night I paint colours on the wings of moths. Oh, I am not a witch as men know witches. I loved men once, for a short time at least. Well do I remember that day, when the gods sat in their garden drinking wine, and I was with them, and one came running to tell us that the new god, the one who tolerated no other, had been slain. Men had done it. They had nailed him to a kind of tree. Then we all praised the glory of men and drank in their honour and feasted for a night and a day. But boundless was our horror that morning when another came and cried, 'He has risen! He has risen!' In terror we fled to the very ends of the earth, but one by one all that company fell and perished beneath the shadow of the cross. I am the last and I too am no more."

Therewith she dropped to the floor with a thud, and was still. Something within me told me that I should feel remorse and shame, but I felt nothing. My soul was dead, like a dried, brittle husk. Dumbly I wandered about the violated room, picking up the books which were old when Ur of the Chaldees rose fresh and new. They were all written in the same tiny, neat hand. I knew I could never know all the wisdom they contained, yet I thought I would take a few and study them. I selected three, which were small and could fit into a pouch or bag with ease. Then I descended the stairs and left the house, and all around me the land began to die.

At first even in dissolution it was beautiful, the leaves on the trees growing golden and brown and swirling to the ground as if it were fall, but then the branches withered and the trunks decayed, as if consumed by some invisible fire. I turned and saw that the house too was in ruin, as if centuries were passing over it in a vast torrent. First the thatch was gone, then the doors and shutters, then the walls themselves began to fall away. The three books I held crumbled into dust in my hand.

All around me the trees bent and collapsed, and the flowers curled like burnt hair and were gone. The grass became straw on the ground, and the underbrush thinned and was no more. And then the birds and beasts came streaming out of the forest, across the clearing and toward the east, away from the town. First ran mice and weasels and foxes and rabbits, then boars and dogs, then hart and hind, then the great bear, and all over flocks of birds flew, all in the same direction, all in terror. At last unheard of shapes came, things half like men and half like goats, things like snakes with the wings of birds, a lion with the head of a man. And these spoke, and these cried out to me, "You have killed the Mother! You have killed the Mother!"

I turned and fled to where my horse still stood, and the beast eyed me in fear. I rode throughout the night, and by dawn I came to the village, and the land was desolate and the sky filled with dust. All was barren. Not a tree, not a blade of grass grew anywhere. Not a bird sang. The wind was beginning to raise dunes.

The people of that place fled before me in a long line, their belongings on their backs, their cloaks drawn over their faces to ward off the wind and sand. Already the sun seemed vengefully hot, and the streams and river bottoms were cracked and hard.

"Bors! Bors! Where is Bors the Mayor?" No one answered and I raged and rode along the column, until I found him. He like the others carried a bundle with him, and his face was slack with horror and hopelessness.

"Bors!"

"You! Why have you come back? What more evil can you bring us?"

"I have slain this one who was a bane to you. Now pay what you promised."

"Pay?" he trembled.

"Pay!" I screamed. "Pay you fool for what you hired me to do!" I drew my sword. My horse reared up, and people scattered away. Bors tried to reason with me.

"We are poor folk now. I pray you have pity."

The refugees streamed around us now, in the same suffering indifference.

"You showed no pity. You used me to perform a foul deed you were too cowardly to do yourself."

"Ah, but sir, then avoid even more foulness. Money is the great evil of the world. What want have you for it?"

"The great evil of the world is in your mind, and I shall split your skull and expose this evil to daylight unless you pay what you owe."

Again he trembled, and with fingers which could barely work together he opened a purse to take out a coin. But my sword snatched the little leather bag from him, and he turned and ran and fell and ran again. I tossed the purse from my sword tip to my left hand and cursed. The bag bounced off the metal stump and fell into the dust. I had not yet reconciled myself to having one hand. The reflexes of a lifetime had yet to be driven out. I dismounted and picked up the bag, and none dared disturb me. I climbed again into the saddle and rode along the row of people, until I came to the innkeeper. He carried no package on his back, but Peter the servant and the stableboy struggled under large ones. I took out a coin and threw it as hard as I could in the innkeeper's face, and he gasped and clutched one eye. I left him kneeling in the dirt, feeling around for the lost gold piece.

And at the very end of the procession I came upon one small figure, a straggler who had fallen behind the others, who was choked and blinded by the dust. It was Matthew. I drew near him and he looked up at me, half in horror, half in incomprehension.

"Boy, I am leaving now. You alone of these unworthy folk I wish well. Find a new land and live there."

"Sir...Sir Julian...where will you go now?"

"To the east, I think. Tell me, what lies to the east, beyond the Valley of the Hand?"

"Oh Sir, go not there. Beyond the valley there is a range of mountains, and beyond the mountains there is the edge of the world, and the abyss which has no bottom. There is a great face carven on the side of the cliff, and it regards the sun as it rises each day, and the stars as they hide in the depths from the light. It knows all things which are to come, but to look on its face is to die.

I pray you, go not there!"

"Have you ever been there?"

"No."

"Then I shall go and see these marvels. Farewell, Matthew."

I rode for a day and night against the raging sand. I had seen no place fiercer, no place hotter, no place more hostile to man in all my travels. I felt the pouch of money by my side, and I thought of the green valley that had been, and I felt helpless and vile and dead beyond any resurrection. Judas must have known the feeling, I am sure.

I rode until the lands were no more, until I had passed through the wrist of the Hand and the valley was gone. Exhausted, parched, I came to a tiny, muddy stream and drank deeply. I pulled plants and ate their bitter roots. I rode on.

I came to the hills and passed over them. I saw no abyss, no stony face save for the bard cliff which looked not into an abyss, but over a grassy plain divided by a wide river.

There were lands beyond.

6

The Castle of Kites and Crows...

She lifted the lifewand and the dead began to speak.

—Andreas

"Sisters, shall we dream of him again?"

"We shall."

"This one means all. Listen: I have dreamed of him as a bird, a tiny black speck against a sullen sky, and I have dreamed that he flew until the sky was no more, until above him and below him and all about stretched the starless reaches of the infinite. His wings grew weary, and yet he could not rest. He dared not. To stop striving for even one instant would mean falling forever into the depths from which no one can ever return. So desperately he flew on, without hope, until at last a point of light appeared before him and he had hope. And the light grew, and resolved itself, and became a window, and from that window came the sounds of laughter, and the flickering brightness of a hearth fire."

"I too have dreamed of him. The vision is mine also. I saw him enter the great hall through an upper window. Far, far below him men sat drinking and making merry. Dancers danced and minstrels sang for the amusement of a lord and a fine lady, and this lord and this lady knew great joy, heeding not at all the little bird fluttering in the rafters. Here it was safe and warm. Here there was happiness always. The bird would stay. He made to alight upon a beam, but ere his feet touched wood a frigid wind blew in from out of the darkness, and the fire below diminished, and the candles went out. At that moment the dancers were still and the singers silent, and all looked up with unspoken dread, as if a spirit mightier than all of them was passing through their house. And the gust seized the frail, exhausted bird and bore it off along the length of the roof to another window, out into the void again, until the rectangle of light behind had become again a point of a light, then winked out. It was only then that the wind let him go, and once more he flew, helpless and in despair, ignorant of direction in the space beyond reason and time."

"So he was, Sisters. So he shall be always."

"How so?"

"Shall I speak the future of Julian? I know his wyrd."

"No! No! Speak not!" I cried, and in the act of shouting awoke from an evil dream. I had dozed off again in the saddle. I looked around me, confused for a moment. I was riding along the bank of a brown, winding river, and damp ghosts rose from its marshy shore like mist. I knew where I was and whence I had come. Tarnished and one-handed I had ridden, maimed arm hidden

70

beneath a plain black shield, out of the place of dusty death, over the edge of the abyss into a new land which had been green and would be once more, but was not now. It seemed that even as I arrived the warmth of summer departed, as if autumn followed at my back.

The river ended in a field of mud, and when my horse could not make its way I dismounted and led it by the reins, the both of us in up to our knees. Leagues sloshed upon leagues, and slowly the ground hardened once more, drying as it rose away from the swamp. Finally, at the top of a gently sloping hill I came to the hall of a lord.

I shall say little of him. His name was Udreth of The Silver Hand, and he treated me with kindness. He invited me into his house, bade his servants attend me, had his own squire polish my begrimed helmet, mailcoat, and shield, and brought me to his table to sup with his noble guests. Yet I shall speak little of him, for he lived not long.

The circumstance was this: As we sat at a table there came a crashing from without, cries of alarm, and one burst into the room, a giant in red armor with a red beard and a voice that boomed, "Who will fight with me? Who will be your champion?" He cast the servants and guards aside like small children, and had cleared a space when one of our number said, "I claim this fight."

And they fought, and the knight of Udreth's household was slain. Another came to avenge him, and fought with the one in red, and was underthrown. Yet another rose to defend the honor of his lord and his comrades, and fought, and fell, and another, and another. Then the stranger roared, "Enough with boys and old women! I have had no sport yet. Who is the greatest among you?"

A giant came forward, as massive as the intruder, bearing an axe no ordinary man could have lifted. "I am he."

For the first time there was a true contest, and the Red Knight and the giant struggled back and forth across the room, overturning tables and sending lesser folk scrambling for safety. But in the end the giant was wounded in the knee, and he fell down, and the next stroke was to his throat.

"Let there be no more slaughter!" cried Lord Udreth. "All shall not lay down their lives for my sake. If you seek a fight with me, then you shall have it."

The Red Knight said nothing as Udreth took up sword and shield, and he spoke not as they contended, nor as he drove his blade through Udreth's heart. When those left alive saw this they let up a sigh of despair, and broke all form. Some of them charged the Red Knight from all sides, but he slew many as he slew one, with the same supernatural agility and strength. Others sought to escape, and they jammed desperately through the doorways. These too he hewed down, until at last I faced him over a heap of corpses and tumbled benches. I was not of this house, and I had tried to stay out of this feud, but now the Red Knight pointed to me with the tip of his sword and said, "It is you, not these others, that I came to fight."

With resignation I drew my own weapon from its scabbard. "Then I shall defend myself," I said.

"Not here. It shall not take place here. Come to my castle in the wood. Follow the black birds, the kites and the crows."

"When?"

"You shall know the time, and you shall come to me. It has been foreseen."

And with this he left, and the hall was filled with the sound of maidens weeping over the fallen.

II

I was guided through the lands I crossed by a kind of recognition. The shape of a certain hill, the twisted trunks of three trees huddled together in a field against the wind, a new configuration of stones revealed by a sudden bend in the road— these things were already dimly familiar, as if seen in some nearly forgotten dream. I knew that my wanderings were directed, that they had some purpose, and that I could take no other path but the one that led to a certain end.

I had long since lost count of the days, but I knew that the month was October. It felt like October as the snow fell lightly out of the grey sky. There were few towns in that part of the world, and in them no surplus of food, but whenever I spied a lone house, or a cluster of them, I had a meager meal, begged, bought, or stolen from people whose language I could not speak. For many days, perhaps even weeks, I saw no one at all and subsisted on what dried meats I had with me and water from brooks and puddles, and for the most part hunched against the damp wind and starved. Above me from time to time black birds flew north, against the season, and I followed them, for their way was mine.

One steely morning shortly after dawn I topped a rise and descended to the edge of a river, and there I saw the first human being I had beheld in a good while. He stood in a boat beneath a narrow wooden bridge, a bent, snow-haired old man. He seemed to be fishing with a rusted piece of chain.

"Stranger," I asked with some hope that I could get an answer, "know you of a castle hereabouts, wherein dwells the Red Knight of The Wood?"

He looked up at me and laughed through broken teeth. He spoke a crude Latin.

"You're on the right road. There is a wood ahead, but you'd be wise to turn from it."

"Why? What danger is there?"

"You'll find only the Devil in that wood, I tell you. So go somewhere else."

I was neither startled nor afraid hearing this. It seemed fitting, I thought, that I should meet the Devil at the end of my quest.

"But is there a castle in the wood? Do you know?"

The old man said nothing more. His attention was back to his fishing. The chill brown waters flowed around him in silence. I waited a minute, then went the rest of the way over the bridge, in the direction of the forest.

Two more hills stood in my way, and I climbed over them before I came to the wood. First the fields were filled with scrub, and the scrub grew into saplings as I passed deeper into them, then into young trees, until at last the trunks of a thick forest rose over me, silent and black, and a roof of branches swayed in the wind like the fingers of a million hanged men. The way grew very dark, enshadowed in gloom, and I felt as if I had strayed into some long deserted cathedral, or a giant's tomb. The path wound and twisted and left me altogether, and I rode lost beneath the massive boughs throughout the day, until evening came and I found the castle. So overladen with vines and moss was it that it seemed at first to be a natural part of the landscape, but as I gazed upon it and the twilight fell deeper, a light appeared in a window over the battlements, followed by another, and another, until the castle stared down at me like a beast with glowing eyes.

I knocked at the gate.

"Ho there! You inside! What place is this?"

There came shuffling footsteps, and a small barred window was uncovered. A grizzled face looked out, and a voice from within growled, "Away! This place is not for you! Begone!"

Above me, nestled among the rooftops, hundreds of black birds flapped and ruffled their feathers, disturbed by the shouting. They spoke to one another in their own tongue, a harmonious gobble like the murmuring of spirits when a witch passes by.

"Open up!" I demanded. "I have business with the lord of this place. He has summoned me here."

"Summoned to the Red Lord's feast? Well, well, well, that's doleful sport indeed we're to have." The guard let out a low laugh, more a dry wheezing than anything born of mirth. A heavy bar thumped to the ground, and the gate swung inward.

The keeper of the portal was a short, stout, very ugly man with warts and tufts of hair spread across his face. He might almost have been one of the dwarfs of the Northmen, but he seemed less quick. I dismounted and led my horse after him as he shuffled, seeming only half aware of what he was doing, across a snow-packed inner courtyard to a heavy inner door.

He took the reins from me.

"Go in," he grunted. "It's unlocked. I'll watch the animal."

A little dubious, I obeyed him, and pushed on the thick oak. The door gave way before me without effort, swinging on well-oiled hinges, revealing a hallway and another door. The outer one had been plain board, but this one was polished and intricately carven with figures of nymphs and satyrs cavorting in a manner that in another time and at another place I might have called sinful.

The carven door also swung open at my touch, and the light of many torches flooded out over me. The heat from the huge fireplace at the end of the room made the ice on my hair and beard drip. My hands, feet, and face burned as sensation returned to them. My eyes were dazzled, but as I came to see again I perceived a company of perhaps thirty at table with a rich meal laid out before them. All but two were dressed in hooded robes, the hoods drawn up, and those two sat at the head of the table on elevated thrones, a man clad all in red fur, and a lady in flowing black. The man was tall and broad-shouldered, a thicket of rust-colored beard hanging to his chest. The lady was not young, not old, with a face that hinted of beauty. She wore a silver crown on her head; her skin was pale, her eyes a dreaming grey.

The lord motioned me to sit. A place had been prepared for me. He spoke no word until I had tasted his wine and his meat, and then his voice boomed with the blast of battle trumpets, and it echoed and re-echoed down unseen corridors in the depths of the castle.

"It is good that you have come, for it is not without reason, Sir Julian, most aptly named after the Apostate, that I have summoned you here."

I put down my cup. "What? How is this? Had I not come to Udreth's hall by sheerest chance I never would have met you."

"It was not by chance at all," he said.

"And why have I been called here then? What is your design?"

The big man shrugged. "My design? Your head will be cut off this night, or mine. We shall see."

I rose to my feet in amazement and alarm, but as I did every one of the hooded company reached into his garments and drew forth a dagger. Thirty pommels banged down on the table, yet thirty throats remained still.

And the voice of the lady was heard for the first time.

"Sit down, gentle knight," said she. "After you have eaten and regained your strength you shall be tested, as has been planned for a long time."

"Tested? How?"

"As you have already been told."

I addressed the Red Knight, saying, "Am I to kill you then? Have you brought me all this way by whatever means you have used just for that? Of all the things I have seen or heard in all my wanderings this is the strangest. Have I come to a second Bedlam? Are you all mad here?"

"Madness is the order of the day," the lord replied. "Even God is mad. We follow divine example."

"You blaspheme!"

"Since when, Julian," smiled the lady, "has the good name of God on High been of any concern to you? You and He have parted ways, have you not?"

"You seem to know everything," I muttered, and sat down. I said no more and ate. Under different circumstances I might have savored the food, but then I did not. The others dined also, in silence, and when all were finished no servants came to clear the tables.

The lord rose and left the room. After an uneasy moment in which I did not know what was expected of me, the lady bade me follow her out the way I had come, into the yard. There, she said, the contest would take place. The hooded ones came also, taking torches down from the walls.

"Tell me," I asked, "what is required of me?"

"If you win," said she, "many things are required of you. If you lose, nothing more."

"Your wisdom is like Solomon's," I said bitterly.

As we came to the courtyard the torchbearers spread themselves out around the edges of the open space. My horse had been prepared in the proper trappings for a joust. I was given a long wooden lance and a helmet with a visor to replace my simple steel cap. I mounted, took spear in hand, and waited, looking expectantly toward the lady, who stood in silence. The impossible impulse to escape came over me. I wanted to dig spurs into flanks and bolt off *somewhere*, but I was hemmed in. The gate was still closed, I would have to fight, and I knew from what I had seen in Udreth's hall that I could never survive.

Just then the gate opened, and the Red Knight entered from without, astride a powerful roan steed draped in red cloth. He himself wore painted armor, and a scarlet banner flapped from the end of his lance. He trotted around the courtyard once, surveying me, then he lowered his lance and visor, and charged without warning. Almost too late I countered him. My horse shrieked as we met the enemy with a crash. My shaft splintered on his shield, but his point glanced off mine and passed by unbroken. As he turned to come at me again I looked around desperately for a page with a fresh lance for me, but there was none. I should have expected as much.

The Red Knight's spearpoint drove at me again, and as best I could I fended it off with my broken stick. I fenced with half a lance, beating his thrust aside, thankful that the courtyard afforded him little room to get his horse up to a gallop which would have made his attack unbeatable. I swung at him absurdly, missed, nearly lost my perch in the saddle, and the unspent force sent the wooden handle flying from my grasp. Now I had only sword and shield against my foe, and still no weapon was offered me, as would have been in civilized sport. The Red Knight bore down upon me, and with the greatest luck I fended him off with shield alone. His lance caught behind my shield, bent, and snapped, but the force was enough to make my horse stagger to its knees and to send me somersaulting to the ground.

I landed unhurt on the hard snow, shieldless, sword still in hand, and sprang to my feet just in time to raise my blade aloft and catch that of my enemy upon it. Sparks flew as the two edges bit into one another. The Red Knight howled in triumph and rode around and around faster than I could turn to ward him off, trying to get behind me, trying to make me dizzy, and I could do no more than just stay alive from one instant to the next, with all hope of attack gone. He beat me back and down, and my legs buckled beneath the force of his strokes. I dropped to my knees, exhausted, and I knew that his next blow would be the last.

But to my astonishment he never delivered it. He reined his horse to a stop and dismounted. I stared dumbly. He stood before me and commanded, "Rise Julian."

And I rose, just barely able to stay on my feet.

And he knelt, removing his helmet. He cast his sword away. One of the hooded ones jumped to avoid it. Metal clanged against stone.

"Do what you must," he said, and he spread his arms out from his body.

I raised my sword, then paused, utterly dumbfounded.

"Can you not kill a defenseless man?" laughed the Red Knight. "May death never be handed to you? Must you win fairly always and earn the blood of another? Does some strange sense of honor hold you back? I must know."

"It is not honor which holds him back," laughed the lady. "It is fear. He fears some subtle treachery of magic."

"Nay!" snorted the Red Knight. "It is only out of fear that he can kill at all. I resist not and he stands there as if enchained—"

With one stroke I cut off his head. It was a motion of the arm, not the will. I was aware of the action only after I felt the impact of the sword's edge against his neck the bone snapping, the blade passing free.

The head dropped to the ground, and the body fell forward. I stepped aside quickly to let it fall, and then amazement came to me once more.

There was no blood. Nothing spouted from the severed neck. The corpse lay still for perhaps the count of three, and then, to my further horror, to my complete incomprehension, began to move. Hands groped for the head, and finding it, the fingers entwined themselves in the hair. The thing—I could no longer think of it as a man—rose unsteadily to its feet. As the head hung at the level of the right knee, it spoke with the same thundering voice I had heard when I entered the hall.

77

"Mother Witch Eternal, he has passed the test."

The Red Knight staggered blindly into the castle, carrying his head.

I turned to the lady, but it was she who spoke.

"Yes, Julian, I am a witch, but how can you be surprised? You are not unacquainted with witches."

"Be quiet!"

"No matter. Your past may be forgotten. The future alone concerns me. I ask you this, knowing already the answer: Were you not at the Holy City when the army of the faithful burst in? Did you not yourself partake in the slaughter of the pagans, and the women and infants of the pagans, those who were born in lands where the gospel never reached? Did you not do this and much more, all for the glory of God? And does not that same All Mighty and All Merciful God damn men for sins of weakness and ignorance when He himself made them imperfect and prone to weakness, and taught them not so that they remained ignorant? Did He not allow the serpent to enter the Garden, make no move to stop it, then punish severely his beguiled servants?"

"Lady, as you said, you know the answers. All these things are true."

"Then I ask you, Julian, are these actions of a loving God?"

"I—I—don't—"

"*Know!* But you do. This knowledge is the heritage of all men. You know they are not, and yet more shall you know. God is mad, Julian. He babbles on his throne of light, and the sound of his gurgling fills his angels with fear. He sends them forth with flaming swords to raze the cities of men, and when thousands upon thousands have been slain, and the smoke of their pyres rises into the heights of the sky, when pestilence and famine slay thousands more, then God laughs and roars like some mindless beast, 'THIS IS PLEASING TO ME!'"

"Why do you tell me these things? Why have I been brought here?"

"Because you are to join us in our war against the Father. He has grown weak in his madness, so preoccupied with dreaming new ways to torture men that he will not notice when the very gates of Hell fly open and the armies of his old Adversary issue forth. They are with us this night—"

"Here?"

"Look! Look beyond the gate!"

I turned, and beheld at first nothing but the forest and its attendant shadows. But then the shadows began to writhe, to assume life and separate out from the darkness of the wood. At the edge of the trees a vast sea of faces appeared, all hollow and white with eyeless sockets and sunken cheeks. They wore helms of rusted metal, held up tarnished swords, shields, and spears with their bony hands, and walked toward me on skeletal legs. Without the sound of a single footstep this host came closer, till the vanguard stood in the arch of the gateway, and then all of them vanished at once and the wood was empty. Only the wind swayed the treetops.

"This is your army? Phantoms?"

"On the last day they shall walk the Earth in resurrected flesh. They are souls, Julian, the souls of every warrior who ever battled against God, and with them the demons who were cast down of old. This time the victory will be theirs. Ours. Yours, if you will join us."

"Lady, who are you that says these things to me?"

"The Queen of Fay, driven from her kingdom by the scourge of the cross? Do you believe?"

"I believe—"

"Then do not believe, Julian. Belief comes too easily. Know then that I am Mary, once virgin, raped by a jealous God and made to bear a child that was his and never mine. When he was done with me he sent me out from Heaven to walk the face of the Earth undying until time itself shall come to a stop. And I, like the wiser ones before me, have turned against him. Join us now, Julian. It will be glorious in the end, when the universe is remade!"

I stood silently for a long time, while the torches of the robed men guttered in the wind, and the two horses stamped their feet and neighed uneasily. I trembled as the inevitable words within me fought for release.

"No," I said slowly, "I do not wish to join you. I want no part of further strife. I have fought too long and am weary of battle. I seek only a place where my soul can rest, beyond all pain and labor and fear. That is all."

"There is no such place, O poor, lost, foolish knight. The other gods are dead, and against the Tyrant there can be only war. You will be crushed between the hammer of God and the anvil of the Devil when the day of Armageddon comes. Embrace us. Become one with us, and you shall live."

"No, this cause is not for me."

"Then you must go, to find your fate and perish by it. Slaves we have enough already. We need your will, whole and free, for this mighty undertaking."

I assumed I could leave. I walked over to where my horse stood and led it by the bridle out of the castle. As I passed the gatekeeper he suddenly cried out in alarm, "Dawn! Dawn is come!" And they who had been standing quietly all this time let out a cry of anguish, dropped their torches into the snow, and fled behind the carven door.

The lady came to me, and as she did her step ceased to be graceful. She hobbled, bent over, and when she drew near I saw that she had changed. She was no longer even slightly beautiful, but wrinkled and foul, her nose bending over her toothless mouth almost to her chin.

She held up a bony fist and said, "I could take your soul like this and crush it, aye, strangle it until all life is gone. But I shall not. Go your way and wander your way until we meet once more on the last day. Then ask no mercy from me. Now mount quickly and be gone."

I obeyed her and climbed into the saddle. I rode a short way, then looked back.

The castle had vanished, replaced by a huge *face*, a hell's mouth stretched wide. Within I saw towers and battlements all aflame, and mountains, rivers, and plains of fire. I saw the souls of ten thousand million warriors in unending torment, and among them the lady, again young, and beside her the Red Knight who held himself by the locks still.

For the last time I cried out, "Lady, who are you?"

"It will be glorious, Julian! Glorious!" came the reply, and then she was gone. Behind her, far away, filling the skies that were not of Earth, was the face of another, a mountainous Dark One who sat awash in a lake of molten metal with a sword in his hand. When I gazed upon him I knew the truth of all. I knew that if God is mad, and the signs show that he is, his Foe is mad also, and there can be no hope for the world between them, for creation is but a battleground for two maniacs in their death struggle.

The face, the great face enclosing all, bellowed with the collective voices of all within it, and the forest shook. The hot breath beat on my back as my panicked steed galloped away. I fled, sick with the knowledge I bore, seeking an escape when I knew there could be none.

I fared through the still darkened wood for a long time. Night lingers there longer than it does in fields cleared by men. Often the trail was lost, and the way was never straight. Then at last I spied grey sky ahead and emerged into open ground as dawn dimly brightened the east. I met a peasant coming over the field who was somewhat afraid of anyone who would come out of these trees on the morning after All Hallows (for so the night had been) and I asked him what land this was, and which lay beyond. He told me and I rode past him until I came to a highway, to a bridge, and a town. I stopped, bought food, rested, then continued on my journey. At length I came to another wood, and when I was alone in its shadows the voices inside my head began to stir.

"Sisters, the dream is over."

"It is finished."

"Is it?"

I cried out and they were again silent, and I went on my way to the reaches where all maps end, where charts dissolve into hordes of monsters.

7

The Riddle of the Horn...

"The Ice King is abroad tonight," the man who had just entered the inn said as he held his hands out before the fire. As the light flickered over him his frozen beard cracked, and snow fell from his clothing.

"Aye," someone agreed. "Near Himmel's Fork a great oak was uprooted by the Ice King's sword, which is the wind, and it fell down the cliff onto the river. There it shattered into a million splinters, but the surface did not break."

They talked on, as if about some specific person, not a figurative lord of winter. My curiosity was awakened.

"Who is this king?"

There were a dozen men in the room. All were silent and genuinely astonished.

"You mean you do not know?" the man who had spoken first said at last.

"I mean I do not know. I arrived here but this evening."

"Then listen, stranger, and listen well, for all must know the tale of the Ice King if they hope to survive even a single winter of his reign. Of old there were two unworthy brothers, both of them very wicked, both of them magicians of fabulous power. One of them was filled with hot fury, the other vicious, cruel, delighting in slow torture as his brother delighted in total devastation. More than anything else they hated one another, and they fought a vast war with all the nations of the earth as their pawns, drawing strength from the forces akin to their natures, from ice and from fire, from winter and from summer. One cast oceans of flame upon the lands, which consumed men, beasts, and forests. The other poured snow and dropped mountains of ice from the clouds. They would have destroyed the world, had not the enchanter Merlin, in the days before he was famous, when he was newly born and old and very wise, put a stop to their struggle. He was more powerful than both, and he brought them to their knees before him. But even he could not kill them or take their magic away completely, so instead he weakened them as much as he could and placed around the neck of each a horn, which if blown will bring about the destruction of the one brother at the hands of the other. So now each of them roams the world in pursuit of his brother, seeking to capture the horn without losing his own that he may triumph."

"And how is it, as you said, that the Ice King is abroad in this land on this night?"

At this some of the listeners laughed. Some shivered and shook themselves.

"Can't you tell? Is your skin steel that you feel not the cold? Have you no ears to hear the wind howling down from the ice

84

fields in the mountains? On a night such as this, I tell you, no man, Christian or otherwise, should be out of doors, for on such a night the King rides with his host seeking mortal folk. With his touch he freezes them, then carries off their souls to be used as stones in his castle in the place called The Center of The Storm, from which all winter winds blow."

I raised an eyebrow. "In my own country we have the season, yet no one has heard of any Ice or Fire Kings." I cursed myself inwardly even as I said this. All those around me became angry at the assumed insult. I had implied that they were liars. I needed no more trouble. I had enough already, and my tongue had gotten me into it.

"Do you think us fools, hook-hand?" one of them spat.

I tried to patch things up as best I could.

"No. Pray, forgive me. I am a stranger here. I have been in this country but one day. How can I claim to know better than you who have lived here all your lives?"

In my nervousness I had driven the hook on the stump of my left wrist deep into the table at which I was seated. With my right hand I pulled it free. Everyone winced when it came out with a thump, but they seemed pacified. Embarrassed, I hid the hook in my lap under a fold of my cloak. The room was silent then, except for the crackling of the hearth fire.

In any case, no one had a chance to say much more, because it was then that my first woe caught up with me. With a crash and a gust of frigid air which reached even where we were gathered, the outer door of the inn burst open and a voice I knew thundered, "Has anyone seen Julian, the apostate knight, whose hand was bitten off by a devil, the one who has spilled blood in Vitushall? Our task it is to chase after and slay him."

I leapt from my seat, shoving astonished folk out of my way. I had no time to snatch up my shield. My sword I fortunately had with me. I had been too much on guard to take it off. Even as my pursuers entered the room from one end I was out the other, scrambling through the kitchen, knocking over a cursing cook and spilling the pot of soup he carried, then wading through an enclosure filled with chickens and pigs until I was outside in the snow. I reached the stable while there was still shouting and confusion behind me, grabbed a saddle and threw it over my horse, then tore it off again when I saw I had no time for that, and rode the unbridled steed bareback into the wind and darkness with ten furious knights close behind me.

Indeed, I had killed a man in another town. He was an arrogant braggart of high birth. For two hours I sat across a room listening to him as his wine cup brought more and more incredible lies out of him. According to his account he had conducted the Crusade all by himself, personally slain every pagan Satan had ever smiled upon, and at last, as if that were not enough, been singularly honored with a miraculous vision of the Virgin in which he had learned of his own future as the one who would teach righteousness to all Christendom by means of an epic poem he would be inspired to write. He called for a harp and one was brought, and he began to sing—or croak really since his voice was fit only for a swamp at night—a verse or two of his allegedly wondrous creation, whereupon I could stand no more and demanded of him why his hands lacked the hardness known to all but the pampered, why his face showed not the touch of the desert heat, why he described wrongly many things in the East which I had seen (he thought the Sphinx was a kind of dog) and why, above all, his poetry was such drivel.

He screamed curses at me in a manner quite unlike one worthy to be chosen by the Virgin for anything, and drew his sword. I had been on the road for a long time. I was alone, friendless, and no one present knew me. My clothing was tattered, my mail tarnished and broken, and this young fool would not believe that I was a knight at all. He said I had robbed the dead, that I was no more than a beggar to be cursed and kicked and hanged on a pole by the crossroads.

He came at me with his blade swinging viciously and amateurishly, and I had no choice but to fight him. As a trained warrior I fought, not with my mind but with my arm and eyes, and I did it as in battle, responding too fast even to think. I would have wanted to prick and disarm him, slaughtering only his pride, but I parried and thrusted instinctively to prevent my opponent from skewering me, and made short work of him. As he lay pale and gasping in the arms of his stunned friends, with his life's blood pouring unstoppably onto the floorboards, I fled, before they could recover their wits and charge at me as one.

But in time they did recover, and they did come, and that was how I came to be clinging precariously, with my fingers numb as they dug to the roots of the mane, to my unsaddled horse on the bitterest of all January nights, racing through knee-deep snow over roads and fields I had never seen before, with death at my heels in the form of a crew of vengeful swordsmen.

The snow fell so thickly that it seemed to hang in the air like lacy curtains; the wind was a volley of arrows. My ears and face were bereft of feeling almost at once. I was vaguely aware of ice forming in my hair. My head was numb, and yet I was intensely aware of what was going on, terrified and simultaneously furious at the thought of being captured and put to death like some common criminal. I hated nothing more than the prospect of ending my days at the hands of others. It was not that I was afraid to die, but that it was *my* life and *my* fate to be decided, and *my* soul to be sent to perdition when the Judge Eternal stood before me in the end, and I would come to that end of my long journey by my own means, on my own terms, when I knew that my time was up. I would come independently, of my own will and hopefully to some purpose, not in some back country field, slain by apes in repayment for the killing of a monkey.

The only things I could feel were the cold throughout my chest and back and thighs and the motion of the horse beneath me as it bumped up and down over the snow-buried roughness of the terrain. The wind blew and blew, yet its howling seemed to fade from my frozen ears until all was silent and the chase was a thing of dream, my foemen dark, shadowy spirits.

I looked over my shoulder to see if they were still there, and they were. They were out in the open now, and I could see them clearly against the white of the snow and the gray of the sky. How long we rode I can never know. The snow drifted and swirled like waves on a gale-tossed sea. All around me trees bent and swayed, their branches reached for me like a million brittle fingers. Perhaps my foemen called out something to me or to one another. Their voices were lost in the storm. Perhaps I screamed back in something others would call madness, but the night swallowed the sound.

The fields ended. The last farmhouse was behind us and the forest closed in from all sides. Now branches whipped and raked my face. I huddled low to avoid them, but dared not raise a hand— or even a hook—to ward them off, lest I lose my grip. All of us crashed through the underbrush, and suddenly there was sound again. The trees shielded us somewhat from the wind and snow. The voice of the storm was above us and far away, among the uppermost boughs, which threatened to snap and come crashing down. I could hear my enemies shouting, "There he is!" "No, I've lost him!" "There again!" "This way! Follow me!"

My steed ran where it would. I could not control it, did not want to; it served me well. Gradually the shouts fell behind and I was alone with the cold, with the trunks towering above me like colossal black pillars holding up the forest roof, but then I was betrayed. A particularly large and low branch loomed before me, and I was swept from my mount. I might have hung on had I reins and stirrups, but bareback, I was unhorsed in an instant and flung through the air.

I landed in the soft snow unhurt, the breath knocked out of me. I looked around. I was still alone. Not even a trace of the

departed animal. I was as solitary as Adam newly created. But then my enemies were upon me, the racket of their passing on all sides. Some saplings parted and there was one of them shouting at the sight of me. He charged; I drew my sword, the blade pierced his horse and it reared up, throwing him. He disappeared into the wood, dragged by a foot caught in a stirrup, screaming at first and then silent. Another came and our blades met, clanged and sparked. He rode around and around me, seeking to get behind me for a swift and killing stroke. I slashed with my hook-hand while fending off his blows, and left him struggling to remain in the saddle. I broke free from his circle and escaped through thick bushes, under a leaning tree, running where he could not easily follow. In the confusion and darkness and storm, I eluded him. Once I huddled behind a stump as he rode within arm's reach of me, but then he was past and I was able to head swiftly in the opposite direction.

I was sure I was not free of them. I felt as the stag must feel when the hunt is nearly done: hunters all around, the woods alive with danger, any safety only momentary. In an instant they would come together, surround me, and I would not be able to evade so many, or fight them for more than one or two strokes. They would not do me the honor of personal combat, one man to one man. They wanted blood and revenge and nothing more. They would be as relentless as a pack of wolves after the prey has been run down.

The fighting, the riding, and the running through the snow was exhausting. My breath came in painful, hoarse gasps. My heart seemed ready to explode in my breast. My feet were burning with cold, while my hands and arms were numb. I had to look to see that I still held my sword. I could no longer grasp it tightly. This was the end. For all my horror at such a fate, this was the end. I would never leave this forest except perhaps slumped over a horse, my head aloft on a spear. I would fight. I would take any I could down with me into the flames, but ultimately the victory would be theirs.

Strangely there was never any combat. I went on for what must have been an hour or more and nothing happened. I could run no more. I slowed to a walk, then to a stagger. I sat on a log to catch my breath. I began to feel comfortable. My feet no longer bothered me. The wind was far away. I wanted to lie down in the white bed of the earth and sleep.

The hilt fell from my stiff fingers, and the sword dropped into a snowdrift with a whisper. The sensation alerted me. I snapped out of my reverie, picked up the sword, and got to my feet. If men could not trap me, I swore, neither could the elements. I would not be so beguiled. I had to keep moving, I knew. I stamped my feet, hoping for some feeling, but still they remained leaden weights. If I stayed in one place, if I dozed off, the cold would finish me as surely as any nine men (for that many remained, so I thought). An icy death with winter my murderer was less appalling, but I wanted to live. It was not yet my time.

A while later I came upon one of my pursuers, then another, and another. There was no fight. Not a weapon was raised. In the darkness I must have circled around and returned the way I had come, back toward them, or else they had gotten in front of me. I had no idea, but I found them and their horses lying dead in the snow, frozen hard as wood as if they had been there for a long time, or had been blasted like Sennacherib's army by some sudden and lethal breath.

It was unnatural. There was no other explanation. Eventually I discovered six corpses, all in the same condition, and I had little doubt as to the state of the missing three. It was then that I was reminded of what the man at the inn had said about the Ice King hunting souls in the night. Still I was not safe. If anything, my peril had increased. I walked on, filled with expectant dread.

And the wind blew and blew.

The night would not end. The hours came and went in slow succession and dawn, I was sure, was long overdue, but there was not even the faintest glow in whatever direction might be the east. It seemed as if the lamp of the sun had gone out, leaving the earth condemned to darkness and cold forever. I thought of the prophecies made by Christ in Matthew's gospel, of how there would be such gloom right before the end of all things, and I wondered fancifully and half believing—could this be the time of judgment? Yes, it would be fitting. I with the stain of a rash murder on my soul, I the cause of ten more deaths, would face my disappointed Creator without any preparation.

I wandered on, not daring to return to the inn, even if I could have found it, or approach any inhabited place thereabouts. Surely the alarm was out by now, and swords and spears would greet me at any door. So I bent forward against the wind and shivered in my stolen second cloak and fur hat. Gloves also I had taken from the dead men. These seemed to help a little, but not much. I had to look down occasionally to reassure myself that my feet were still on the ends of my ankles, for I had no feeling below the thighs. And all around me the night laughed, the throat of the sky spewing down its bitter breath.

A snowdrift was not a snowdrift; from afar I saw it,

definitely a half-buried wall, part of a ruined fortress perhaps, something behind which I could find shelter from the wind, if only for an instant. But when I came closer it was sloping, soft, and white. My eyes had deceived me.

Before me, with increasing frequency, flickered ephemeral towers and battlements and gates, like mirages in a desert. I knew them for illusions at once and thought this my last dream. What had truly come to pass? Had I ever left the log where I had once sat down, where the sword had fallen so easily from my nearly dead fingers? Had I escaped the ten riders in actual fact, or had they felled me with their swords? Was this the last imagining of a failing brain as I lay face down in the snow, my life's blood a brown stain in the uncertain light? How could I know? Perhaps my exhausted body had invented such a fantasy to delude and satisfy the will, so the limbs would never be called on to labor again.

The trees of earth, those which were solid and not phantoms of the snow, thinned out as I left the forest and moved into open country once again. It was foolish for me to do so, but as soon as they were out of sight—and they were almost at once—all directions looked the same and the only real thing was the agony of the cold and of further motion. The wind stung my face with renewed fury, sweeping long and far over rolling hills and fields, no longer broken or held back by ancient trunks. I was without destination, like a corpse bobbing on an endless sea.

The wind alone was my guide, and I seemed to suffer less if I kept it to my back and went where it would have me: always downhill, into some vast bowl of a valley, into the mouth of the night, into the blizzard's belly. And around me rose shapes fantastical before my weary eyes, whole cities of ice and snow, filled with rustling crystalline spirits, and there were mountains, castles, frozen rivers like beaten silver highways, and beasts known only to madness and to dream—snow dragons, mantichores with teeth of ice, horses of white cloud, birds with wide and lacy wings, a mile-long serpent glittering with jeweled scales and yet semi-transparent, as if it had been carven from a single perfect piece of glass. These things became more substantial, more real, and I less. I was in their country now, and to them I was the fading dream. This was not the world of mankind any longer.

Suddenly overhead the sky lit up with flashing sheets of lightning. No thunder followed, just a glow like pagan Valkyries riding home with the souls of the slain over their saddles. Then faintly, in the aftermath of the light, my faltering ears seemed to detect hoofbeats clattering across the hidden arch of the sky, and also the jangling of bridles and stirrups, the wordless shouts of voices, and the barking of hounds.

Again hours seemed to crawl past and the dawn still refused to come. After a time, I don't know how long, I found myself in the courtyard of a palace, with no memory of having entered. Perhaps the wind had blinded me and I had stumbled unknowingly through an open gate, and now, partially shielded by the walls, my sight had returned. Or perhaps I had merely blinked, and in the space of that instant the walls had grown up, and the towers also, all of them glowing with that same light I had seen in the sky, with diamond roofs aflame as if beneath the bright gaze of the moon. Before me a great keep stood luminescent against the gray sky and the white storm. Was this another vision, or a solid thing? There was a door like that on the front of a cathedral. I touched it and found it to be made of a light, smooth metal. It yielded and swung wide, and I entered through an arched portal and left outside whatever doubts I had as to where I was.

The winter wind had brought me to its master. I was in the hall of the Ice King.

He sat against the far wall between two clear pillars, on a throne of glowing glass, as if he had poured all the lightning on which he rode into it for safekeeping. He was short and hunchbacked, almost a crooked dwarf, his face mapped with countless wrinkles. I thought how grotesque he would look astride a horse. His skin was pale and his hair and beard the purest white, and yet he was not decrepit with all his years. He was eternal. He had conquered age, and time itself knelt at his feet.

Behind him stood his knights leaning on their glistening silver swords, fifteen stout champions, their beards, like their master's, hoary with aeons and frost. Behind them hung a tapestry of sewn snowflakes on a wall of jagged, curving ice, more like the inside of an arctic cavern than a room.

The King showed surprise at the sight of me. He rose, leaning on a thin, intricately carven staff and climbed down the steps before his throne, hobbling toward me. He swayed sideways as he walked. His motion reminded me of a crab. At his side a pale gray horn hung by a strap, thumping against his leg as he moved. It must have been a nuisance, but I knew that the people at the inn had spoken truthfully and he couldn't take it off.

Bent as he was, the Ice King came to the middle of my chest when he stood before me. His beard curled a mere span above the floor. He looked up and spoke, and his breath was a chilling blast, even to my numbed face.

Before he uttered any words, the King laughed cruelly. Then he said, "Foolish warm one, how good of you to come and give yourself up to me!"

Then he hopped back a pace clumsily, more like a toad than a man, as if nearness to me offended him, and he continued.

"But—in a way it is not so good. You have ruined my sport. It will be no accomplishment to take you here."

I had to think quickly, and could not. My mind was still befuddled with wonder and dread, and I wished I had met my death honestly, on the swords of the ten earthly knights, rather than here at the touch of the Ice King.

Almost as if to answer my thought, he took a little tinkling bell out of his pocket, and at the sound of this shapes came to him from the far corners of the hall, rising from the floor like smoke.

Once more he laughed. "You'll walk with these my minions before long."

First there were ten known to me, the knights who had sought my life. Their ghosts marched slowly and with resignation past their new master, looking neither to the right nor to the left. If they recognized me, they showed no sign. When they reached the far side of the hall there was a tunnel which had not been there before—it had opened up while my attention was distracted—and this swallowed them up. Then came three female dancers, whirling, as delicate as snowflakes, and they rose into the air as softly as burnt leaves in the smoke of an autumn fire, and in the shadows above they were gone. After them were fifty or more sailors, lost somewhere on the ice floes of an arctic sea, walking stiffly, as rigid as the physical bodies they had left behind. And more came, until I had seen hundreds of folk, all felled by the Ice King's hand. Then he rang his bell again and the room was empty again save for the King, myself, and his grim lords.

"Enough of this. Enough," he said. He walked around me several times, stroking his beard as he looked me over in rapt fascination, like a learned doctor who has discovered a new and curious tree. He came to a halt in front of me once more, banged his staff impatiently on the floor and barked, "Well, I cannot hunt you here, so there's no sport at all."

And he reached to claim me as his own.

"Wait! Majesty!" I said, and his hand paused. "There is a challenge yet. I challenge you to—"

"To what? Swords? Axes? Mace and shield? I am master of them all. Shall I joust with you?"

"None of these things." My heart raced. My mind was scant seconds ahead of my tongue. I was running along the only possible avenue of escape, and I could not see what lay ahead. "We shall cross wits, Majesty, not swords."

"Wits? What mean you?"

"Riddles. I challenge you to a contest of riddles." It was an impossible, impetuous thing. As a young man, when the long and inactive winters had come, I spent the days in my father's castle over the chessboard, at song with the lute, writing poetry, and also at riddles. As a child I had been called the Wicked Clever One because I knew more riddles than anyone else and could invent ones that no other could answer. But his now was not a game.

"Ha! Riddles!" snorted the King. "Yes, I am very good at riddles. So good am I that the rules of our contest shall vary from the ordinary. It shall not be that you ask me a riddle and then I ask one of you, and the winner shall be the one who answers the most correctly. No, you shall ask all the riddles—fifty—and if I fail to answer even one, you may have your life and whatever you wish of me."

I knew by his manner that I was not being given any vast advantage.

The King scrambled up the steps and onto his throne, then sat, faced me, and waited for the first riddle. And, testing his reflexes like a swordsman with an unfamiliar opponent, I spoke my first:

"A wondrous creature am I,
With a hoard of gold between my horns.
I build my fortress among the mountains,
Among the clouds that sometimes mask me.
But my foe climbs over the mountains and banishes the clouds.
I flee before him into the dark cloak of my mother.
The eyes of my little brothers wink out.
Name both of us."

The King sighed, as if profoundly bored, and then the sides of his mouth curved up a little bit. Perhaps it was a sneer, or the beginnings of a smile, or just a twitch. He held out a closed hand, then opened it and released gently into the air two shining orbs which hung suspended before him. One burned like a little torch. The other was silver and gold and rugged, and it merely glowed.

"You have correctly answered my riddle," I said, and the miniature sun and moon vanished.

My second riddle was this:

"My birthing song is the clangor of battle.
Strife has shaped me.
I am a great treasure, a thing of valor,
An instrument of mighty deeds for him who holds me.

94

Yet if I myself am broken and slain none shall avenge me.
Another shall stand high in my place, my glories forgotten.
Women are not for me, nor I for them.
I must enjoy only the company and bold deeds of heroes.
One end of me is like God's tree.
In his sign I have always conquered,
Cut the mail and shield of my foe
With my great tooth.
Name me."

Again the King's expression seemed to say he regarded this as simplistic. He snapped his fingers, and out of the air appeared a two-handed sword, beautifully decorated.

"This is Excalibur," he said. "I took it from Arthur when his arm could no longer wield it. When he was cold it came to me."

Thus was my second riddle answered. My third was that of the unicorn, and he answered it, my fourth of the whale and he answered it, my fifth of the basilisk, my sixth of the holy stone of the Tigris, and these too were known to him. I drew all I had from my store of riddles, and all of them failed me. Some of the most difficult ones, ones which had stumped the court for a month—for I had once held out that long, reminding the lords and ladies each day that they had not yet unravelled my words—caused him to frown and ponder a few seconds, to wrinkle his brow as if in deep thought, then burst out with an answer that was always completely correct.

When I came to the forty-ninth riddle and he solved it, I knew he was toying with me. He smiled patronizingly, like a master against someone who has never played a game before. This wasn't even practice for him, but something as easy and unthinking as breathing. I think it was in jest that he answered my last question the way he did. I had given up. I knew the situation was hopeless, and so straightforward and direct was my final riddle:

"From my men drink mead.
From men I drink blood.
On the head of my master I am a mighty ornament,
An armament feared in battle.
Sometimes men kiss me.
Sometimes I call them to fame and to their deaths.
The doom of Roland came from my throat.
Ask what is my name."

Without any hesitation the King asked, "Yes, tell me your

name."

"Your Majesty...taunts me...It is over. You have won."

"No, no, your riddle has defeated me. You have won."

I had never been so astonished. Hope awoke—and then I knew this for another and more subtle deception.

"Do what you will," I said.

"Do what *you* will. I am yours to command."

Still unbelieving, I said to myself: Nothing can be lost, for everything already is. When the lion comes to the edge of the cliff the hunters expect him to jump, but sometimes he does the unexpected and charges with a fury they never imagined he possessed. It is a hopeless assault, but fearsome. Despair brings added strength.

And boldly I walked up the steps to where the King sat. The knights stirred, but he raised a hand and they lowered their swords once more. He was finding the game amusing. Imagine how a cat would feel if suddenly the wounded mouse got up and danced.

I knelt before the feet of the Ice King.

"Majesty, the answer to my riddle is Horn, and it is my wish to lay my hands on your sacred horn and swear fealty to you and serve you all the days of my life and beyond. Mankind has cast me out, so I come to you that I may ride with you until the Last Day, and be revenged upon my enemies."

Now for once I was a step ahead of my nemesis. It was his turn to be amazed. He had started in alarm when I mentioned his horn, but he still sat there staring at me. And he was still sitting when suddenly I lunged forward and grabbed the horn.

Of course the strap didn't break. I yanked and the King tumbled forward onto me squawking like a speared chicken, and together we rolled down the steps. The fifteen knights had their swords on high in a single motion, but they could not strike lest they wound their lord, so the two of us wrestled and before they could even attempt to untangle us I had the horn away from him. I rolled to one side, nearly strangling the Ice King with the strap, and even though the coldness of it burned my lips I put the instrument to my mouth and blew as hard as I possibly could, until all the breath was out of me and I limply let the horn drop out of my hand, ready for the guardians to slay me if they would.

But they did not. The whole palace shook with the note I had blown, and the King and the knights looked up in fear. I was forgotten. Without meeting any resistance I was able to crawl free of the King, get to my feet, and run a short distance. Then I turned to see what held their attention so.

The roof of the hall was melting. Water dripped down onto

the face of the King and froze again, forming weird streaks on his cheeks and icicles in his beard. And then the roof exploded in a million fragments, then into teardrops and vapor, and a stairway of pure flame descended and another entered the room, one as old and bent as the Ice King but otherwise his opposite, dark, without hair or beard, burnt smooth as forged iron. When he opened his mouth clouds of flame billowed. The fifteen raised their swords and charged him, but he held out his hand and when they touched him each vanished in a puff of steam. All around the walls of the palace, the pillars, and the floor were all melting and flowing away, trying to escape the unquenchable heat. The snowflake tapestry vanished faster than the eye could see. The throne fell down over the King and joined the boiling lake which was forming in the center of the room.

The air was filled with steam and I could see little. I fled from that place, lest the fires consume me as the cold nearly had. When last I saw the Ice King he was in the arms of his hated brother, locked in mortal combat, the two of them rolling and tumbling as he and I had.

Again I passed through the walls of the castle unaware, only this time because they melted before me. The snows of the surrounding hills became torrents, suddenly pouring down upon me. I desperately sought the high ground. Now I was in the lowest place, in the middle of the newly born lake. Even the sky seemed aflame and all creation was running, running, splashing over me. My fingers found a boulder and I clung to it for a long while as the waters raged around me, as mud and smaller stones were washed by. Then I felt it coming loose. It had been undermined from beneath, and I got clear before it rolled down the slope. Somehow I prevailed against the current and fought my way out of the swirling whirlpool to the top of a hill, where I could stop and rest. As far as I could see there was flooding, as all the snows of winter yielded before the searing heat. In the distance other hills stood aloft like islands.

Far below a horn blew, another horn. The Ice King had copied my own stratagem, and a second doom was sealed. The fires went out, and steam ceased to rise from the center of the waters. Everything was still.

A while later the sun rose on a barren land, devoid of forests and the workings of men. The inn where I had stopped, the houses I had passed, and the castles of my enemies all had been stripped away. Only on the tops of the hills did anything remain where the Creator had originally placed it. Below, Noah's flood had come again.

The waters receded enough by afternoon for me to leave that

country, and I did, walking until dusk when it began to grow cold once more and my soaked clothing brought new pain. But this time I did not have to go very far before I found sanctuary in an abbey of Hospitalers, whose self-assigned task it was to shelter and succor all who came to them. They muttered among themselves in wonder when they saw that I had both frostbite and burns at the same time, and came to them in garments frozen stiff as wood, but they carried me to a bed, healed me with sweet oils, and brought food and drink.

I am unable to say how long I dwelt among them, but I do know that when at last I left the air was balmy and comfortably warm, and there were but a few patches of old snow on the ground between which tiny blue flowers bloomed.

So now the tale is done. What moral? There was in the abbey a learned man who insisted that all things have a greater meaning, that life is but a symbol of motions on a higher plane. Nothing, he said, is random. Nothing is without purpose. Yet I blundered into my adventure and out of it, seeking only to save my own life. I came to the only place a wretched fugitive could have come on such a night, and my escape was miracle enough. A meaning? A purpose? When others, as the ballads tell, pass into Faerie, or into the lands of the dead, it is for some lofty purpose, to learn some deep wisdom, or to rescue a loved one, or to save a kingdom. It was not like that with me. My life will make a poor amusement if it is ever told. There is no form to it, no order. No conclusion, no moral, no answers. Only more questions.

8

Divers Hands...

I

"In what battle was it, Sir Knight, and to what foe did you lose your hand? Did you slay him who maimed you thus?"

The speaker was seated before me, a short, hooded man with a copious gray beard. I could not see his face in the fading twilight. He was the last one to come that day into my tent, at the crossroads fair in the mountain country beyond the empire of the Greeks, which is called Byzantium. The circumstance was a strange one: I, Julian, of various names and titles, long since lost to chivalry and my God, was reduced to beggary, shunned by the folk of every land. Who would trust this grim, hook-handed knight in tarnished mail, whose shield and surcoat bore not the emblem of the cross? What is he doing here? Is he really a man, they would ask, or some creature out of the darkness? Why goes he not with his comrades, to the east to fight the pagans? At the fairground, in that tent in a strange land near a strange city, and speaking a tongue I knew but rudely, I seemed to fit in, at least for the moment. I could not admit to myself that mere existence had become an end in itself, and each hour of peace a worthy goal for a long quest.

To make a living I told tales of my travels and of the adventures of others, and sometimes when these failed I invented, but no one could tell when I lied and when I didn't. Ever popular was my sojourn in the land of darkness, where dwell folk marvelously transfigured, so that their heads grow beneath their shoulders, and their ears, appended to their arms, stretch wide like the wings of bats, enabling them to fly. Also there were the salt maidens of Antioch, whose tears filled up their entire forms, so that they were left pillars of salt, like Lot's wife, when they mourned a blasphemer struck dead by the Apostle Peter. As each tale concluded, the listener would drop a coin in the bowl I had set out—and the telling was rewarding in another way too.

Being a storyteller is like confessing to a priest—nay—more like the fool in the fable who buries his head among the reeds and whispered *King Midas has asses' ears.* Everyone knows, but it is a fanciful thing. Who believes what is said by the wind in the reeds? Thus one can be unburdened of truth. So I told the questioner the true answer:

"Long and long ago it seems, but not very long ago in fact, there was a knight who met the Devil face to face in a ruined hall deep in the forest, and there he gave himself to him, to ransom a maiden who had been wronged. This was, by his faith, and his faith was a terror to him thereafter, the only chivalrous thing he had done in his entire life, for all his ideals, all his training, all his

100

deeds. And for this he was damned, so that the Devil did not take his soul just then, so sure a thing it was, but instead commanded him, 'Go wander the world which shall this day be made anew, and forever be a stranger, until at last you come to me.' And in his travels he met an evil thing, which in the guise of a lady comforted him, but in truth drank away his blood and his years. When the thing was slain, as needs it must be, the knight woke from a blissful dream in those false arms, and was confused, and in misguided wrath killed his deliverer, and for this was again damned. Then, on one of the occasions when he wished his life would end, but knew it could not, lest the Devil have him at once, he sought the Vale of Mistorak in the farthest East, and there conversed with a spirit, but bought those words with his own flesh, and that is how he lost his hand."

"And was the bargain well made?" asked the listener. "Was the answer satisfactory?"

"If it were, would I be here in this tent telling such wild tales?"

The hooded one wheezed what was supposed to be a laugh.

"I have no coin for you," he said, "but in exchange, a tale of my own. There was a king, whose name was Tikos, who ruled over a very ancient land. To the castle of his fathers came all the great lords of the world at one time or other. Alexander came there as a boy, and saw the wonder of it, and when he grew older turned his armies away from it, toward the east. But at long last, through treachery wrought by the priests of a new god, against whom the old gods were powerless, the people seized the king and mutilated him according to their custom, cutting off his right hand so that he might never again raise a sword, cutting off his left so he could hold no scepter. Thus was the king reduced to misery and scorn, until he found a way to gain his revenge. He swore himself to a new master. He became *Nekatu*."

"*Nekatu?*"

"As such he had vast powers, including prophecy. It has been prophesied that the knight of your story will come to the castle of the king of mine, and learn what that word means."

With that, he rose and left the tent. The flap waved like a flag with his passing.

"Wait!" I sprang up and went after him, bursting out into the evening air. It was intensely cold already, as it gets so quickly in the mountains. Beyond the peaks, the sun had set in a splash of gold. Overhead, the stars were already out, and I was sure the chill wind I felt came from between them, from beyond the mortal earth, where winged demons freely traffic. Such a demon my listener must have been to get away so fast. There was no sign of him anywhere.

Nekatu, he had said. That was the first time I ever heard the term.

That night as I slept I was haunted by evil dreams, at first, a recurring vision of a meadow strewn with the newly slain, all of them rising up as I approached, their wounds unhealed, to fight again in hopeless misery. Their cries at last drove me from the dream, and I awoke, bewildered for an instant, finding my tent an unfamiliar place. Then I listened to the night noises, tethered horses stamping in the cold, the crackle of campfires, a dog barking, someone singing. Beyond all that, an owl hooted.

I slept again, and this time I was riding through a dark wood, where every tree seemed to lean low with the weight of monstrous menace crouched in the branches, and inhuman faces peered fleetingly between the trunks. I had seldom known such terror in the waking world. My horse wanted to rear up and bolt, and only with utmost effort could I retain control. I gave in to the animal's instincts some, letting it speed up to a trot, then a canter, and finally a full gallop, as its panic and mine were one, and we thundered through the forest in a rain of great clods of mud thrown up by the hooves, and still there was the feeling of suffocating dread, and the half-glimpsed forms between the trees. Then I turned around in the saddle and looked behind me, and saw that I was indeed pursued, by another knight clad all in black mail and a black surcoat, mounted on a black steed, with his visor raised and a bare skull for a face. Then I screamed, and awoke again into the tent, and there was absolute silence in the camp, with every ear turned my way. Was the strange knight wrestling with a demon in his bed? I knew I would have to leave in the morning, before the tale grew in the retelling and reached the ears of a priest, and too many questions were asked.

Just before dawn I dozed off again. I was still riding through the forest, the apparition just behind me, and I was exhausted, as if my dream self had been fleeing on the foam-flecked dream horse all the while I had been awake. The terror was still there, and every instant seemed my last, until finally the forest broke into an open plain where two rivers joined. Where they joined stood a walled town, and beyond it, with a river girding it on either side, was a lone mountain. Three of its sides were sheer cliffs, but on a fourth a road wound down, crossed a bridge, and entered the far side of the town. Atop the mountain perched a castle of black stone. As soon as I spied this place it seemed a great weight was lifted from me, and another glance over my shoulder revealed that my nemesis had vanished. I let my horse slow to a walk, and as I approached the town and castle, the sun rose behind me, out of the forest, banishing all evil.

The last thing I saw—and I don't know if I imagined or truly dreamed it—was the hooded stranger rising from where he sat over a steaming cauldron, stretching his cramped legs, while within all the things in my dreams, the knight, the horse, the forest, the castle, and even myself, sank slowly through the broth to the bottom and there dissolved away.

I had no more visions that night.

There were people milling about when I awoke the third time. When I emerged from my tent they steadfastly refused to look directly at me or speak a word, even if questioned. And I knew not to persist in questioning. Some were breaking camp, piling unsold goods into carts, making ready to go even before the fair was over. I didn't have to ask the reason. An ill omen. There would be no luck in this place, and perhaps a curse for those who lingered. Next year the fair would doubtless be held somewhere else.

I didn't linger either, but instead packed what supplies and money I had into saddle pouches and rode away, leaving my tent where it stood. I couldn't take it with me in any case. For all I cared, the old bread-seller from whom I'd bought it could have it back. He might want to wrestle a devil in there sometime.

I knew that in such dreams, from wherever sent, something of import had been revealed, if a little vaguely, as is the manner of dreams. But such things cannot be without meaning. Indeed, as had been prophesied, I rode west, and that very afternoon came to the forest I had seen. It was not as sinister as its dream self, but always in the periphery of my sight there was a suggestion of a shape that set me ill at ease. I glanced back now and again to see if I was followed. I was alone, but my steed was as nervous as I, and difficult to control.

Beyond the wood was a plain, as I had foreseen, and two rivers met, and a mountain reared above all. One could only reach the castle atop it by passing through the town as if the castle were the innermost keep of a larger fortress surrounding it.

Soon I came upon peasants bringing their crops to market. The folk on this side of the forest seldom dared venture to the other, so they were not the same who had been at the fair, or so I hoped. There were all sorts going the same way; two priests—and I recoiled unconsciously at the sight of them—a boy with a mandolin slung over his shoulder, obviously a minstrel, and every variety of low-born person, afoot, astride mules and plow horses, or in carts.

As the traffic increased there were even a few of the wealthy in their ponderous, solid-wheeled carriages, surrounded by troops of men at arms. It occurred to me to seek employment as one such, but first I knew I must discharge whatever supernatural obligation had been laid on me, the dreams would continue, the skeletal rider overtake me as I slept, and at the very least I would awaken mad.

There was a soldier at the town's gate leaning lazily on a pike, asking each man what his business was. A farmer would drive up with a load of cabbages, announce that he'd come to sell cabbages, and be passed through with a bored wave. The nobles in their carriages would be known by the signs of their houses, inevitably on a banner carried by one of their horsemen, and not challenged at all.

In my case, it was not that simple.

"What do you want here?" Seeing that I wore a mail coat under my cloak and a steel cap on my head, and carried a sword, and eying the plain black shield that hung by my saddle, and all the while knowing by the most cursory glance that I was a foreigner, the guard stood up attentively, and raised his pike to block my way.

An equally cursory glance on my part revealed no other guards nearby, and none of the men at arms attending the carriages were close enough to come immediately to his assistance, or even ascertain at once what was going on.

So I reached up with my right hand—my only hand, the hook being hidden beneath the cloak—and pushed the pike away. At the same time I feigned a rage and glared at him.

"You filthy churl! How dare you question your betters?" My Greek was rough, but I was understood. The pike dropped limply away, and the fellow's mouth hung agape. He didn't know what to do, and alone he dared do nothing. So I took rein again in hand and spurred my horse quickly into the city before he could recover his wits. Almost as quickly I wondered if I had done the right thing. Would the guard brave his master's wrath and report his incompetence? Well, the die was cast, as Caesar had once remarked, and I had done what I had done. If my strange saga were known, I surely would not be welcomed here, but first I wanted to know what sort of place this was before seeking out its lord and making my way to the castle.

In the main square something was going on which wasn't standard trading or entertainment.

A large crowd had gathered and there was much excitement. I stood up in my stirrups to see more clearly. It was an execution. A man was being drawn and quartered between four separately harnessed oxen. Even over the yells of the mob I could hear his shrieks. As he hung there above the ground, and hooded executioners stood by with switches ready to prod the animals on, another, presumably the Master Executioner, had slit his belly open, yanked out an end of intestine, and begun coiling it around a stick. With every firm, jerking turn came another scream. Then one of the prisoner's arms slipped from the ropes and I saw why—he had no hand, so the wrist slid right out of the knot. Gesticulating furiously, the master rose from the disembowelling, kicked one of his assistants aside, and retied the rope, below the elbow this time.

As if this sight reminded them of something, the crowd began to shout with one voice a single word: "Nekatu! Nekatu!"

I sat down, startled. That was the second time I had heard the name, or term, or whatever it was, and I liked the circumstance even less well than I had the first. I took care that my own lack of a hand was concealed. I doubted this was the criminal's offense, but instinct counseled caution.

Disgusted, I rode around the edge of the square and along a narrow street filled with booths. Behind me the shouts of the crowd came to a crescendo, then stopped.

Now, most cities I have seen are vast caverns of wood and stone, and this one was no exception. Night begins early in a city. Even the great capital of Constantinople is lighted only around the palace and guard houses, and in a few principal squares. The common people grope like the blind through muddy, treacherous streets. In this place the upper stories of the houses leaned over the back streets, the nearly touching roofs shutting out all but the light of noontide. As I rode it was well into the evening, the fading sunset reflected only from those high gables and rooftops which caught the glow.

I came to a gap in the buildings, where I could get a full view of the castle on the hill beyond the town. Now it was silhouetted starkly against the western sky. Even as time passed, and the light faded even more, the place remained dark. Not a torch was lit in a tower; not a lantern glowed from any window. It seemed simply impossible that it could be deserted with a thriving town at its feet.

"Hist!" someone whispered. "Don't be staring at that! Ye'll bring a curse down on yer head."

I looked down, astonished that anyone would speak to me in such a manner. It was an old woman, her hair a tangled white explosion, with a bundle of sticks on her shoulder.

"And what ill can come from looking at the house of your lord? Woman, do you speak treason against him?"

Her face all but split apart with an irregularly toothed grin.

"Our *lord*? Ha! Our mortal lord lives here in the town. Only the wicked call *him* lord!" To make herself more clear, she pointed at the castle with her free hand.

"Does Satan himself roost up there then?" I laughed back at her.

" 'Tis no subject for a jest, good sir. That one they quartered today—that's what happens to people who take too much interest in evil places." She crossed herself hastily.

"For merely looking at it?"

She grinned again. Now I was sure she took me for a fool, for all my higher birth.

"He *went* there. He was *Nekatu!*"

As soon as she uttered that word, the exchange was no longer a joke. I leaned over in the saddle and faced her intently. Despite the gloom I could see her eyes well enough to tell she was suddenly frightened of me.

"I have heard of this *Nekatu* many times. Twice since I came here. Old woman, there is gold in this for you if you will kindly tell me what—may the saints preserve us—everyone is talking about. What is *Nekatu?*"

She put her hand to her mouth and said nothing. Ah, I thought. Her tongue is suddenly tied in knots. Thinking to loosen it, I reached into my purse for one of my few coins. But the leather thong was too tightly drawn. I couldn't get it open with one hand. So without giving it any thought, I slipped the tip of my hook between the thong and the bag to work it loose.

And the woman screamed. At the sight of the hook she dropped her bundle and ran down the street shrieking "Nekatu! Help! Help! Another one! Nekatu!"

Instantly what seemed an empty alley filled with people. Some grabbed at my horse's reins. I drew my sword and slashed, and there was a howl of pain, but by then dozens of others had swarmed all around. Hands were pulling me from the saddle. My horse reared in terror, which only helped them, even if a few skulls were split beneath the hooves. I tumbled over backwards out of the saddle and into the muddy street, striking furiously with sword and hook.

This had a temporary effect. No one was holding me when I hit the ground. I struggled to my feet. Whirling steel kept my foes temporarily at bay. None of them were armed with anything more fearsome than some of the old woman's firewood.

This changed almost at once. Nearby mail clinked, and I glanced quickly in the direction the crone had run. The pikes and steel helmets of the city guard were working their way through the jostling crowd.

With renewed fury I cut my way through the wall of my assailants. My horse had run off. I would have to escape on foot. An iron shoe in the groin, a chop at an upraised arm, a raking slash across the face with my metal hook, and I was no longer surrounded. A shout went up from the guards, and all the people regained their courage and surged after me. The chase went along that street into a narrower one, splashing through the mud, pushing passersby roughly aside until they understood what was happening, and joined in. The cry of "Nekatu!" seemed to be a kind of universal alarm, and every citizen stopped what he or she was doing and united against the common enemy.

My mail and my iron-covered shoes weighed me down, and I surely would have been overtaken before long had the chaotic fray not spilled into a lane so narrow that there was barely enough room to squeeze a cart along it—and there was a cart heading straight toward us.

Some of my pursuers hesitated, but I lunged forward with desperate speed. The cart driver drew rein, unsure of what was going on. Before he knew it I was alongside him. I flattened myself against a wall, then gave his horse a long, shallow swipe on the rump with my sword. Of course the enraged animal charged forward, completely out of control, right into the mass of my foes. As it clattered past, the protruding axles of the cart missed me by scarcely a span.

Breathing heavily, but still maintaining the strength which had brought me through countless battles, I came at last to the far end of the town, where a gate led to the bridge over the river, then to the winding road up the one less than utterly sheer side of the mountain. This gate was barred from the inside. Now the bridge itself was fortified, and a small number of soldiers thereon could surely prevent an enemy from climbing up onto it from barges. This side was otherwise completely inaccessible. The thick, slippery wall of the town dropped straight to the water's edge, leaving no more than a foot or two of muddy bank. In any case, I'd seen no indication that this was a time of war.

Not hesitating to ponder this idiocy of siege design in a town that seemed completely crazy anyway, I placed both shoulders beneath the massive wooden bar, and with all my strength forced it up until it rose free of its supports and fell to the ground with a thud. The gate swung outward and I staggered backwards through it, onto the bridge.

By now those who hadn't been trampled by the runaway cart had found me again. With long strides I ran across the bridge and part way up the mountain. Then I turned to look. They weren't following. The crowd now filled the gateway, but none would venture forth. A tangle of faces stared up at me, sullen and quiet. It only seemed fitting that people who so irrationally feared men who were missing hands, and who so shunned the castle around which their town was built that they condemned to death anyone who went there, should behave in so ridiculous a way. I was sure they were all lunatics. With a contemptuous snort, I turned and made my way up the mountain at a leisurely pace.

It was only after I had gone a ways and the castle loomed huge above me, blotting out the stars, that it occurred to me that the people might have been sensible after all. Could there be some danger lurking among those towers such that one going the way I was would be insured a more frightful doom than anything the executioner could contrive?

If so, I was in a terrible situation, like a man who cannot swim trapped on a burning ship. I could not return to the town. There was no way to go but up, into the castle I had first glimpsed in a dream. In that dream it had been a place of relief and refuge, but now I was not so sure.

There was a little door beside the main gate of the castle, with a heavy metal iron for a knocker. I clanged the thing until the sound must surely have echoed throughout the whole land.

There was a stirring within.

"*Nekatu*," I said.

A bolt slid aside and the door opened.

That is how I found refuge among the *Nekatu*.

II

"The phrase '*nekatu*' literally means 'messenger,' not in Greek, but in the older language of these people. As you see, I have made good my promise. As soon as you arrived here, you learned the definition."

The same hooded stranger who had come to my tent the night before now led me up a winding flight of stairs, and into a large room. I couldn't tell how large. He carried only a small oil lamp, and nothing was lighted. The castle was clearly in a state of considerable disrepair. I couldd dimly make out fallen beams, stones, and tattered draperies scattered about.

He put the lamp down on a bare wooden table, pulled out a high-backed chair, and indicated that I should sit. The only sounds were the scraping of the chair, the clank of my shoes, and the soft pad of his slippers. He stood and I sat absolutely still for a moment, and the only sound was a slight fizzling from the lamp. Then there was something else: a faint pattering, like the scurrying of rats. At first I thought it to be that, but there wasn't enough scratching. Too soft, without claws. More like many people drumming their fingers nervously on wood.

I watched my host's every move with utmost suspicion. All this had been his contrivance. He wanted something. I was being brought here as surely as a fish on a hook. To make the point that I was not utterly helpless, I did not sheathe my sword, which I had carried in hand all the way up the mountain, but placed it in clear view in front of me. It clattered, and for an instant the tapping sound in the background stopped. Then it resumed, somewhat closer.

The hood fell back, and a thin, bearded, ageless face was revealed. Atop silvery hair rested the thin band of a golden crown.

"King Tikos, I presume."

"The unhappy knight of the tale, I presume." Another chair was dragged, and he sat down across from me. "But let us set aside all pretense. Look at this."

He leaned forward into the light, pushed up both sleeves, and held his wrists up to the lamp, so I could plainly see.

"Look very closely," he said.

I let out an inadvertent grunt of astonishment. There was a thin line across both wrists, and he turned both hands over to show that these lines went all the way around. No one could have scars like that. They were *seams*.

"Sorcery! Not even the greatest doctors of physic...."

"Most not-so-noble knight, if your tale is as true as I think it is, you are not wholly godly yourself."

"That is...true. But how?"

"This is one of the many powers of the *Nekatu*."

"Messengers?"

"A kind of brotherhood, set apart from the rest of mankind. This is why I have brought you here, why I sought you out when I saw you in the fair and noticed that your left hand was missing."

"Are you some kind of ghoul that you are fascinated by mutilation? Go to the wars in the east, and you'll get your fill."

"No! No! You fail to understand! I offer you a great gift. Look again!"

He reached under the table and drew from someplace a wooden box. The hinged lid came open. Inside there was a left hand carven out of a single piece of crystal, glittering with a thousand facets. It was a stunning piece of work, something with which to ransom empires.

I was not at all sure that it was a trick of the poor lighting that the thing seemed to move. Had the fingers been entirely outstretched? Now they seemed somewhat curled.

"By a most secret art," he said, "I have learned to make these. Contrary to what the philosophers will tell you, that which glitters has substance. Each ray of light captured within the crystal is a living thing, giving the hand itself life. This hand I have exposed to the stars for a hundred nights, giving it the life of the *Nekatu*. When joined to a wrist it becomes as living flesh in all ways."

"Joined? How so?"

"It natually adheres, as you shall see. Take off that hook and bronze cap, and be healed and whole again."

The intensity of his gaze, my exhaustion, and the perils I had passed through must have bewitched me, for I thought of little else but having a living hand again, even if there would be a seam around it. I forgot the treacherous, extreme outrageousness of my situation, and childishly obvious fact that the King was not doing this out of charitable commiseration over my wound.

Hardly realizing what I was doing, I pulled the hook and cap off my left wrist, exposing the healed stump. Tikos took the arm in his hand—I did not resist—and joined it to the crystal hand over the flame of the lamp.

I felt no pain. First there was a numbness, then a tingling, a sort of melting, as the flame licked over the wrist and hand, and the substance flowed like hot wax. Even as I watched the crystal lost its lustre, the facets smoothing over, the color fading. It was turning into flesh. I seemed far away from everything, drifting in abstraction. I wondered in bemusement if this were tried on a Negro. Would the hue be right?

When the King let go, the hand seemed as if it had grown there. Thrilling at the sensation, I flexed the fingers, then made a fist and banged with all my might on the table. The sword and the lamp bounced.

"A miracle! I am restored!"

"Yes, miraculous. By the way, are you hungry? I doubt you've eaten."

I made no answer. It seemed such a silly question, like the hues of Negroes. Who could care about food now?

King Tikos snapped his fingers and a tray was set before me. My heart skipped a beat when I saw that it was placed there by *hands*, but nothing more. They floated in the air as if creatures were reaching through from some invisible world into our own.

"*Christ and Satan!*"

"Swear by whomever you like," laughed the King. "Why not Jupiter, Thor, Mithra, and Ahura-Mazda also? It'll do you as much good. Those hands, I can safely tell you now, are simply *Nekatu*, like yourself, only in a far more advanced stage of development. The body withers away—it is unimportant—and is absorbed entirely into the hand. Why has this not happened to me? I remain whole because the Master, whom we all serve—yes, even you now—wills it. I recruit new slaves for him, even if sometimes, like that fool in the town today, a few are lost. He tried to run away."

With a howl of rage and despair, and every curse I could think of garbled together, I grabbed my sword and lunged across the table at the laughing monster, bent on total dismemberment. But before I could even get to my feet a frigid shock ran up my left arm and through my body. I staggered numbly for a second, the sword dropping from senseless fingers, then collapsed forward onto the table, smothering the lamp. That was the last thing I remembered.

For a second night then I was tossed like a cork on a sea of nightmares. At first there was complete darkness, and a feeling of being long dead and very *soft*, trapped far underground, and clawing my way to the surface, until all the putrid flesh of my body had been sloughed off, and only my diamond-hard *hands* emerged from the earth. Then the scene changed and I saw myself lying where I had fallen on the table, my left arm, with that accursed hand, dangling over the edge. Again came a numbness at the wrist, and a sensation of melting.

The thing dropped off, landing on the floor upright on its fingers, like a cat dropped from a rooftop. It stood there like a living thing—which indeed it was—and there was an instant of confusion and disorientation: I was wrenched from where I lay, drifting, falling, floating upward into warmth; and then I was looking up into the gloom at an enormous table with an unconscious giant sprawled over it, and the stump of a left wrist hanging over me.

My soul, my self, was now a prisoner in the hand. I was not in control. Another mind was at work. Following a way the fingers knew, I was carried away from the table and my body, into utter blackness as the hand passed through a tiny crevice in the wall. I could "see" nothing else until I/we/it emerged on the outside of the castle. All the while the sensations of fingertips on damp stone were intense, very real. Then there was the vast panorama of the town and surrounding countryside viewed from a height, and a brilliant full moon in the sky.

The hand wanted to avoid the light. It stayed in the shadows as much as possible as it climbed down the outside of the castle wall, each finger seeking and finding holds sufficient to sustain the weight of the thing. Like a monstrous spider it crept over the stone until it was just above the door through which I had first entered the castle. There followed a sickening, terrifying drop through space as the grip was released, then a jolt as the hand landed upright, as it had done beneath the table.

It crawled down that road up which I had come, scurrying as fast as a rat. For all the distance and its small size, it was at the barred gate of the town very quickly. The closed gate posed no obstacle. The rough outcroppings of the city wall were as sure as the rungs of a ladder. Up and over we went with practiced skill, and once more there was a drop, and the fingers sank the second joint in mud. Still the hand was not stopped. The fingers spread out, then curled, squeezing mud, then spread out in a kind of swimming motion until the fingertips reached more solid ground. This gave way to a paved street, and the filthy fingers paddled silently along the cobblestones, remaining always in the deepest shadows.

"Sight" was a confusing thing. At times I seemed to view the five fingers working, as if I were a tiny observer seated on the back, just behind the knuckles, and at other times the hand would stop, raise the index finger like an eyestalk, and I would get a sweeping view through that.

My walking self, Julian, the man who had been duped, had no idea where we/the hand intended to go, but there was a definite mission in the motion of the fingers. The hand came to certain intersections, and the index finger would scout about, then I would be going down a particular street, to a specific destination.

At last there was a wretched hovel propped between two brick buildings. A board was missing from the door, so the hand could enter without difficulty.

Within, the pattering which was definitely not a rat crossed the floor, steering a wide curve around the glowing coals of the firepit in the middle of the floor. Moonlight streamed through the smoke hole in the roof, and I could clearly discern a person asleep on a heap of straw on the far side of the room. It was the old woman who had carried the sticks.

Stealthily the hand made its way through the straw then began to climb the tattered blanket she had wrapped herself in. The hand began to climb the blanket onto her shoulder. The index finger stood straight up, again the "eye" of the creature, while the second and third fingers pinched cloth between them, as did the little finger and thumb. With these two grips the hand inched its way on top of her, then crept across her rising and falling body. I could feel her heartbeat beneath my fingertips as I moved down onto her breast, over the collarbone—

It was obvious what was intended, I desperately wanted to stop, to curl the fingers into a fist and drop into the straw, to shout a warning with all my breath. But I had no breath. My voice and lungs were back at the castle. I had no will, no control as the fingers slipped around the helpless crone's thin throat. Blood throbbed in her neck, but the skin felt like parchment.

Suddenly, with furious strength, the hand closed on her windpipe. She awoke, sat up wide-eyed in terror, let out a single gurgling cry, and then could utter nothing more. For a minute she writhed in the straw, flailing wildly after her unseen assailant and meeting only empty air, and then she lay still. The horror of the thing was not merely the death, or even my inability to prevent it, but that I had done the deed. As the hand strangled her I felt the muscles of a phantom arm, my arm, the arm of my body back at the castle, straining with the work. I felt the weight of my whole body pressed on the woman, pushing her down until her neck snapped like one of the sticks she had been carrying.

Someone stirred in another part of the room.

"Grandmother? Is that you?" Bare footsteps moved near the firepit, and a handful of rushes was lighted, then carried in my direction. I could see the face of a young girl as she bent over her grandmother, and the contortions of revulsion and mad terror at the sight of the thing still perched on the corpse. The light went out again as the rushes were dropped to the floor. The granddaughter screamed and was answered by shouts from without.

Instantly the hand knew what to do. With unbelievable agility it scrambled up the wall and was out another hole in the rotted wood. Then followed a drop into the muddy back street, and a scramble across to another house, and up a wall. From atop the neighboring roof it watched and gloated—yes, there was a definite feeling of that emotion in the second mind, joined to my own, which I could not escape.

"It has happened again! Grandmother!" the girl tried to explain to others through hysterical tears. "*Nekatu!*"

It was then that I came to understand some of the peculiar things about this town.

III

It was no surprise, but a dreadful, sickening certainty when I awoke the next morning on the table and there was mud on my left hand.

Revenge the King had said. In this way he wrought revenge on those who had overthrown him. No wonder there were no men-at-arms on his battlements. He had an army of *Nekatu* which was far more deadly.

I lurched to my feet and instantly fell. My legs would not support me. I was sick, exhausted, as if I had just completed a vast labor, and I realized that, as the King had said, the hand was beginning to absorb my vitality into itself. I dropped to my knees, grasping the edge of the table with my right hand. I left the other arm hanging limp. The thing seemed asleep. Now, by daylight, my body was my own.

Apparently there were limits. I had to stay alive long enough for the thing to steal my life away. It would take a while. I would have to be kept for a long time. The tray set down by the hands the night before was still there. On it were cold meat, bread, and cheese. A cup of wine stood beside it. This had *not* been there before.

My breakfast was laid out for me.

I spent the day exploring the castle. I could not go into the town, where I would be killed on sight. If I fled over the countryside, making my way down one of the cliffs with only one hand I could trust, I had no doubt the hand could bring me back, or at the very least deal with me the same way it had with the old woman. I could, at last resort, cast myself from the walls, or simply refuse to eat until I starved, but these were indeed last resorts. It is not like a warrior, *any* warrior, be he Christian knight or pagan savage, to surrender before the battle is joined. The enemy must be met, no matter how hopeless the odds.

So all day I wandered through the ruined halls of the castle. I found a library filled with books written in strange scripts. There were also a few in Latin, and these I glanced through. Most were treatises on magic, of vast age. One was dedicated: *To my Lord Nero, who taught me how to begin.* The same Nero who reigned shortly after Christ, and slew the apostles Peter and Paul. How long had it been since King Tikos lost his natural hands? Surely the folk of this town were not his subjects, but their remote descendants.

When twilight was drawing near, I knew my efforts were over for the day. Another night of helpless horror was to follow. But before anything happened I dragged an iron brazier I had found into the room where the wooden table was, then gathered up some dry rushes, bits of wood, and scraps of the fallen tapestries. I meant to keep the place lighted so I could see Tikos when he came to put the spell on me, and slay him if I could. I still had my sword.

Supper had been set in my absence. I ate while the familiar pattering passed back and forth behind the walls. Long shadows crossed the floor.

There was a footstep behind me.

"Ah, now that you've dined, it's time for another errand," said King Tikos.

Before I could even turn around, the cold blast overwhelmed me.

Many more died that night, but not in the town below. The mission was far stranger. I was in the company of a whole brigade of Nekatu, perhaps as many as fifty. Together we climbed up the outside of the castle, to the top of the tower. There a flock of black hawks were waiting, as still as carven gargoyles. Each hand climbed on the back of a bird, the thumb and forefinger hooked around the neck, the rest grasping the body. The feel was very familiar. I've handled falcons often.

There was a more terrifying drop than before as the bird I was riding fell into the abyss, heavy with its burden, struggling for flight. It flapped desperately, then caught the air and rose clumsily to join the others, all of them lurching in an equally heavy manner. Below, the fields and hills rolled. Moonlight gleamed on the two rivers. We followed one of them to its source in the mountains beyond a forest, then over the mountains until we came to the manor of some lord. The birds waited patiently on walls and window ledges while the passengers dismounted and went about their business. The hands worked in pairs this time, not necessarily left and right, but always in pairs. I was with a huge black member—answering my question about Negroes. Together we came to a chamber in which a man and a woman slept. Now the black hand did something which I had witnessed the first night, but had never been able to imitate. It floated in the air, as if attached to an invisible body, as those bringing the tray had done. It slid a sword from the scabbard which hung from the bedpost. All this while my own hand was climbing up the side of the bed, inching up a blanket. "A more advanced stage," the King had said. A Nekatu which still had a human body, a newcomer like myself, had not yet all the powers given to that fiendish brotherhood. I could not yet rise and float. I had to crawl.

The murder was done. I/the hand in which my self was trapped crept to the face of the man, then clamped tightly over his mouth while the black hand slit his throat from ear to ear with the sword. The lady slept through the whole deed, so swiftly and silently was it performed. Again I felt the weight of my whole body leaning over the bed, gagging my victim while my accomplice slew him.

The sword was placed gently on the floor and the two of us returned to the windowsill, there mounting our bewitched steeds. As if at a signal, the whole flock took off at once, bearing the army of *Nekatu* back to the castle of King Tikos. I was not told, but I knew that what I had participated in was not unique that night. In twenty-five rooms wives would wake up, soaked with blood, and scream as they found themselves sharing beds with still warm corpses. Could King Tikos hear the screams? Was he somehow nourished by the terror and death?

Once more I found myself in that room by the table, and a breakfast had been prepared for me. Where did he get the food? No stores could keep fresh all that time. Did he send *Nekatu* to rob butchers and bakers? Well, that was the most innocuous thing they would ever do.

I hated myself as I ate. It was all I could do not to vomit as I remembered what had happened. It was time, I told myself, to leap to an easy death, before more innocents perished. *I* was not innocent. I had many times longed for death. But then the familiar terror came…After death—damnation, the eternal torments I could escape only for that brief time I lived. Like all men, I am ultimately selfish. I would sacrifice the whole world to escape Hell even for a short while. I could kill myself only on a sudden, saving impulse swifter than thought. If I reasoned what was right, just, and the moral thing to do, I would forget all about rightness, justice, and morality, and be paralyzed.

That day I continued to search the castle, hoping to find some secret thing by which I could justify myself.

And I was rewarded. There was a small door beneath what had once been a long bench. I made a torch out of wood, weeds from a courtyard garden, and scraps of cloth, lit it with flint and steel from the pouch on my belt, and descended into a vault. There I found twelve stone coffins, each of them with, curiously, an opening of about a span cut into the top.

No, not curious at all. A span is measured by the spread of a man's fingers.

Within were *Nekatu* of "a more advanced stage of development." When I slid the lid off the first coffin, I grew faint at the sight, but quickly gathered my courage. There lay an ancient, withered corpse, little more than skin stretched tight over bones, save that on one of the arms the shrunken skin blossomed out into a perfect living hand.

The fury of loathing gave me strength. I hacked at the thing with my sword, severing the hand, cutting again and again until the fingers were scattered and the whole body was a ruin. The skull splintered; the ribcage collapsed into slivers and chips. Only when nothing remained recognizable did I stop, sweat-covered for all the dampness of the vault, breathing heavily from my labor. After a pause I went on to the next one and destroyed it as thoroughly, but more methodically.

I was encouraged that my left hand was my left hand as I did this work. It did as my muscles commanded, and aided me in my task.

That night, however, the King again appeared from nowhere—I still had no idea how he did it—and more evil work was done. The army of *Nekatu* was abroad once more, and I noticed, and despaired as I saw, that some of them were crisscrossed with imperfectly healed scars. One or two even "limped" as they crawled on broken fingers. But they did what their master bade them. This time we came to a monastery, and, after stealing candles from the chapel altar, each of the *Nekatu* crept into a cell and burned out the eyes of the monk therein.

IV

When next I awoke, my vital essence was so drained I could not rise. I was getting rapidly weaker. My flesh was wasting away. Already I was as gaunt as a starving beggar, increasingly like the shrivelled corpses of the *Nekatu* in the coffins. Doubtless before long I would be unable to move at all, and many hands would carry me to those same or similar coffins, and place me in one of them. Only with utmost effort could I crawl to the chair, eat, and live for another day. Now I knew I could never fling myself from a parapet. I'd never reach the wall. So I sat there throughout the day, as sunlight shifted from window to window along the south side of the room.

I was very cold, Somehow I found the strength to rise after a while and light the brazier. I could think of nothing but warmth. For warmth, in my wretched condition, I would sell my soul. But my soul was already spoken for, so I had to provide for myself.

Thus I sat as evening fell, leaning against the back of the chair, my sword before me on the table, both hands in my lap, right on top of left in vain hope of restraining it. Beside me, the brazier sputtled and crackled. The smell of smoke was comforting, my single tie to earthly things. Whenever the flames burned low I fed them bits of straw, cloth, and splinters of rotten wood. A heap of fuel was within arm's reach.

King Tikos arrived. He did not come into the room; he was merely *there*. I thought the white spot in the air was a trick on my tired eyes, but it grew and took shape, and he was in the room with me. His slippers padded softly on the floor as he walked. All but soundless, a horde of *Nekatu* kept pace with him on extended fingers. There were more of them than I had ever imagined. They poured from the cracks and holes until the floor was covered. There were easily a thousand of them. How foolish to think my tiny group made up the whole army!

"It is time," said the King, "that our brother be brought fully into our fellowship. No waiting in the vaults for him. The Master is coming this night to claim and transform him."

He was speaking to the hands, not to me. I was merely an object to be dealt with. He paced back and forth as he spoke, the *Nekatu* scurrying this way and that after him like thousands of crabs come out of the sea just long enough to devour a drowned sailor the waves had washed up.

"We must wait, brothers. Have patience. The Master will come when the Master feels it is time. In the Master's world, beyond our own, time is not as we know it. I have been there as none of you have, and have seen, so believe me. Shapes and sounds and colors are all wondrously transformed, unrecognizably different. Senses are confused. One *hears* the color white, tastes the sweet tang of terror. A scream is like a soft caress *within* the body. Space, and time, and distance? These do not exist where the Master dwells, any more than depths exist in the world of a drawing on a page of parchment. Can one of those figures stand up, and walk out of the book? The Master can. You and I shall be able to also, in the end, when this world likewise belongs to the Master. That is why I worship him. That is why he is greater even than the God who created this universe. The Master walks between many universes. *Whence comest thou? From walking to and fro in the sum of cosmos, and up and down in it, between the planes and angles.* That is why the Master is the Master.

"And yet," said the King, pacing back and forth in the semi-darkness amid the thousand disembodied hands, "and yet I do not fear the Master where I now stand, for he needs me, to become material in our world. To take on solid substance. *And the word was made flesh, and screamed among us.* He is not as powerful here as he is in the void between the voids."

I listened to all this with the dull incomprehension of a pig in the slaughterhouse overhearing the talk of two butchers. Surely Tikos was mad to talk of anything beyond the sphere of the Earth, the moon and sun moving around it, and the fixed stars in the spheres of the firmament beyond, but then I was surely mad to be dreaming this nightmare in which I now existed, and the whole world was mad to allow such thoughts to come to be, and God was mad, as I knew well, for having created it that way. *And the Earth was without shape and form, and darkness was on the face of the deep.* Ah! If only the Father had been truly wise, and not meddled!

"The Master comes!" There was a rippling of the air, like foam on the sea an instant before a great whale leaps from the depths. For the first time Tikos spoke to me: "Watch! Watch, Sir Knight, and listen, and observe the last thing you shall ever observe with mortal eyes and ears. Tonight on this night of nights, the last of the harvest moon, the Master comes into this chamber, and you will be within our grip. *Ours.* I am part of the Master. This is the ultimate secret. Now, as I have promised, you truly know the meaning of the word *Nekatu*. A messenger, a servant of the Master, a finger of his hand."

Literally. As I watched the whiteness in the air returned and surrounded the King. He stood still. A thousand hands paused on five thousand fingertips. Four columns of whiteness began to materialize around him, and as they did he lost his own shape. He was flowing together, arms melting into his body, his two legs become one. Like wax. A candle. *Lighted.* Fire. Dimly the association anchored in my mind.

A finger of the Master. Exactly. That was what he had become. The four other fingers appeared beside him, and he—the index finger—was lifted off the floor as the Master reared up. The Master was a huge hand, that of a giant as tall as the castle if any body had been present. Something reaching through the air out of an invisible world coexistent with our own.

The hand climbed up on the table. It was the size of a horse. The wood creaked under its weight.

All time seemed suspended, and in my abstraction, I noticed a curious thing. The finger which had been King Tikos had a red welt around it. Was the Master a kind of *Nekatu* of a larger world, not complete without the animate finger which was the king, or which he had become? Was this the ultimate bargain to which the maimed and outcast king had agreed so long ago, through which he gained his continual revenge?

Joined together, a voice in the back of my mind chanted. Candle. Wax. Welting. Fire. Wax. *Fire.*

Now my left hand, that which was *Nekatu*, had come alive. The rest of my body was too weak to obey any commands, so the hand was on the table, crawling toward the far end where the Master stood on fingertips a foot across, dragging me with it. Now my awareness was entirely in my head. The hand didn't need me, and moved of itself.

So I was pulled forward, across the table, toward the grasp of the Master.

I leaned forward. My chin touched the hilt of my sword, which was still on the table in front of me. With impossible strength the *Nekatu* hand was dragging me up out of the chair, onto the table. It passed the overturned oil lamp from the first night.

Fire. Wax. Melting.

In the remote regions of my mind, where thoughts were still my own, the idea came. I laughed at the brilliance of it. I was completely detached, my awareness floating. What was happening was not *really* happening. It was an intellectual exercise. I had always been good at things like chess. There was all the time in the world to carefully consider. Soon, someday, I would try—

I lost myself wholly for an instant, and *was* in the *Nekatu* hand, unheeded, but feeling the attraction of the Master, the call to union, a kind of lust—

—and was again myself, and in less than a spilt second the thoughts, the little voices, melted and turned and twisted upon themselves: Fire. Wax. Fire. Candle. Fire. Fire. *Fire....*

The unexpected: a convoluted stratagem—again I slipped into blackness, was in hand for a longer interval, and the call was far, far stronger—and flashed back, perhaps for the last time, into the body and mind of the man Julian—the convoluted stratagem: while all attention was on my left hand, the *Nekatu*, the right hand was doing something.

In the realm of philosophical abstraction, detached from time and space, as an interesting exercise, the fingers of my *right* hand, my human hand, curled around the hilt of my sword as it lay there on the table.

With a sudden *thwunk!* the right hand brought the sword up and around and down, crashing into the tabletop, aimed at the *Nekatu* hand, but clumsily. It missed by less than the width of the blade.

The hand stopped, startled. The Master stood there impassively. The thousand *Nekatu* on the floor remained motionless.

The grip on my left arm was relaxed for an instant. I was free. My body fell backwards into the chair, and with desperate effort I thrust the left hand into the flaming brazier.

The *Nekatu* hand recoiled. The Master stumbled backwards, and toppled off the end of the table, landing with a heavy thud on the floor, crushing those beneath him. Now a lifeless hand hacked apart during the day feels nothing, but a living one at night is different—and the Master directs all his hands, feeling as they feel.

Feeling as I feel. The hand did not go for my throat. The Master now writhed with the agonies of those he had crushed in his fall, and I, linked to them as a *Nekatu*, felt the same. I was in the fury of this pain that I was able to put my left hand back on the tabletop, then with my right, with the sword I still held, strike the mightiest blow ever struck in all the battles of mankind. I could have felled whole cities with it. The blade crashed down, through the wrist, just above the place where it joined the *Nekatu* hand. Honest agony followed. I was severed from the Master—it was mortal blood that flowed now from the stump. Only my own body.

I screamed, and in screaming woke fully into myself. Thick in the midst of the fight, instinct took over. The Master stood up once more, trembling on his pale, flabby fingers and began to crawl back up onto the table. I hurled the brazier at him, and again he retreated from the flames. I lifted the table with my bleeding stump, and the hand that still held the sword, and flipped it over on top of him. I sheathed the sword, and hurled handfuls of kindling onto the heap. There was some oil left in the lamp which now poured out and kept the fire going until it could catch on the wood.

All this while the *Nekatu* stood motionless on the floor, waiting for commands. I trampled them with my iron shoes.

All this while blood was gushing from my left arm. It was only as I fell forward, to the very edge of the flames now licking over the upside-down table that I realized my death was moments away. To this day I am amazed that I was able to do anything as rational as reaching forward with the bleeding arm, forcing it into the fire, and closing the wound. This new pain somehow gave me strength enough to rise to my feet and stagger down the winding stair, through the door, and out of the castle.

I was mad. I screamed. I howled. I laughed. I was as far from myself as I had been on the midnight missions of the *Nekatu*. There was that remote part of me which knew what was going on, but the rest raged in a frenzy of pain, fear, and sub-bestial fury.

Do you believe in miracles? *Speak not! Any words are lies! You know!*

Was it not a miracle that when I came to the bottom of the mountain road, with the castle burning fiercely behind me, the people of the town opened their gates and let me pass? "He is dead," I said, not knowing if the Master even *could* die. I think they feared me more than King Tikos. I think they took me for some new demon more terrible than the old. They opened the gate before I could blast it with a thunderbolt. They brought my horse to me. To appease my wrath? To get rid of a dread savior delicately before his unknown will be known? They saw my wounded wrist and knew I was no longer *Nekatu*, and they saw the glare from the castle above. Was this not a miracle?

Was it not a miracle that I found myself, when for the first time in a very long while I could think coherently, riding across a meadow far to the west of the city, beyond the mountains, a place I had once spied from the air, it seemed, in a dream?

And what else could it have been but a miracle, which brought me at last to a monastery of blind monks, who discovered by feel the wound on my arm, and said, "Look brothers, he is afflicted even as us," while carrying me to a bed and stumbling to fetch medicines?

Later, when again I was reduced to beggary, I refrained from telling stories, lest I somehow forget myself and accidentally relate how I lost my left hand twice.

9

The
Unknown God
Cried Out...

A secret birth at midnight, and all the world shook.
    —Titus Ambrosius, *The Nativity of Evil*

In my blacker moments, I find it hard to convince myself that
I had a friend once, but it was so. I met him in a tavern—or was it
on a ship, in a field after a battle, or along a country road?—and
after a while it seemed as if we had always been together, parted
for no more than a short time and now reunited. I dwelt with him
in his castle in the middle of a wood, by a mountain called the
Owl's Beak.

Emile was his name, *Sir* Emile to be correct, since he had
newly become a knight, then inherited lands from an uncle who
had fallen in the Crusade with all his nearer kin. He was half my
age, and knew far less, had travelled hardly at all, and still
professed to believe absolutely in the goodness of God and the
Virgin, and the redemption of the cross. People sent him relics
from the Holy Land, and he treasured them. He confessed his sins
to his captive priest twice a week. I might have called him a
simpleton, but I think, as far as anyone can come to understand
these things, that it was his very simplicity which attracted me. I
wanted him to restore some of the innocence that had been so long
gone from my own life.

I helped Emile get his bride. He loved a maiden; he wore her
veil on his helmet at tourneys; but her father thought him
unworthy (not rich enough), so it came to pass that I held the reins
of two horses one night while Emile scaled a tower and
"abducted" his lady, who had to be restrained from mischievously
giggling on the way down.

"Sir Julian!" she said when she saw me. I was standing in
darkness, so I think she recognized the hook on my left wrist
before she saw my face. "Aren't you too grim and somber a fellow
to partake in something like this?"

"Hush! Mount and ride before your father's men hear us!"
whispered her lover.

He lifted her onto his saddle in front of him, clasped a hand
over her mouth, and we were off. Afterwards there was a half-
friendly joust and her father was wounded only in his pride, and
he acquiesced.

And then my friend was gone. One of his guards saw him ride
out of the castle in the middle of the night. He left no word, and he
did not return.

Therefore, to find him again, I committed that same sin
which King Saul did before his last battle. I consulted a witch. But
I am already called apostate and had no divine favor to lose. I
climbed to the top of the Owl's Beak and spoke with the witch

who dwelt there in a cave, and I told her my tale, more of it, I suspect, that I intended to, for she had no quick answer.

For a long time the ancient woman sat at the mouth of her cave, looking out over the darkened world. It was a long time, I am sure. As I sat by her, I watched the Great Wain run part of its course around the north star.

At last she said, "Julian, I think you ought to pray."

"*What*? To whom? I'll have nothing to do with your Satan—I have met him before—and the other—"

"Did I say anything about Satan? You are the first to mention his name. You should pray to the unknown god, the one we witches may glimpse but dimly, who may, because he is unknown, still have the capacity to help all the world's wanderers, even to love them."

"But you don't know. Could he as easily hate them?"

"He is unknown. Hush, and listen. When I was a young girl, the Emperor Hadrian—"

I let out a grunt of surprise.

"Are you more astonished," she asked, "that I am a thousand years old, or that I am a pagan?"

I could find no words.

"No matter," she went on. "Hadrian had a youth, whose name was Antinous who was more dear to him than any other."

"Sodomites?"

"If they were, it is not important. Of all the people in the court, Antinous was the only one who wanted no power, who represented no faction, whom greed had not yet touched. Therefore he alone could be the emperor's friend. But it happened one night while they were deep into Egypt that the river Nile, which is a god, demanded a sacrifice. A crocodile, walking upright like a man, appeared to Antinous in a dream and opened its huge jaws, saying, 'I hunger for the life of Hadrian, unless some other will die in his place.' At once the boy arose and went to the river, and waded in, and was carried away by the current. All the world trembled with the emperor's grief, as it will when one so mighty knows such sorrow. He prayed to all the gods he knew, and sacrificed, that Antinous might be restored to him, but got no answer. So, in his despair, he prayed to the unknown god which resides in the darkness and can never be seen or described by any priest. He built temples wherever he went and put no image in them, hoping that some day he could return to one of them alone, and there meet Antinous."

"Did he ever?"

"I don't know. Late in life he was heard speaking to Antinous in his garden, and he would listen as if someone were answering

125

back, but when his servants spied on him, they perceived him to be alone."

"Then how can I know that the unknown god will help me?"

"As I said, you can't. But will any other?"

I climbed down the mountain just as dawn touched its peak and the witch retreated into her cave. The forest was just beginning to awaken as I came to it. All the trees were filled with birds singing in a wild riot of sound.

In an open glade I knelt and prayed to the unknown god, before whom I had not sinned, that at least I might know what had happened to my friend. And as I did, I felt something stir deep within me, and I took that as an answer, an acknowledgement that in the course of my search, something would be revealed.

Therefore I returned to the castle, packed what gear I would need for a long journey, and departed, first telling Emile's bride to have hope. But the signs did not give me cause for hope at once. When I asked after the missing knight, no one had seen him, and I was regarded with suspicion. Once, out of the corner of my eye, I saw a highway warden cross himself as I rode past.

I don't know when it was that I noticed something strange about the countryside through which I was passing, but after a time it occurred to me that the day was unusually quiet. When I had first come down the mountain, the birds sang with all the chatter of a late summer morning, but now it seemed that the trees were empty, and there were no cattle in the fields, and no dogs barked. In the towns I passed through there were only a very few folk about, and almost never did a man call aloud to his neighbor or women lean out of their windows and gossip.

After I had gone a good distance, the sun set, and the night was very dark, even though the sky was clear. I camped by a stream, with a low, rolling hill at my back. Since I was in friendly country, I did not worry overmuch about revealing my presence, so I lit a large campfire, since the air seemed unseasonably cold. I ate some dried meat I had with me, also bread and cheese. I had a half-empty wineskin too, but decided to save it for later, and drank from the stream.

Then, when the fire had burned down some, I knelt by the edge of the stream, and prayed again to the one whose name could never be known, and who might, for some incomprehensible reason, care for all those who walk upon the earth. I begged for the return of my friend, and for an answer to the mystery which is living—how could it be that I had had such a friend, and lost him, and that all the days of my journey through this world had come about as they had?

I had been praying for about an hour with my head bowed, when something made me look up.

There was a man standing in the stream. Or on it. With the light of the fire behind me, I could not see well into the darkness. As the figure moved, there was no splashing of his footfalls. He seemed to drift, like a puff of smoke.

I rose and backed away. I loosened the peace-straps from my sword hilt. But I did not draw the sword. I wasn't sure enough to be afraid, or awed, or anything but undecided.

I watched the stranger intently as he approached. Still, because of the light, I could not see his face. I could tell he was dressed in a loose robe and a peaked hat.

"Greeting, good sir," I said. "Will you share the fire with me?"

Still slowly, very deliberately, he came forward. He said nothing.

"You—" I began to babble nervously. "Are you sent? Have you come to—? Have you a message for me from—?"

There was no reply. When the man came within the circle of the firelight, I could see that he had no face, and thus no mouth, and that was why he did not speak. In the place of a face there was a black oval, not a mask, not a burnt sore, but an absolute, limitless void sinking into his head in all defiance of perspective and dimensions. I feared that if I looked at it for too long I would be drawn into it, out of the universe altogether.

He walked through the fire, obliviously, without scattering the kindling wood. He reached out with a very ordinary hand to touch me.

I screamed from terror and against terror, a battle cry to drive all thought away. My sword flashed out. I held up my hook-ended arm to shield my eyes from the awful sight of that hollowness. I felt the blade strike something half solid, and pass through, its momentum unspent. Thrown off balance, I tumbled forward.

Almost loosing my footing for a second, I recovered, whirled about, and sought my foe. There was no sign of him. I was alone. The fire crackled as before.

When at last I slept that night, I fell at once into a dream in which I had returned to the castle of the Owl's Beak. There, to my astonishment, Sir Emile was waiting. He smiled broadly when he saw me and called out my name. I dismounted and ran to embrace him, but when we came together I felt none of the bulk of his body. He crumbled away as I touched him, like sand, until there was nothing but a heap of dust scattered over my feet. All the while his wife looked on and screamed and screamed....

When I awoke the fire had gone out, and the wind had blown ashes onto my face. And I wondered, which of these three things was the sign I had prayed for, the terrible figure in the night, the dream, or the ashes?

I travelled again for a day and a night, always alone, through empty fields and still forests. I came to a village which was absolutely deserted. I stopped once at a windmill where the flapping arms still turned, thinking that surely someone would be there, but no: the stone wheel ground on, and the gears spun unattended.

All through the day the sky was overcast. That night there were no stars, and if any moon was up the clouds hid it. Toward dawn it began to rain, lightly at first, but building up to a raging tempest. Lightning cracked and flickered across the sky like giants dancing on legs of fire. Trees swayed and twisted in the wind.

It was in the midst of this storm that I saw something moving slowly over the ground. I spurred my horse on toward the shape, at first a mere suggestion of grey on grey, then a spot of a darker brown, something definitely alive, definitely creeping along. It resolved into a simple two-wheeled cart covered over with a canopy of dull cloth pulled by an ox.

I rode around in front so that I could see the driver, then reined my horse. The beast was uneasy, halfway panicked from the storm, but I held it firm.

I saw that the driver was a tall, hunched-over monk. Beside him sat a layman, simply garbed, but wealth was betrayed by several rings on the hand that held his cloak shut. In the back of the cart another figure huddled beneath blankets, the face hidden in a hood.

I held up a hand to draw their attention.

"Hail," I said.

"Brother," said the monk, "as I am a Christian, I don't doubt that it will hail, and rain cows, and perhaps a whirlwind of blood will tear the world apart, but before it does we'd best be on to the inn. This is no time for idle talk."

"What inn?" I had to shout to be heard over the wind and the clatter of the rain on the top of the cart.

"Up there a ways." He pointed in the direction he was going. "We had to backtrack. The bridge over the river has washed away."

I pounded on the door of the inn with the curve of my iron hook. The monk banged with his staff and the other man with his fists. A little panel behind metal bars slid aside, and someone looked out, then unbarred the door. We carried the other traveller in from the back of the wagon. It was an old woman, seemingly delirious, and blind.

The bald, fat innkeeper seemed amazed to see us.

"There has been no one for days," he said. "They've all gone away."

"*Away?*" I asked.

"At first a few of them talked about it. They said they were being called. Someone was calling them to some place. I didn't understand it then, but afterwards, when the last of them were gone, I knew they had gone to *him.*"

Now the man's eyes were full of fear, and he trembled so that I didn't think he could speak another coherent sentence, or remain standing there for very much longer.

"Brother," said the monk. "I think you ought to fetch your best brandy, or wine, or something. You need a drink more than any of us, and not just to warm you. And when you are calmed down, tell us what has happened."

He gulped, tried to look brave, and left the room.

"Ah, a good man," said the monk. And turning to me: "Now we should be introduced. I am Brother Francis of the Brown Friars. This one with me is Nicholas Block, a learned doctor—"

"—of Miraclology," the other man said. "We study miracles, what happens, how it happens, what is revealed."

"It's close to blasphemy," said the monk.

"But the intent is pious. We seek to understand the workings of God using the intellect he gave us—"

"Enough of that now." To me again: "And you, sir?"

"I am Julian, a knight. I am searching for a friend I have lost. Who is the old woman?"

"That unfortunate soul is Alicia. She has been afflicted since birth, but to compensate, God has spoken to her many times. She has visions, and in one of them she was told to go to the place for which we are bound, and there know an end to her troubles."

"I want to document such a miraculous cure," said the doctor.

As if she had been prompted, the crone stirred in the chair we had placed her in. "Uhhh?" She sat up straight and turned her head this way and that in a jerking, birdlike motion. "I dreamt that a mouse crawled into my ear and whispered that I should go to Inglegarth, beyond the deep river...."

"That is why we are traveling. There is no question that strange things have occurred in this region. My abbot has sent me to determine if the manifestations are of heavenly origin, or Satanic."

Or neither, I wanted to say, but had enough wit not to.

"Yes, that's it," said Block. "News has been very infrequent, but I talked to a couple of pedlars who had passed through. One said the Virgin has been seen, and a spring now flowed from where she had stood. The other told of a woman who gave birth to a baby with the head of a lamb, which died almost instantly, but spoke three words before it did. I am sure that if I learned those words, and came to know their meaning, all the secrets of creation would be unlocked."

"Either way you gain something," I said.

"Don't make sport!" scolded the monk. "It is true that unusual events have taken place—"

"Yes, very unusual indeed." It was the innkeeper who spoke. He had returned with some cups and a bottle of wine. We all drank.

"What have you seen?" I asked him.

"Much. One night flocks of chattering gargoyles swarmed over the windows, trying to get in. They were like slender, hairless apes with leering faces and bat wings always in a blur of motion. We all yelled at them, and a few waved torches and knives. I had a roaring fire lit in the fireplace to keep them from coming down the chimney. Still, they wouldn't go away till dawn. And that morning, the first few said they were being called away, and they went. The next night all seemed well, but after I had retired I heard footsteps in the hall outside my chamber. I sat up in bed and listened. It was a light, scraping sort of sound, more like something being dragged than something walking. There was a knock on the door. I tell you, my heart almost stopped then. And a voice said, 'Message for Master John.' John, that's my name. I got up and opened the door, all the while sure I was mad for doing so, and found a rotted skeleton just outside. I screamed at the sight, and my screams echoed through the place, but after that all was quiet. There were no guests to wake. They had all gone, leaving their things behind. I don't know why. Good sirs, you can't imagine the terror I felt. What if, somehow, all the evil, all the nightmares and terrors there could ever be, were caught up in a flask, and somebody, by a wicked deed or thought or something pulled the plug out, and it all spilled over the world? Either that, or I was sure it was Judgment Day, and somehow I'd been left behind. I went downstairs. The next thing I knew I was seated at this very table by this very fireplace. I think I slept. I'm not sure if I was dreaming, but the next thing I knew there was someone in the room, whispering that I should go with him. I would know the reason for everything, he said, and I would be beyond any earthly woe. I looked up and saw a man standing over me. There were no eyes in his head, only black pits, bigger than sockets. You could put your fists through them. I turned and ran away screaming, back to the bedroom. I don't think I ever got there. When I awoke that morning I found myself on the stairs. My nightgown was ripped from where I stumbled. The building was empty, and the front door was open."

There was much talk of miracles that night. Brother Francis told how he had once been met on the road by an apparition of a woman carrying her head in her arms. He crossed himself and spoke the name of Christ, and when the thing did not vanish, he knew it was holy, and, led by it, he came to the tomb of a forgotten martyr, where on certain days thereafter the sick could be healed, and those who waited for cures sometimes had strange visions. Nicholas Block believed that all perceived things are made of three essences, the earthly, the spiritual, and that of fire.

"Your friend, the other knight," he said, "was obviously akin to you in the spiritual essence, and it is your fiery essence, which rules the passion, that makes you long for him and seek him out. But just think: if you or he were somehow melted down like a metal into the pure essences, and reconstructed in the same pattern, the two of you *would be the same*. Your soul, your self, is not as unique and inviolate as you might think."

At this point the monk, sure he had at last detected heresy (I was sure this argument had been going on for a long time), directed a fearsome glare at the doctor.

"Of course," said Block quickly, "such a thing is really impossible, just speculation, and in the hands of God."

Whereupon Brother Francis again became his jovial self.

I told them of my own experiences, sometimes the truth, sometimes utter fabrication, sometimes repeating what I had heard from others. There were lots of forced marches, sieges, and mighty battles against the pagans, in it, and, of course, not a few miracles.

Alicia mumbled to herself for a while, then snored.

The rain continued. Gradually the fire in the fireplace burned down. The smoke made our eyes heavy. Nicholas jokingly suggested there might be a gargoyle stuck in the chimney, blocking it. We all slept by the hearth, huddled against each other for warmth and protection. I muttered another prayer to the unknown god just before I dozed off.

I had another dream, so vivid this time that I could not distinguish it from life, and I never have, and I never have determined where it ceased and waking experience began, *or if it ever ceased at all.*

I dreamed that I got up in the middle of the night to piss, but suddenly the sequence of time snapped like an over-taut rope. The others slept around me, and I stood in the middle of the room for no reason. Then I was on my knees, praying to the unknown god for some final sign and the ultimate revelation. The witch from atop the Owl's Beak was with me. When I looked up from my prayer, she was laughing, or making the facial contortions of laughter, even if no sound came forth. Her eyes were gone, replaced by endless black pits, like those I had seen before. Her mouth also was of the same nature, an oval which wavered and grew until her cheeks were eaten away, and her chin and nose and forehead seemed to hover by themselves. Then her whole face became utterly dark and without form, reflecting no light. She stood there for a moment, ridiculously headless, as if nothing were amiss, but as soon as she moved her whole body became as the face, a mere outline, a woman-shaped gap cut in the air, within which was a pit which could never be filled.

Before I could even think to cry out or run away, the creature blinked once and vanished. The air rushed into the space where it had been with an audible pop.

I was once more standing in the room at the inn, with the others sleeping at my feet. The coals in the fireplace were glowing dimly.

I stared down at my companions for a long time, wondering if I would ever know the company of flesh and blood people again. All of them, for all their failings, seemed limitlessly dear to me just then, so wonderful, closer to me than any family. I felt as if I were on one raft and they on another, drifting apart. I could see them clearly for a long time, but would never be with them again. Somehow I knew this.

I thought of Emile. I spoke his name aloud.

I turned away from the old woman, the monk, the doctor, and the innkeeper, and noticed that the door to the outside was unbarred and open. The night was very dark, and the rain had stopped.

Just beyond the doorway stood a man in a black, hooded cape. I could see his face: wrinkled, sunken cheeks, tangled white beard and hair, and empty black sockets where his eyes belonged. I wondered if that void were not a kind of degenerative disease, which in this one had not yet progressed very far.

He held his hands a little ways out from his sides. Wolves, larger and darker than any I had ever seen, were licking his fingers.

He spoke no word and made no gesture, but he was irresistably beckoning me.

When I stepped over the threshold I felt more intensely alive than I ever had before. I could feel the chill of the air and see the moonlight beginning to break through the clouds as if my senses had been heightened a thousandfold. I could smell the damp ground and the mustiness of the wolves' fur with incredible intensity. The leaves on the trees rattled like the last, dead husks of November.

I walked toward the man. As I looked at him, he alone seemed real. The rest of the world around me, for all the sharpening of the senses, was a dream, a wisp of smoke which drifted away before his being. And I was moved to speak, in the manner of an Old Testament prophet. The words came of their own volition, without any act of my will.

"I think you are an angel or a demon," I said, "and I am not sure which I am more afraid of. Then, you could be neither, and I might fear you most of all. But I think you are a sign sent to me by the unknown god. Of this I am sure. It is my fate and his command that I follow you."

"I have summoned the great masses, but you are one of the few who have called out to me, not once, but several times. Then come with me." His voice was a soft dry whisper, like the rustling of the leaves. He raised his hands, and two of the wolves rose with them, growing and changing their shapes. They became intensely black, like his eyes, again, like the whole body of the witch-woman, more wolf-shaped rents in the fabric of creation than living things. They seemed two-dimensional, and yet their depth was infinite. The fabric continued to tear, and the shapes were those of immense stallions. Then they regained some substance. They were beasts again, wearing saddles and bridles of curious workmanship.

The stranger—who was not a stranger at all, but the one who had visited me by the stream; even if now much of his face was restored—climbed onto one horse and I the other, and we rode over the soggy fields, through banks of low-lying mist, and along a muddy highway. We came to the ruins of the bridge that had washed out, and our steeds did not hesitate. They galloped over the water as if it were stone, and sparks shot from their hooves. And yet they made no sound.

Beyond was a land of reversed light and shadow. The sky was a brilliant white, but all the trees and stones, and later deserted towns and curiously crafted castles on the hilltops, were dark. Little patches of brightness hid beneath the leaves and behind the stones, where shadows would normally be. But the stranger ahead of me remained dark, and our horses were the color of midnight. I had on a blue surcoat over my shirt of chain-mail, and I also wore green hose, and these remained blue and green.

Onward we rushed up a long, steep hillside, into the rising sun. The sun was black, as black as the eyes of the stranger and the vanishing face of the witch woman, and it spread its blackness over the sky, dispelling the light, until it reached the horizon on every side. And the bright patches beneath the leaves and behind the stones were swallowed up as darkness flowed over and around everything, like water through the hold of a sinking ship.

For a time we rode blind, in an absolute absence of light. There seemed to be ground beneath us, and the horse between my legs was solid enough. I could feel its muscles rippling as it ran.

When we emerged into a land beneath an ordinary, star-filled night sky, the shock was such that I had to shield my eyes with my hand, all the while holding onto the reins awkwardly with my hook.

We drew to a stop, dismounted, and the horses shrank into wolves again, then into dogs, then to mice, then they vanished. I stood with my companion in the middle of a circle of fallen stones, some so covered over by weeds and earth that their shapes were merely suggested by the contours of the ground. But as I watched, they became more prominent, and stood up, and others seemed to rise like steam out of the soil. Soon there were upright columns with other stones laid across the tops of them, like the Giant's Dance on Salisbury Plain in England. But the development did not cease there. Walls rose up, and towers, and vaulted arches, until we were surrounded by a vast complex of buildings, unlighted, and filled with shadow.

"This is the Temple of Darkness," he said. "We who call out to the darkness or are called by it worship here. Come."

I followed him by the sound of his footsteps through a corridor until we emerged into an open courtyard paved with smooth slabs of stone. In the middle of it was an oval pool with a stairway leading down into it. The pool contained no water, but it was not empty. It had no bottom I could see, but instead an utter void filled it, like the blackness I had seen in the faces of the various apparitions, including the one which accompanied me now. The stars in the night sky were not mirrored in the surface of the pool.

"I—"

"You want to know why you are here, and who I am. To answer the first, you are here because you called out into the unknown darkness, and it heard you. To answer the second, I am Tiresias."

"The blind prophet?"

"At first I was blind, but in the sorrow of my blindness I looked deep into the darkness which was my eternal companion, and I understood it, and heard it speak. And I gave myself over to

134

it, to the absolute black stream of midnight. Now I have seen throught it, like a man who enters a forest and is lost for a time, but then comes out on the other side. I have the sight of darkness now. In a way, I see."

"And you worship it? As a god?"

"I surrender to it, and I serve it, and for this reason it causes me to be reconstituted over the years, and I emerge out of the darkness in the shape I wear, and for a time I live again, until its purpose is fulfilled."

"And what is its purpose, ultimately?"

"Julian, are you stupidly arrogant like all other men, or do you somehow realize that this world of yours, and all its gods, are like chips of wood, like sawdust floating on the still sea of darkness? These pieces cling to themselves, and think their world is solid, but it isn't. One ripple in the Unbeing, and all is washed away. But, look. We are no longer alone."

Even as he spoke, a throng of people came out of the recesses of the temple, from corridors and portals, from the shadows beneath the eaves. I knew some of them: the monk, the crone, the innkeeper, the doctor, the keeper of the gate I had met a few days before—the fellow who crossed himself behind my back. I recognized that man from his uniform, the monk by his robe, the old blind woman by the way she hobbled. The doctor still had his rings. But none of them had faces left, nor did many others in that crowd. Only a few of them had huge, empty sockets like Tiresias, and perhaps a mouth which was endlessly black and uncomfortably out of proportion.

As I watched, this strange procession moved slowly to the stairs leading down into the pool, and one by one the people descended. As they touched the surface, each of them became an entirely dark, human-shaped hole in the universe, and they spread out, losing all semblance of form, until they melted into the pool, which remained as smooth as it had always been.

"What is happening to them?"

"What will happen to all eventually, and to you before very long. They are becoming one with the very darkness, the very unknown you called upon in your prayers. They lose their selves utterly."

For the first time in all this series of events, I said something that I am sure was my own thought, not something drawn forth from me by the Darkness.

"How horrible...."

"Is it really? Does not every drop of rainwater long to rejoin the great ocean, to be completely a part of it? There is peace in that. When you prayed, when you asked for an escape from—how did you once phrase it—'the hammer of God and the anvil of the Devil,' for something which is neither salvation nor damnation, you spoke directly to the Darkness, and this is what you brought upon yourself. And someday it will swallow up that God and Devil, and all will be void and without form, and quiet as the pool."

"*No.* I won't. I can't." I knew again that it was I speaking, free of any restraint, for I knew that I feared oblivion more than anything else. Can a man even conceive of such a thing? To spend forever in Hell is one thing, but still you are yourself, even as a wretched wanderer is himself, and clings to that fact when he has nothing else.

"Julian, there is nothing to be afraid of," someone said, and when I heard *that* voice I turned from Tiresias in terrified astonishment.

Sir Emile, my dearest friend, stood at the top of the stairs. His eyes were gone, and it seemed all of cosmic space was in his head, and I wanted to ram two fingers in, grasp him by the inside of the skull, and drag him out of this lunatic place. I was sure that if I did, his head wouldn't rattle.

"No! Please! Stop! Don't!"

"Why are you so excited? You should be glad to come along. Julian, there is no pain here."

"*What do you know about pain? Life was good to you!*"

"I heard the darkness calling, and I answered, and I came, and here I am. It was so obvious. I never tried to resist."

And he smiled, that quiet smile I had always known—the ends of his moustache perked up—and the sight of that brought more agony than any torturer's iron. This *thing* smiled like my friend! This *thing* spoke with his voice! This *thing* had been my friend!

This thing very calmly stepped into the pool and became a silhouette, and flowed like oil poured into a vat, into the darkness and was no more.

How can I say what happened after that? My mind snapped like the time sequence, like the over-taut rope, and I went mad with grief, and I took on the guile of the madman. Craftily I watched and made no further protest as each of the others went into the pool, until Tiresias and I were again alone.

"Since they have all done it with no ill effect," I said quietly, "I shall go with you. I believe now. Yes, you are right. This is what is best for me."

"Then, since you come of your own will entirely, I do not have to touch you, and give you the mark of Darkness before you go." And he smiled, and his mouth had no teeth in it. The abyss between his parted lips spread and joined that of his eyes, and swallowed up his face until only an empty oval remained. And he had the mark of Darkness on him, and his will was the will of the Darkness.

He walked slowly to the stairs, and paused.

He was waiting for me to descend first.

I walked slowly to the stairs, and paused. And the craft of the madman aided me.

"I—I—am still...afraid. I want you to show me how the thing is done, that there is nothing wrong with it. Will you give me this last proof? Oh, don't think that I shall run away. I know full well that I cannot leave the Temple of Darkness!"

Nodding, he stepped down into the pool, and at the very instant he became a black outline, my sword all but leapt from its scabbard of its own accord and slashed right through him.

And met no resistance as he melted into the surface of the pool.

I was alone in the temple, and I knew I had accomplished nothing. Therefore the madman that I was was moved to call out, "Help! Help! I am still afraid. Tiresias, come back and take me by the hand, and lead me into the Darkness! I can't do it by myself!"

Somehow, he who was a servant of the Darkness, and who could be reconstituted when It saw a need, heard me. There was a flickering by the steps, and some of the pool seemed to crawl up, and take shape, and become a man.

And then my sword slashed out again, struck a solid neck, and went through.

There was an amazed scream which shook the whole temple, and a head dropped to the pavement—the sockets had blind, white, rolled-up eyes in them—and I reeled back, deaf and stunned by the sound. And I screamed at the top of my voice, rejecting the unknown god, spurning the Darkness, proclaiming that I would always be Julian, damned and apostate or not, and I would never give up my *self* to anyone, to any thing, to any shadow or ghost. The walls gave way around me. The towers trembled and fell. The crashing masonry fell on me like feathers, like ash, like puffs of wind.

I fainted, and I awoke, and I looked up to see the outline of the place shimmering beneath the stars. And I fainted again, and slept for a long time.

When I next opened my eyes, it was morning, and I was alone on a dusty plain. There was no sign of the temple, or even the stones. Or of Emile or any of the others.

And my heart was filled with sorrow.

That is my adventure, as much as I can make any sense out of it, or find any meaning in what happened. Did I truly awaken? When? As I left the inn, or not even yet? I still fear the dark, shadowy places, and I wonder if I should be like the Emperor Hadrian, and build temples all over the world, and place no image in them, in the hope that someday I might go into one of them, and meet my friend.

But I am terrified of what I may learn when I find him.

10

Into the Dark Land...

For three nights I had dreamed of the lady in white, the hillside, and the hooded rider, and on the third night, at the darkest hour just before dawn, I awoke with the realization that it was my fate to view all the strange secrets the world kept hidden. And I, who had fled from Christ and all his works, I who had done unholy things, I, Julian, called Apostate, second and lesser of that name, prayed in that darkness to whatever *other* gods might listen, that the veils of life might be parted from me, and a new world revealed. Then I slept and dreamed again, and because I dreamed it the thing happened, and because it happened I dreamed it. Past and future, cause and effect all turned back in confusion, like the serpent swallowing its tail.

On the fourth side, led by my vision, I sat on a grassy hillside watching the rider approach. The sky was unusually bright, a full moon shining through thin clouds, against which the branches of trees stood out like intricate carvings of black jade, each leaf and twig clearly outlined. An owl swooped low over the valley, rising with the slope of a second hill opposite me, searching after mystery.

I saw the horseman coming from a long way off, as I had in my dreams: first a hint of movement in the distance, then a speck, then a shadow, a shape, and the thudding of hooves, all before the man reached me.

"Will you come with me?" he said, "Sir Knight, the tale of your deeds has preceded you. There is need of your peculiar skills in a place beyond the sight of your God. I offer an adventure."

I had no words. In the dream I had spoken none.

"Will you come with me?" he said.

And I mounted my horse and together we rode, overtaking the owl in its flight, at full gallop across the valley and up the other hill. The moon seemed rising to meet us, and a fancy came to me that it was an enormous eye, the iris dilating to the far reaches of the heavens, through which we passed into another existence altogether.

By the light of this moon my shirt of mail, my helmet and scabbard, and the dull bronze cap in which was set the hook where my left hand used to be all shone like purest gold.

Atop the ridge we paused and looked down into a second valley, this one filled with mist rolling and glowing below us like some enchanted smoke, as if a sister to the moon were being birthed therein. My companion raised a hand. He spoke a word. I listened, at first hearing the cries of night birds, a dog barking far away, and my own heart. There was no wind. Then out of the mist came a deep sighing which grew into a muted roar like the surf at the edge of an endless ocean. The clouds began to stir in the depths of the valley, and dimly, distantly, I spied rising out of it a dark point, a glistening cone, a cylinder, a sheer tower. Another rose near it, and another, and another. Rooftops broke the surface, then a long line of battlements. A huge, arching gate reared up like a giant's mouth.

I lost all sense of time, but after an interval a city stood before us, gleaming like a sunken hulk dragged up from the bottom of the sea, revealed to the night sky.

"Behold Kelasdrene," said my companion.

"Is this the same of which the poet sang, *Kelasdrene the phantom, more fleeting than the fog?*"

"*More solid than the rock on which the whole world stands,*" he completed the verse. "Yes, it is the same. I am king of this place, and have no name but Kelasdrene for myself. The very soul of this city is the ruler, and of the ruler, the city. Literally. Remember that. It is important."

As we descended the hillside, the King's hood fell back. He wore a crown of silver; his long, thin face was deeply lined, his beard streaked with grey.

The fog enveloped us, no longer glowing as we neared the gate of the city. Chill vapours rose from a river as we clattered over the drawbridge. Here and there exceptionally dense patches hovered, or huddled against the dripping stone walls, like ghosts of the newly drowned, not yet sure where they were supposed to go.

No guards greeted us. No watchmen stood on the walls. The massive gates hung ajar on rusted hinges. Much of the grandeur of the city vanished as we entered it, now replaced by a sombre brooding. There was a feeling of decay over all. The very towers seemed dead. Only at very great intervals was there a light in any window, and these were always very far off.

Somewhere, indefinably beneath us, a great bell tolled. I felt an unnatural chill pass through my body, as if it were more than an ordinary sound, and now I was under its spell forever, trapped by venturing close enough to hear it.

At first the city seemed entirely deserted, even if there were a few lights, but then I glimpsed a face in a crack between two shutters, a scurrying form in an alleyway, and heard someone scuffling along the ramparts above us.

And still, from the heart of the city, the bell tolled.

"I have never seen such a place as this," I said at last, and then paused, fearing I had given offense. But the King took none, and spoke:

"Kelasdrene—I, I am Kelasdrene and it is I, and I know—is a ship without anchor, adrift in time and space. This much you must have already surmised. But did you know also that I have been present when the name of Julian was mentioned, when you were a memory, a legend, and then a dream? I have been ahead of you in time. In doing so I have become more like you, you more like me. We share the brotherhood of history's phantoms."

Still without being hailed in any way, we rode into a narrow and especially dark street, and the King dismounted. I could barely see him against the glistening wet pavement as he tethered his horse to a post. I did likewise and followed him on foot. The fog was denser than ever, and by its very grey it relieved the utter blackness. Against it I could dimly make out the form of the man leading me.

I could see nothing on either side or above, but after a time I sensed that the walls were even closer and we were in a tunnel. The stones underfoot were no longer rough, but smooth like polished marble. We walked on. I think we were actually indoors, but the fog was still with us. It seemed that only the two of us existed in all of dim creation. The only other reality was the floor underfoot. The dampness in the air was forgotten.

We resumed our conversation, as if there had been no hiatus.

"Then you must know to what end I will eventually come," I said, intensely excited, since I knew that in this life things are not random, but for a purpose, and surely something was about to be revealed. I felt fear and hope together. Surely I was long since damned by God, but this place was beyond His sight, was it not, outside the universe?

"No, oddly I do not. The ending of the tale is not clear to me. Stories never end, it seems. We wake from them, but they wait for us, ready to resume when we dream again the dream which is living. Just this morning, if such a term can apply to this place, I looked out my window over the plains of Illium, and Troy still stood. I saw nothing of the conclusion of that story. Another time I came to the shore of an endless grey ocean, a place where bare rock met the unceasing waves, and the sun was red as blood overhead. Again, no ending. I am carried adrift on this stone ship like any other. I am not the teller of the tales."

This struck me as mad, distracted talk, and I wondered if the King's mind were diseased. I asked him a more direct question: "Why have you brought me here?"

"First, to mourn for my daughter, who was to have reigned after me, and taken the soul of the city to be her soul. But before that even, we must sit and eat."

Even as he spoke we came to a table at which two places were set. I was sure we were inside a building now, but the fog continued to hide everything around us.

Places were set, but there was no meat or drink. I looked in askance across the table to my host. He merely pointed to my right.

I turned, and a wine cup floated out of the darkness. I took it, and felt a firm grip released, but saw not the hand that held it. I turned to my left, and glowing against the gloom was a silver plate, on which lay a cooked fish. This also was brought by an invisible bearer. As the King was being served, I thought I spied a black hand and sleeve eclipsing him for an instant as a dish was set before him.

All this did not help my appetite. Was the food unearthly? Would I sleep for a thousand years after a single bite or sip? Or would I be turned to stone?

The King ate without waiting to see if I did or not. Cautiously I joined in, with no ill effect, but not tasting much, considering the darkness, the chill, and the sheer strangeness of the experience.

At last I saw a light approaching from behind the King. A lantern. When it was directly behind him, he turned around in his seat and took it, placing it on the table between us. This time I was sure there had been a black human figure present, and I heard the soft pattering of slippered feet retreating. He was not attended by spirits.

"Ah yes," he said. "You desire more light. So let there be light, as someone else once remarked."

As he spoke, as if by his command, even though his voice had scarcely been above a whisper, more lights appeared around us like stars in a clearing firmament. First two or three, then a dozen, then a hundred.

And all this while the deep-voiced bell tolled beneath us.

Slowly the hall became lighted well enough for me to make out shapes, then details. It was a vast room. I still could not discern the ceiling far above. Here and there between hanging draperies, and in and out of a forest of pillars, faceless men in black went silently, rapidly, tapers in hand, lighting lanterns.

The bell still tolled.

As the light grew stronger I saw that the lanterns hung on the doors of tombs, all of which were open. Dank drafts from within made the flames flicker. A few went out and had to be relit.

And I knew my long and dreaded doom had come, and now I sat in the anteroom of Hell.

As it turned out, I was wrong. It was nothing so simple.

The bell tolled.

Now the last part of the dream came to me. Seeming to float

on the air, but in truth borne by dark-stained hands, the lady in white, whose form I had scarcely glimpsed before, came out of the distance, until she was scarcely ten cubits from where we sat, and I could tell she was too stiff to be alive, or even a corpse.

"My daughter has arrived," said the King aloud. "Let all lights be lit."

At once the room was ablaze. A thousand lamps flared up at once. A huge vessel of oil roared into flame. My eyes were dazzled; I covered my face; I thought myself dead in the land of the dead.

When I could see again the fog was entirely gone, and we still sat amongst the tombs, surrounded by hundreds of the folk of Kelasdrene, all of them garbed in black, and also with their hands, faces, and even their teeth painted that colour, so only their eyes were in contrast. Facing us, held upright now in the hands of the multitude, was a crude wooden carving of a woman, garbed in white, and wearing a queen's crown.

I looked in astonishment from face to face, and no one seemed surprised or dismayed. I concluded they were *all* mad. Was this the afterworld of lunatics? No; many were holding back tears. All faces showed resignation, but intense grief also. Even the King's.

"You must understand," said he, "that in Kelasdrene there are no burials and no corpses to be buried, which is why the tombs are empty at our funerals. My daughter, who was the hope of our people, without whom all will surely perish once I am gone, is only *represented* by the statue. In truth we have not even the comfort of her remains to dress and prepare. She has been carried off by Escheoun Vatu."

The name meant nothing to me, but again, as if my thoughts were being read, an explanation came. One whom I took to be a priest, for his robes were more ornate than those of anyone else, and bedecked with black jewels, stepped forward and told a tale of Kelasdrene and Escheoun Vatu. And a lesser priest followed him, and another. And another came, and spoke on, until there had been ten tales and ten tellers. They began with a time shortly after God first opened his eyes to gaze upon the Earth, when the first of all magicians was born in the light of that half-sleeping gaze. This was before the age of Adam and the garden even. The Church tells none of it, and the Jews hint only a little in their secret books. Most of this lore is lost to mankind outside of Kelasdrene. This first magician, whose name was Kelasdrene, took a drop of his heart's blood in his hand, where it dried into a scarlet pearl. From this, using only his fingernails, he carved the city as it once was in its prime, sublime and beautiful. Then, fearing the wrath of the jealous Creator, he masked his work in a

144

golden fog, and placed it in a pocket beyond the universe, where he could rule unopposed as king. From him all the kings of Kelasdrene descended. Out of the breath of his mouth all the folk of that place sprang. It was his soul and his heartbeat which sustained the city, and that of his heirs. And it was a flaw inherent in his scheme of things which caused the coming of Escheoun Vatu.

This spirit was the Lord of Death, who ventured into Kelasdrene from the void beyond the end of the worlds, enshadowing the city from the most ancient times. Perhaps he was admitted at the foolish behest of the people, who wished to worship a god like no other. No one can be sure of this, for it happened very long ago, before there was ever a Redeemer or even an Abraham. It was before any such memories that Escheoun Vatu broke the chain anchoring Kelasdrene to its place in time and space, setting it adrift and even more apart, so he alone could prey off it, summoning the folk into his kingdom with the irrestible tolling of his bell, which rang now for the daughter of the King. His curse was more deeply rooted than any wrought of mere sorcery.

By the last priest a curious thing was mentioned, that those taken by Escheoun Vatu suffered not, but fell into a kind of endless sleep without dreams. Thus there was no true Hell for the subjects of Escheoun Vatu, nor was there any Heaven.

And again I asked, as ideas and possibilities swirled within me, "Why have I been brought here?"

And the King answered, "To be our champion. Your task it is to venture yet living into the land beneath our land, to the place where the great bell rings for our souls, and win back our queen. I think"—and at this he lowered his voice and gazed at me knowingly—"that at the end of the quest you will find your own reward. It is told that such a deed may only be accomplished by exchange. One soul taken away, one given in its place."

Deeply I felt within me that this was the part of the dream I had never dreamed before, always interrupted by waking. This was the end of the tale, as had been pre-ordained.

I would make this journey.

The bell of Escheoun Vatu rang on.

II

Now after many strange prayers were prayed, and the statue of the queen was placed in one of the tombs, and still the tomb

was left open, and the deep bell rang throughout the ceremony without pause, slowly, as if the eternal tides of the sea caused the motion, the folk of Kelasdrene began to drift away by ones and twos, taking their lanterns with them, until at last the King and I were again alone, and the fog closed in around us. The vessel of oil sputtered as the last fuel at the bottom was burned, the dying flames casting huge shadows up the walls.

The King took me by one hand, and led me to the tomb where the statue had been placed.

"You are ready to go now."

And I thought of my weary wanderings through all the lands of the Earth, my sorrows, my wretched, sinful, desperately unavoidable deeds, my anger at the Judge Eternal who made my lot thus, and condemned to even more when I railed against him, and I said, "Yes."

Then the King spoke four words, and the bell beneath seemed much louder. I remained where I stood, but the cramped space within the tomb seemed distant. I could not see his face clearly, even though now he held both my true hand and my metal hook, and was gazing intently into my eyes.

"*Elam.*"

I felt his grip loosen, and then he was no longer with me. At first there was only darkness and fog, as there had been in the city outside. But still his voice was clear.

"*Aelam.*"

Now I was falling and twisting through impossible angles, and the bell thundered in my ears. Lights like the lanterns, like the stars viewed from beneath the sea, fled ever downward, leading me on.

"*Olam.*" His voice was like the cry of a herald on a distant mountain. Still, as if I were underwater, the mud at my feet sprang up in knee-high clouds at my every footstep, then settled slowly. I was running, without any sense of motion, without any effort, down a barren hillside. The bell was so loud it was the only true thing, all else peripherally imagined, nay, not imagined, but impossibly dreamed. Above me the night sky was clear, and the stars shone brightly, arraigned in constellations I had never seen before, which no man has ever seen while he walks the Earth.

The hillside levelled out. I came to a ruined wall, and a gate, and passed through.

"*Thhoh!*"

This last word was more felt than heard. Silence. Surely the bell still tolled, but where I was no sound travelled.

I was in the kingdom of Escheoun Vatu.

I, Julian, called Apostate after a more distinguished

147

predecessor, had evaded the grasp of my God, and was in the country of Escheoun Vatu. Triumph! Now, since I was not of the blood of Kelasdrene, I could evade Escheoun Vatu too. But before I did, I had a task to perform. In thanks for this boon, I had to fulfill my part of the bargain with the King and his people above.

I wandered across a completely empty landscape until it seemed I knew no other action. So bare was the soil that an occasional stone seemed as rare and as extraordinary as a mountain on the great Steppes. Somehow I never seemed to tire, but the place was not timeless. There were days and nights of a sort. The sky would turn a dull grey and provide a sort of twilight, then darken again, and the strange stars would come out. There didn't seem to be any regular intervals between the two periods. Imagine black butterflies and white ones trapped in a bottle, flapping back and forth, swarming over one another, battering themselves against the glass. These were the days and nights in the land of Escheoun Vatu.

Basically my sojourn below was a long walk. Many poets and painters have depicted the Christian Heaven and Hell in the most elaborate terms, with many levels and stages, with marvels at every hand. Indeed, once I saw the latter in a vision, and I know. Perhaps Escheoun Vatu was less imaginative. Still league followed league of desolate waste. Perhaps his land was as yet so unfilled that nothing more was needed to contain the souls in it. I forgot all dangers and my quest. I tried to make a game of counting paces between those rare rocks at least the size of melons, but lost count. Distance was no more coherent than time in that place. It also occurred to me: the dead of Escheoun Vatu are truly dead, knowing no joy, no pain, no movement. It has always been obvious what hands shaped the towers of Satan's palace of Pandaemonium, what backs carried the stones. Escheoun Vatu simply lacked the labour force.

At last the desert came to an end, and there were sparse grasses over a still, flat, and empty landscape. Then it was no longer empty. I came to a wall of white stone. The quiet of the land seeped into me, and I felt no urgency. I examined the thing at leisure. It was smooth, neither warm nor cold, but solid to the touch. All over it, so that never a span remained bare, were carved stone flowers, and in the middle of each flower was a face. They were not standardized faces like you see on tomb brasses, where the master craftsman commands his apprentices to have three knights, two ladies, and a burgher ready by the end of the month. Each of these was an individual, wrought with infinite delicacy and care, so that no two were alike, as no two humans are alike exactly, even twins. One may have a blemish and the other not.

One may have eaten more, and grown greater of cheek. And I knew that these were not carvings, but the souls themselves. Each of them slept, their faces utterly blank, without fear or sorrow, or even an awareness of contentment.

In this wall was a plain gate of iron bars, which swung on silent hinges. It was unlocked.

I went in, and found myself in a garden, lushly overgrown with flowers and trees. A placid brook ran through the middle, but the water made no sound. There was absolute silence, utter peace. I wanted nothing more at the first sight of that garden than to lie down and rest, never to reawaken, thus escaping my life and my God. But before I could do this thing I had to remove one last concern from my mind: the queen-to-be of Kelasdrene. I would find her, bring her to the edge of this land, where she could go on to reach her father, then turn back.

I wandered a ways among the trees before I noticed a new wonder. It was like my adventure of the Island of Faces all over again, with shapes of men and women hidden among the leaves, the branches, and swelling with the bark; only there was no pent-up fury here, no suffering. I thought it would not be so terrible a thing to be part of some enormous bough or trunk. Also, unlike the Isle, there was no wind blowing voices through the branches. There was no wind at all.

After the forest ended I entered a field, and here more folk lay. I could tell which had been there the longest. They were slowly turning into beds of flowers, with blossoms growing out of the eyes and mouths, then the whole face, and where they had been thinly spread over the body they became thick, until little of the original form could be seen. Others, newly arrived, seemed at first glance to be just resting among the grasses and flowers, perhaps wearing a garland, but no more.

One of these was the white lady of my dreams, whose image I had seen in the darkened room—the daughter of the King. She was motionless, her face blank, as if her soul had already seeped out into the soil. Flowers were tangled in her hair and the bright faces of them peeked out of her garments, but her face was as yet untouched.

Surely this was the greatest marvel of the realm, that the dream of three nights, obviously a sending of Escheoun Vatu himself, should be so well fulfilled. But there was another astounding thing also. I was at the very centre of the garden, with the lady at my feet, and right before me, swinging back and forth in what seemed to me utter silence, the only moving thing except for myself, was the great bell I had heard before, mounted between two pillars. There was no bell-ringer. It moved of its own volition, perhaps six feet off the ground.

As if it were whispering to me to lie down and let all things flow from me, the urge to abandon my quest was far greater in the proximity of the bell. All but overwhelming. I actually did go so far as to kneel down, but then my gaze fell on the princess, and I remembered the sorrow of Kelasdrene. It seemed like a vague thing, no more than a whispered summary of a dream, but I remembered it. I have lost all my chivalric ideals over the years except this one: I have never been able to utterly shake my sense of duty. I was on a quest. There was a deed to be done, a promise to be fulfilled.

So, I told myself, I would bear this lady up and carry her to the ruined wall at the edge of the waste. I knelt, and worked both arms under her, careful not to stab her with my hook, all the while using it to break roots, separating her from the ground, I pulled. More roots broke. She was a dead weight, but free.

Then there was a sound. If a pile of bones were tied together into a net or loose drapery, then suddenly lifted and spread out, the bones would rattle. That was the sound I heard. The shock of the noise brought me out of my dreamy stupor. I was alert for danger.

Rising up to one side, farther away from the bell than I, was a thin shape. A man, but so fragile in appearance that beneath his billowing cape—billowing with some wind from within himself—he hardly seemed material.

Besides the cape he wore a silver helmet with a visor. A skeletal hand raised the visor, revealing a faintly sparkling mist within, but no face. Still I sensed there was something there, eyes, a mind, an intelligence. This could be none other than Escheoun Vatu himself. I wondered how many had ever seen him while they yet lived.

The other hand held a long, thin sword, a needle of grey-white bone.

"Put that one down, and you shall sleep by her side."

The voice was like rustling leaves, but I did not hear it. It was inside my head, directly in my mind.

"I have sworn to take her away. When I am done I shall leave myself in her place."

"Why should I accept only one, when I can have two?"

Neither the King nor I had foreseen that.

And Escheoun Vatu came forward slowly, rattling, billowing, his sword pointing.

I set the lady down and drew my own sword, which was made by mortal hands out of ordinary steel.

Our blades touched, and a numbing shock ran through my

arm. My weapon was hurled from my grasp by a mere flick of the other.

I backed away from the death god, toward the bell.

"Why do you avoid me? What is there to fear? Soon you will be beyond fear."

Still I backed away. Still he advanced, rattling.

"Is this not what you truly came for?"

At that instant time seemed to stop, and I thought more things than a scholar can write in a hundred books. I thought that even rage and pain are true feelings. They are living. To be without them is to be as insubstantial as a puff of steam, rapidly dissipating into nothing. Could I, who had lived so intensely, come to this? I think it was fear and courage working hand in hand which made me realize I really did not want to die, that the very notion was a childish, cowardly recourse. I wanted to go on, no matter what the circumstances. I knew I had to continue my defiance of all things. There was also my duty. I had to accomplish something. I had known for a very long time, since the beginning of my wanderings, that more than anything else I feared dying for nothing in some futile gesture, and leaving great deeds undone. Horatius at the bridge is my idea of martyrdom, not Christians in the lion pit. If I were to touch the tip of the bone-coloured sword just now, the lady would remain where she was, Kelasdrene would pass away, and what would all my previous adventures have amounted to, when weighed together?

Nothing. Meaningless oblivion while still living is far worse than a well-earned death, and that would be what my life would become, even if only in retrospect. The prospect of knowing this appalled me.

Escheoun Vatu slowly approached. I backed under the bell itself, ducking down to avoid the swinging edges.

I was within reach of the death god. He drew his sword back for the final stroke. I caught a subliminal glimpse of the blade flashing my way.

At that very second, almost without knowing what I was doing, I leapt straight up, into the bell. I caught the clapper with my arms and pulled myself up. I slipped my hook through the chain which held it, and clung desperately. I was slammed into the side of the bell by the weight of the clapper, just as Escheoun Vatu's sword passed beneath my feet. Ribs cracked, and all the breath was knocked out of me, but mostly because of the tangled hook I held on. Of course my legs fell limp in my weakness and pain, and my feet hung beneath the edge of the bell. My opponent could have gotten me with a second stroke, and that would have been the end.

But he didn't. I hit first one side of the bell, then the other, and the second time my right elbow smashed into the metal. In a sudden burst of pain I let go, and with the hook only to support me it came loose, and down I tumbled, minus hook, with the stump of the left wrist yanked raw.

Escheoun Vatu stood completely motionless when I landed at his feet. The bell had stopped. I had muffled it with my body. Thus he could no longer call the living into the land of the dead. He was powerless.

III

I took the lady in my arms and carried her out of the garden and across the waste. As we neared the end of it she began to feel warm, and slightly less limp. Then she stirred. The flowers fell from her hair. I set her down beyond the ruined wall, at the base of the long slope. There she opened her eyes, and sat up.

I was too ecstatic at the wonder of this thing to think of anything else, and thus I was like the hero of the old tale who forgot to change the black sails of mourning for white, and thus brought on tragedy after his triumph.

"Look!" she said, pointing up the hillside. "It's Father!"

Indeed it was. He came lurching stiffly down toward us. I hailed him, but he made no reply. Even when he was very close he stumbled by, taking no notice of us. His face was devoid of any awareness, his eyes turned up so that only the whites showed. His head bobbed loosely on his shoulders. There was a rope around his neck.

When we got back to Kelasdrene we learned, amid weeping at the uselessness of it, what had happened. The King had watched our progress in a magic glass, in which living souls appeared as tiny candle flames. He had expected mine to wink out, and that of his daughter to be relit. When the bell had stopped ringing he had wondered, but not known, the true meaning of it, for he was too distraught with sorrow and the suspense of the venture to think clearly. When he saw both of us beyond the wall, alive, he cried out that he had been betrayed, that we were attempting the impossible and the full wrath of Escheoun Vatu would be upon the city. Therefore he had hanged himself to set things right, to exchange his soul for that of his daughter.

That is exactly how I refused to allow myself to die. But the King's deed took greater courage than I have ever had. He is the true hero of this tale.

Riddle me this, said I to myself, what does it mean? Does it mean anything? I think it is a taunt from on high. No, no, you can't quit the game now. Your very nature won't let you, and by that you are trapped. You'll go on and on. Your life and your sorrows are not over yet. You amuse us too much with your rebellion, Julian, and with your despair. No rest for you.

On and on. Riddle me this: Did I wake or dream when I rode from that timeless city afraid that I might emerge into a world a thousand years beyond my time, only to look over my shoulder as I rode and see beneath the bright midnight sky, beneath the moon, galloping up the slope I was descending, a one-handed knight and a hooded rider?

One night I could not sleep, and I rose, and wandered away from the inn where I was staying. The night was clear, the air a little cold. It felt good merely to walk beneath the stars, breathing that air.

By the side of a road I met a man of the East who was held to be holy by folk who had never heard the name of Christ. He sat with two companions by a fire. He wore a purple robe, the others, brown ones. Their heads were shaven, and their round, yellow faces seemed to glow in the flickering light. Cordially, they invited me to join them, and we drank tea together. For a while we spoke of unimportant things, and for a while longer we said nothing at all, but sat and watched the stars wheel above us. I remarked that in my country one of the formations around the North Star is called Karl's Wain—the chariot of Charlemagne. One of the companions said that in his those stars were thought to be the bier of a king who had been treacherously slain when an enemy in the form of a metal bee flew down his throat and cut out his heart with its wings. His many wives, forever weeping, vowed to bear him across the heavens until those very heavens ceased to turn.

Still later, this same man sang a song of his country in his own language. I did not understand the words, but it was clear that he was as far from any familiar place as was I.

The stars turned some more. At last I asked of the holy man, "Is it possible to never die?"

"And live forever?" he laughed. A broad smile spread over his face. "Yes, it is. In fact, I have already done so. A single year ago I slept in a cave and dreamt that I was a pilgrim, and I wandered over the entire Earth, touching every corner of it, following every river to its source, climbing every mountain. I sought the secret of eternal life in all those places, but, not finding it, I fell down by the edge of the sea and died. Then a golden bird came out of the dawn and took up my spirit in its beak, and, wheeling about, carried me toward the sunrise, to the great hole in the world ocean where the sun emerges every morning. But the sun had already risen, so the bird could descend without fear of the flames. It placed me in the pool of unending life, which is in the land beneath the sea. The pool is no bigger than a bowl you hold in your lap. There cannot be much immortality, lest the balance of things be upset.

"As soon as I touched that water, I became a tiny fish swimming in it. For a thousand thousand years I swam, exploring my abode. For a thousand thousand more I floated, contemplating the sun as it passed up into the world every day. For likewise as many years I went mad with boredom for, as you may imagine, the life of an immortal fish in a pool that size, when there is not

155

even the need and challenge of seeking food, lacks variety. Then I meditated, until my awareness became as dissipated as the steam which escapes from our kettle, and all of eternity passed me by and I was oblivious to it. But then a blue-faced god with stars in his hair came walking through that land, and, reaching into the pool, seized me and ate me. The pain of being ground between his teeth returned me to consciousness, but since I had been immersed in that water for so long, I could not die. For a while I resided in the stomach of the god, and later, as he stood upon the upper world, I passed out of his bowels. I became part of the soil, feeling the sun and rain, and grasses grew out of me, and vast trees, until finally the dew from those blades and those leaves ran together in the shadow of those boughs and I became as you see me now."

"But that is impossible," I said. "How could eternity have passed if you only lay down to sleep a year ago? Are you now a figure in your own dream? What of the one who slept in the cave?"

The holy one paused, and for a moment I feared I had offended him, but still he smiled. His tone had changed, though, and now he was the schoolmaster addressing a student who had shown some promise, but turned out disappointing.

"If I ever meet that one, perhaps we shall debate," he said. He rose to his feet and pointed to the brightening eastern sky. "The whole night has passed away. Now I must go and converse with the sunrise. One more thing I will tell you, the great secret I learned through my experience."

"What was that?"

"Never listen to idle tales. They make you mad and lead you through the bowels of a god."

"Of course," said one of the disciples after he had left, "it is the nature of the madness that one never heeds these warnings."

11

A Fabulous Formless Darkness...

"Oh God of mysteries and doubt, is it in your stone heart to send me on my final journey without any signpost or beacon to mark my way? Let there first be a revelation, an unveiling. Touch my eyes that they may be opened and I may see the inner workings of the world, and know where I am going and why and how. You who set Man above the beasts and kindled in him the desire for knowledge, knowledge before faith, knowledge supreme and secure, must by all that is right and holy grant that knowledge and justify your ways, lest it be said that the mind is but another torment for a soul already damned."

At first they were a single dark speck against the featureless waste of the desert, but as I rode nearer the speck divided in two and became human, a faithful servant kneeling at the side of an ancient and dying lama.

Age and whatever disease wasted him had given the holy man an aspect almost reptilian. Only his huge eyes seemed to remain alive in a face otherwise leathery, wrinkled and dead, sunken deep in his sockets like carefully set jewels. His voice was dry seeds rattling in a hollow gourd.

"I feel your destiny, stranger," he said. "It was destined that I wait here to tell you of it, before I set foot in the new land. In Ta-Neng you shall see the workings of the universe. It is your nature and your task to probe into such things."

He held up a frail twig of an arm. On one of the fingers of the hand there was a large jade ring.

"He wants you to take it as a sign that you have met him," said the servant.

I was unfamiliar with the customs of this land, but I suspected it would be better to have met and spoken with this revered one than not, so I dismounted and gently eased the ring from the already stiffening finger.

Even as I touched him he died. His eyes were still open, and he was staring at me with fanatic intensity. It was evident that at the moment of his departure he had been mad, possessed, or both.

We could not bury the mad lama. The desert was not made of sand, but baked clay, and it was hard as bricks, only occasionally broken into chips and powder, and here and there laced with crevices and gorges. So we left him and the servant sat behind me on my horse, since he had none. I wondered how he and his master had come to so desolate a place and I asked him but he hid behind his imperfect knowledge of my tongue and my imperfect knowledge of his, and would not answer. Probably they had been abandoned by a caravan, but not out of neglect or disrespect. He had wanted it that way.

In time I spoke to the servant, whose name was Yuan, of the strange prophecy. He was shocked at my ignorance.

"Have you never heard of Ta-Neng?"

"No."

"And the Black Faith? What of that?"

"That too is strange to me."

"The Black Faith of Ta-Neng is known to all of this country. Surely...."

"I am of Europe, Yuan, not this country, and where I was born your world is a fable no one more than half believes in."

He set to explaining.

"Ta-Neng is a place all can find but none go to of their own will, except perhaps brave and wise men like my master, who go there secretly at night to gain wisdom through fear. For the Black Faith is a fearful thing, dreaded by all teachers and monks. The adherents worship death and terror and darkness, not as personified creatures, not as gods, but as one basic and irresistable principle underlying all things."

"And do you believe this, my friend?"

"I...I cannot say." And he would not. He was silent for many hours until we came to the edge of the desert and the land was fertile again. He directed me to a place he knew and we stopped by a stream to drink and wash the hot grime of the waste off our faces, and I was given sweet water roots to eat. Then we continued on, into the highlands, until mountains rose around us, their snow-capped peaks glistening against the blue sky like fangs. It was here, as if he were finally beyond the hearing of someone he would not share his words with, that he spoke again of his beliefs.

"Death whispers with a thousand mouths into the ears of every man at every instant of his life. In the storm Death sings; in hail it rattles; in rain it softly caresses. Death and darkness are stronger than life. Their mysteries are far more profound."

And I told him of the faith of Christ, how the savior died and was resurrected, and how he was worshipped in the churches by men who fought against the Saracens and Jews in the name of the God of Love.

Hearing this, Yuan laughed softly. "At this Death is glad, if it can be anything. By such practices Europe is brought into harmony with darkness."

After a while we were among the clouds. They drifted by like fleecy leviathans on an invisible sea, and below us, to the east, intermittently hidden and revealed, stretched the lush valleys, the rivers, and the scattered towns of Asia. Overhead the sun sailed around the side of a cliff, it sank directly behind our destination, the monastery of Ta-Neng, bathing all the walls and towers of the place in a brilliant orange glow. My eyes were dazzled and thus I did not see, until I was in its shadow, at the end of the winding path leading up to its gate, the greatest marvel of Ta-Neng. The monastery was not built, but carven out of the side of the mountain, intricately, beautifully, impossibly, over a thousand centuries or a single night by an army of demons, who placed their own images everywhere on the walls, in the windowsills, over the doors. Countless stone shapes seemed to writhe as I gazed upon them, and when viewed from the side they seemed afire, leaping forth into the fading sunlight with blazing arms, legs and tails. As the shadows shifted they seemed to stare back at us, tittering at the strange and wide-eyed newcomers.

The gate was of jade, and before it stood two burly men like black beetles in their strange armour, yet unarmed, bearing only carven staves. They cried out a challenge and Yuan answered, explaining with quavering voice our situation. But they were so surprised to find at their door a tattered, one-handed knight from a land to them beyond the setting sun, that they would not let us in, despite all entreaties.

"Show the ring," whispered Yuan.

I did, holding my hand out so they could see. At this they grew silent and even more astonished, and after a brief conference at one side, one of the guards called out and the gate was opened from within just enough for him to slip through, while the other stood, staff firmly in hand, to block my path.

I could see that Yuan was trembling. He was ashen with resigned fear.

"You do not wish to accompany me?"

"No master...I mean, my master gave me a command which I have carried out, even though I am greatly afraid, and I...."

"I understand. Take my horse and return to your home."

"I will be able to walk. I thank you, great sir...."

"Then take at least my water bottle and what dried meat I have left to replenish you on your journey. I shall not need them here."

These he accepted, babbling thanks in scarcely coherent language. He slid from his place behind me, took my gifts, and hurried away down the winding path, back the way we had come. A few minutes later I turned around to see how he fared and saw that he was running.

The green gate swung wide, and the lord of Ta-Neng came to welcome me, resplendent in jewels and a billowing yellow robe. He was a tall man for his folk, nearly my height, and he did not look his years.

160

He walked upright with assured strides, and only in the deepest wrinkles of his face, and only in his eyes was there any sign of his vast age. His head was entirely bald, the scalp stretched over his skull like tight brown leather. When he came forward with hand extended, I dismounted to greet him, and was allowed inside. Someone led my horse away.

I showed the master, or abbot, if a pagan can be called that, the ring the lama had given me, and he remarked, "Yes, my student had great powers of foretelling. It is well that he sent you here."

And I recalled what Yuan had meant about brave and wise men going to Ta-Neng secretly at night.

At once the two of us seemed to be old friends, the abbot and I, and we spoke of many things. A great feast had already been laid out, and I was invited to attend. In truth I saw and heard much that was strange, many rituals of hidden meaning, prayers chanted to the four directions, all the lights in the hall put out for a while as a low, murmurous song was sung, and libations poured out the windows to appease I knew not what, but there was no apparent cause to hold this place or these monks in dread as Yuan had.

During the meal I sat by the side of the abbot and he questioned me at length about the places I had seen and the land I had come from. I told him all he wished to know, and after he had heard it he was silent for a while. He drained a cup of wine and ate a leg of fowl, musing over what I had said. At last he came to a conclusion as the tables were being cleared.

"It is all a dream, Sir Julian, that you have wandered out of."

"What is?"

"Europe. The sun rises there when it sets in Asia, and when the men of Europe rise and work those of Asia are asleep, dreaming. Europe is a dream in the mind of Asia."

"Or it could be that Asia is a dream in the mind of Europe."

At that he only smiled tolerantly.

I dwelt in pleasant tranquility for many days, often alone in my room with my thoughts, but more frequently in the company of others. I was welcomed by the monks at any time. I participated in their daily routines and in their discussions, and whole worlds were shown to me.

There was a complete world on a rafter in the corridor outside the feasting hall, painted by a little old man standing atop a ladder. It was a beautiful and intricate piece of work, a miniature no longer on a side than the distance between the artist's wrist and elbow, but in it there were hundreds of figures, and when he bade me climb up the ladder with him, the painter showed me what he had done more closely, telling of the lives and deeds of his characters, and the histories of the walled towns between his mountains, and there was a world there. Some while later the abbot took me to the top of the highest tower of Ta-Neng, and the sky was clearer than I had ever seen it, and there was another world stretched out before me, as vast as the one on the rafter. And I saw how, as he had once said, the great and small dance together as lovers and become one.

He was a very perceptive man, this abbot. I never knew his name; I called him only, as all the others did, 'Master'. He was surely the greatest philosopher the earth has ever known.

One night he said to me, "You struggle under the burden of some great sorrow."

"I am afraid of death," I replied.

"Is that so strange a thing, that you have crossed half the world to escape?"

"I am afraid not of dying, but of living beyond it." And suddenly the floodgates of my soul were opened, and I told him all my sins and terrible deeds, how I had turned my face from God and from the Devil also, and stood now like a helpless child between two onrushing armies, and when I had exhausted my store of woe I weakly rambled on, repeating stories told by priests about the torments of the damned.

"This Hell created by your loving God is indeed a terrible place," said the Master. "Would it comfort you any to know that there is nothing beyond this life except silence?"

"It is not comfort I need, wise one. I am a warrior. I am used to pain and I do not fear it. The terrible thing is *not knowing*, going into the endless dark without any tangible evidence of what I shall meet. I don't know, I cannot know...."

"But you do know. Your priests have described it all for you, to the minutest detail."

"I'm not sure I entirely believe them."

The Master smiled.

"We can delve this night into these mysteries. It was for this purpose, after all, that the dying one sent you. He was, as I have said, a foreteller, and it was known to him that you desire the certain knowledge of which you speak. He knew also that you have the will and strength to go very far."

"Yes, I think I have. But I do not understand...."

"Come, and you shall understand much."

Again he showed his tolerant smile.

I followed him wordlessly through the hallways of Ta-Neng. My mind was filled with questions. Was I now to understand the dark principle underlying all and come to believe what Yuan had called the Black Faith? I felt a certain tension, an excitement as if I were going into battle, or a joust, but I did not fear. The Master was leading me and I trusted him more than I had ever trusted anyone before.

We came to a bronze door on which two armies of dragons were devouring one another, and passed beyond it, down a narrow, winding set of stone stairs worn by the feet of many generations. The stairs led to a tunnel, which also went downward, sloping, and breaking into more stairs whenever the way was too steep. We were going into the very bowels of the mountain. At last the tunnel opened into a vast cavern, like the inside of a buried cathedral, and from the opening in the side of the rock we descended more stairs to the cavern floor. Above me the roof was lost in distance and darkness. The place was lit by a ring of torches around its circular walls, and everywhere shadows flickered and danced.

But I paid little attention to these things. The huge disc below held my gaze. It was as wide as a courtyard and made of a smooth white stone, perhaps a kind of marble, and it was perfectly round. Around its rim were placed statues of a beautiful, glazed stuff the eastern folk called porcelain, the images of kings and emperors, and also little castles and towns. From above, from out of the darkness, hung a long cable, on the end of which was a metal weight. It was round, but not a ball, more like an inverted teardrop, the point downward. The thing was a pendulum, swinging back and forth on the cord, reaching one side of the disc and then the opposite, always passing through the centre. Yet so subtly constructed was it that the path of the weight was never quite the same. Always it came to a place just a little bit further along the edge, so that eventually it would cover the entire circumference.

The pendulum drew closer and closer to one of the statues, even as I watched striking it, and there was a tinkling like broken glass.

I looked to my companion for an explanation, and he said only, "Somewhere a king has fallen from his throne."

"But how can you know this, to arrange the statue thus?"

Yet again he smiled, and his tone was that of a teacher explaining something for the twentieth time to a slow schoolboy.

"Nothing has been arranged. Because the image on our clock here has been shattered, a king has fallen from his throne and his dynasty likewise has been shattered."

"Then this is like no clock in all the world. But how is it a clock? How can it measure hours?"

"There is indeed no other like it. There can only be one clock like this in a world, and it measures all times and places in that world."

"Is this one of the mysteries you spoke of?"

"The first of a great many. Follow me now."

He stepped out into the face of the clock and I followed him. I nearly stepped on a castle and he scolded me sharply.

"Have care! The walls you topple might someday have protected you. The lord might have become your ally."

The Master vanished into the air like a burst bubble.

Now I thought I was mad. I looked around. There were no trapdoors, no place he could have gone. The stone was solid beneath my feet. The weight on the end of the cord had reached its farthest distance and was coming back. Was it a thing of sorcery? Surely it was. It was also nearly upon me when, almost without knowing what I was doing, I leapt forward to avoid it, over the line of its path.

I felt the metal teardrop pass through the air a hand's thickness from my head. I landed, stumbled, fell flat, then sat up and looked about.

I was somewhere else, and the Master was standing over me.

We were no longer in the cave, or even among mountains. The air was hot, heavy and dry, the sky a dull grey. In all directions a flat landscape stretched, scattered with pebbles but lacking any other feature. It was not a dead place but a lifeless one. Life had never been here.

I got to my feet and faced the abbot wordlessly.

"Shall we go on?" he said.

I followed him. We took two or three steps and the pendulum slashed the air behind me again, and the sky was bright blue. We stood in the cool of morning, and the robes of the Master flapped in the stiff breeze. It was a pleasant place we had come to, a narrow green valley between two hills. The two of us stood on a large boulder, which rode like the hump of a whale above a sea of bright, flat-leaved plants. They resembled nothing more than lily pads out of water.

I had seen far too many wonders in Ta-Neng and elsewhere to be greatly amazed. I did not know where we were, what was happening to me, or what the Master intended. I merely accepted and proceeded to explore.

He said nothing and made no motion to stop me as I climbed down the rock. I walked among the green things a short distance, enjoying the peaceful, beautiful world I had come into, and then I felt the sharp pain of a venomed bite in my ankle. I looked down.

"*The blood of Christ!*"

No, it was my blood. The plants had come alive. From under

each leaf a crab-like shape emerged, of the same green substance, part of the plant itself, a detached limb, containing the mouth, teeth and claws of the ravenously hungry thing. Hundreds of them swarmed over my feet and ankles, tearing at the leather and metal of my shoes. I kicked them off but it was like kicking quicksand. More clambered up my legs, stinging like thousands of hornets. Already I was hellishly dizzy. I bent down to brush them off and there were more of them, on my arms, shoulders, and tangled in my hair. I drew my sword...I still had it; the monks had never objected...and took a swipe, and succeeded only in slashing my thigh.

"Help!" I turned and saw the Master, still standing on the stone. It was foolish to call to him. What could he do? Was I expecting him to wave his arms and utter a spell to save me? I waded toward him through the wriggling green mass, stamping down as hard as I could, crushing useless hundreds, flailing my arms, swatting myself with the flat of the sword blade. My knees began to give way under me. My legs were numb. Walking was like balancing myself on stilts. I drew nearer the rock, reaching out, sword still in hand, and my balance failed. I fell forward, sure to meet my end, when hands caught me. Hands dragged me up into the boulder, and as if by a benevolent charm, like a spent wave receding, the plant creatures dropped off me, scrambling back down their leaves to wait for another prey.

The Master did not have to tell me never to go where he did not. I said nothing. I managed to sit up and, noticing the sword still in my swollen hand, I sheathed it. My companion reached into his clothing and took out a vial, the contents of which I drank. It was a drug to ease the pain. I slept on the stone for a long time, and when I awoke he was still beside me and the sun was low in the sky.

"Shall we climb another step? Are you able?"

I nodded and the pendulum went past us once again, and there was no sky. We were in a great hall of stone, in the heart of some impossible castle that seemed to go on forever in all directions. It was made up of little rooms, like a honeycomb, and as far as I could see all of them were empty and filled with dust. From the ceiling of each a golden bell hung. I opened my mouth to speak, to ask what place this was, when a draft blew past me, and all the bells began to ring, filling the universe with their voices, louder, louder, louder....

I felt a tug on my arm. I took a step back the way I had come, faintly heard the metal teardrop swish by in the blissful quiet, and then stars shone overhead.

It was a deep, moonless night, and we stood dwarfed by

rocky crags. The stones were cold beneath my feet. From my right a frigid breeze was coming, as if from the depths of a cavern. Above, the peaks stood like mute black giants.

The Master pointed to the left.

"In that direction," he said, "lies the world of men. The sun passes over it, as does the moon. If you begin walking that way you will first see a glow on the horizon, and then the sun at noon will just barely show itself, and then you will come to inhabited country. Here beyond the reach of the sun dwell only monsters."

I indicated the direction of the wind. "And what is in that direction?"

"Nothing. The world ends there."

I went to see. Deathly afraid, yet irresistibly fascinated, I dropped to my knees and crawled over a slight rise to the edge. I lay down on my stomach, clinging tightly with hands and feet as if someone were trying to dislodge me, and I inched forward the last short space until my chin hung over the abyss. I looked down to where the cliff vanished in the darkness. There was no land below, only stars against the black sky.

Still terrified, awed beyond words by this sight, I crawled away, down the rise backwards, only daring to turn around and get to my feet when I was almost to where the Master waited.

"Did you find the view instructive?"

"Yes."

"You are doing well. There is much more."

The pendulum swung back and forth, back and forth. Porcelain castles crashed into bits and kings toppled. The Master and I went on and on, from world to world. Once we stood by the edge of a well and he said, "Look," and I looked in. At the bottom, suspended in space, was a cat, playing with a ball. And the Master said, "Look again," and I did, and this time it was clear that the ball was the earth, and the cat was teasing it as it would a wounded mouse.

Once we stood on a mountaintop and peered into the night sky, and beheld a woman sitting above the horizon, spinning on a great wheel rimmed with stars. And behind her there was a man sitting with his arms folded, with planets for eyes. He seemed blind. And behind him there was another, with the head of a boar, and towering over him, dwarfing him as he dwarfed the others was something not at all human.

"Can you understand," said the Master, "that the universe is filled with gods and spirits? They go on forever. More are born with each human thought. Many love mankind and many hate him. Most have never heard of him. Some have and laugh at the knowledge. Others have gone mad. There are so many they can never all be counted."

We went on, to the end. The end was a featureless room without windows or doors. In the middle of the floor was an onyx chest.

"The answer to all your questions is inside," I was told. "No one before opened that box. Few have come as far as you have. Only once before have I ever stood in this room with someone, and then that one, who was greater than I, did not lift the lid. It is my advice that you follow his example."

"But I must open it, if the knowledge I seek is within."

Without hesitating, even though I knew I was on the brink of a far more fearsome chasm than that beyond the edge of the world, I raised the black covering.

And screamed.

And peered down into another darkness without stars, and as I watched a white speck appeared, far, far below, and rising higher and higher until I could see it was a deathmask, a skull-face, a face with features, a corpse's face with hollow eyes ready to devour me, rising on a shooting column of nighted void.

The face was my own.

The blackness poured out of the box like smoke, filled the room, then condensed into the shape of a man only much taller than a man, and the dead, horrible face rode atop it. My face transformed.

The Master screamed in fright.

"Know now what the Black Faith is! You worship a god you never see, and so do we. Only now I see it face to face!"

The thing walked with a light, hollow tapping. It reached out a hand toward my guide and he cringed in terror from Terror Incarnate.

And I did an incredible, foolish, heroically insane thing. I rushed between the two and held out my sword to ward off the unstoppable enemy. I stared into those eyes. Those eyes, which could drink all creation.

Suddenly there was another sword, a black sword touching mine. The two met, fused, and the blackness flowed up the blade into my hand, up my arm, and I felt an arctic numbness. I watched, wordlessly, horrified beyond any will to resist, in abject paralysis as the thing from the box became one with my body, sinking into my flesh like water into desert sand. I felt a loss of self, of body, of will, and I was but one of many thousands of bubbles in the foam of a black wave.

My name is Legion, for we are many....

I tried to speak. A howling gale coming from my throat. I still had enough control of my limbs to turn around, to face the Master.

"*No!* I can see it! I can see it in your eyes! It is still there!"

He ran from me, into the air, out of the room. The pendulum swung. I followed him, met him again, and he ran, from world to world, past the well of visions, past the mountain peak with the gods beyond it, and I pursued him. The act of pursuit helped me become a little more myself. A fury drove me, but also a pain, a pain that so dear a friend should now regard me with horror. This was the thin shred of humanity I desperately clung to.

I came to the rocky land beneath the stark cliffs near the edge of the world. I didn't see the Master anywhere. But he was there, waiting, taking me by surprise, wrestling with my right hand. I made a slash at him with the hook on the stump of my left, but a twinge of something held me back.

He was after the jade ring I wore, and I was able to notice then, for the first time, that he wore one exactly like it on his right hand.

He got mine off and was running toward the edge. I went after him, unhesitant this time, but was too late. I got to the cliff just as he dove headlong over it, my ring clenched firmly in his hand.

Down below a star winked as he went past.

I was filled with grief and at the same time was glad, not for the death of the Master, but for the grief, for by such an emotion I could conquer the darkness and regain myself. I walked away from the brink, down the rise, and to the spot where we had entered this level of creation. Nothing happened. Without the ring I could not pass over the course of the pendulum. He had taken it to prevent my return to Ta-Neng, to save his world from something so dangerous it had reduced him, the greatest of all men, to frantic fear. No, not frantic. His death had been rational, for a purpose.

I headed toward the sunlight and the inhabited lands, wondering all the while where I would find myself, in what world, or on what part of the earth. Perhaps not in Asia at all, perhaps not in my own time, perhaps where I belonged, in a realm ruled by trolls and goblins. All this while the force within me boiled, ready to explode. I could not relax my thoughts. I had to cling to powerful things, to my fear and guilt, to the painful deeds of my past. I dwelt on the faces of my murdered squire, of my violated beloved, of the drowned Lady Catherine, of the horror in the pool in the Vale of Mistorak.

I went over all the torments of Hell as reported by the priests, and I knew that a wrathful God had prepared them all for me.

By this means I held onto myself. At last the storm within me subsided and died, and the strange visions it brought faded, and nothing remained but an empty sorrow. My body was human again, weak with hunger, thirst and cold. Before me the sun rose cautiously over bare mountains, and beyond the mountains there was grass on the earth, and trees grew. I had come into the world again from its outermost edge. There were human beings there, and they fled at the sight of me, for still I bore the stamp of terror, the unearthly, and the holy.

For a thousand days and nights I wandered, until at last I came to Egypt, to a valley of stone kings resting against the sides of two mountains, and I heard them speak with my newly opened ears. Their words were the deep rumblings in the ground, and their sighs the night wind.

"Another century has passed."

"And another is born."

"A kingdom has been overthrown. A pestilence will come to a continent. This night a hundred thousand will perish by its tread."

"It does not matter. There are many kingdoms, many men."

"There's a gnat by your toe."

"What?"

"A man-shaped gnat, a ridiculous insect who asks foolish questions and seeks answers and reasons for the things around him."

"There are no answers or reasons."

When I understood that they were referring to me I fled in abject and fully comprehending dread.

Behind me, the colossi laughed with the voice of an earthquake.

12

Midnight, Moonlight and the Secret of the Sea...

I

I lost my faith on a foreign shore, in the shade of the conscience tree. In the shade of the conscience tree, on a foreign shore, where the sand ran wet with the blood of children.

II

There is something about the number three.... Three encounters started my adventure off.

First: Ragged and tattered and starving I came, my mind filled with a thousand ghosts and shadows, into a land where it was always raining, raining until all color had been washed out of the land, save for muddy brown and the grey of the sky. Nothing grew. The earth slept beneath dead leaves, the branches of the trees bare of them. It was late in the year, almost to Yule, and yet nowhere did anyone sing the carols of the Child Christ, or allow themselves to be seen, or stir unseen. It was very quiet, almost without sound. The constant voice of the rain was too universal, too interwoven with the fabric of existence to be considered a sound. After a while, the ear shut it out.

There I arrived, I Julian, called apostate, second of that name, formerly a knight of God and his holy crusade, shunned and shunning. Once more stepping into Europe and the realm of my own people. I found a newly slain knight lying under his shield in the middle of a meadow, already beginning to decay. Despite the rain, two large black birds perched on his face, pecking at his eyes. I drove them away and stripped him of his sword, his shield, his coat of mail, and his helmet, for I had lost all of mine. I couldn't recall where. In desert or in sea, in waking dream or in sleep.

I found his horse nearby, mounted, and rode away. I examined the shield. On it was the sign of the Endless Knot, and emblem of great potency. But the blow of a sword had dented the metal, scraped away a bit of paint, and broken the knot.

All around me the ground seemed to boil with mist; the air was damp and bitterly cold, filled with pestilent humors and dead souls.

Second: In an ancient wood, where pagans long ago had carved idolatrous faces in the trunks of the trees, near the ruin of a charcoal burner's cottage, I heard a cry of distress. I spurred my steed ahead through the underbrush and came to a clearing, where I found a lady writhing on the ground in agony.

172

"The bite of the serpent!" She pointed to twin wounds on her ankle. "Quick! Tie a string around my leg, lest the venom spread through my whole body." And her speech broke into inarticulate screams, and she moved her head from side to side rapidly in her pain.

I dismounted. Right by her was a huge tree, around which was tied a red cord. Without thinking I yanked it away—it broke easily—and knelt to bind her wound, when suddenly something stirred in the leaves and a tiny, dry voice said, "Did I do well, mistress?"

"You did very well," said the damsel.

I looked down, astonished, just in time to see the snake whiplash away. Then I turned my gaze to the lady, who was gazing beyond me at the tree, and laughing. She seemed entirely recovered.

I leapt to my feet, whirled about, and beheld six old women sliding down from the branches, slowly as a slug oozed rather than as a human climbs, as if they were growing from the boughs like obscene, overripe fruit. Six more were emerging from the roots of the tree, burrowing up out of the ground like worms, mud on their faces, and spitting up filth.

"He cannot stop us," they tittered. "He has not the cross. His magic sign will do him no good without it."

"*Who are you?*"

"Hail, anti-Merlin, brought to us in the fullness of time. Hail, liberator. Hail, fool."

"*Who are you?*"

"Who are we? Who are we?" Their voices slid into chant, into singsong. "We are all the evils of the world, all the lusts, all the fears, all the secrets concealed in the unredeemed dark. A great one bound us with mighty enchantments, and now you have undone his work. What is let loose may never be bound up again."

"*Who are you?*"

"Who are we? Who are we? We are who. We are who. We are who we are." They joined hands, the twelve of them, and danced in a ring around the tree, cackling, and I knew them to be witches, but older, more powerful than a common village hag who sells her soul to the devil for the power to send pains and poison wells.

The laughter of the damsel stopped, and I glanced back to where she had been. A fat toad hopped between my legs and into the circle. One of the crones scooped it up and placed it underneath her clothing, against her breast. Furious and frightened, I drew my sword, let out a battle yell, and charged. They scattered like startled pigeons, running between the trees in all directions with startling agility. For an instant there seemed to be a hundred witches, an army of them; my horse reared and bolted at the sight of them; and then I was alone, in the rain, with the final echoes of my voice coming back to me from the depths of the forest. I felt very cold and exhausted and began to shake.

I asked myself, how can I know this thing has happened, or where it has happened, or whether or not it is a vision of the future? Were my eyes closed to these things, or open? How can I ever know if I wake or dream?

The answers: There were still holes in the mud at the base of the tree, rapidly filling with water, their sides collapsing. On the ground nearby was a broken piece of red twine.

Third: I waded to my thighs in a frigid stream where a bridge had washed out, then clambered up the muddy bank, stumbling over loose stones. I splashed through once tilled fields, now bare of all but a few dead stalks. The rain made little lakes, and the soil ran away in brown rivulets. Beyond the fields, another stream, another ruined bridge, and a mill with its wheel moss-covered and rotting and motionless. Beyond this, roofless cottages and a manor house, which seemed abandoned, but at least might provide me with dry shelter.

The great hall within was empty, and the rooftree sagged. Boards and beams had fallen across the tables. The hearth was cold, and tiny waterfalls were everywhere. I explored other rooms, and found them likewise fallen down and sodden, but then I came upon one which was not, and in it were the four inhabitants of the place.

Three were bald, white-bearded men who wheezed and shuffled, servants to a younger master, or at least one who might have seemed young once before suffering had wasted him. His eyes were sunken, his face all but a death mask. His hair was falling out in patches, and it was streaked with grey. The skin of his hands seemed exquisitely white, like carven marble.

He sat in a high-backed wooden chair, hunched forward with a soiled blanket in his lap, and his three bent servants at his side. He was paging through a mildewed book, carefully separating the damp leaves with a thin knife, so as not to tear them.

When I had introduced myself and explained the circumstances of my coming—or at least as much as I cared to let him know—he said, "You were destined to arrive here, as my savior." And he told me his tale:

"My name is Gottfried. I was called Gottfried the Bold at one time. I was a bold, proud knight, a champion always in joust and battle. I wore a blue lily on my shield, and the scarf of my lady in my helm. Yes, I was to marry a great lady—more than that even, a

174

vision of the Ideal made incarnate—but first I swore, for the honor of my lady and the Lady of us all, by which I mean God's Mother, that I would go to the East and fight in the crusade. There I would cleanse the land of pagan evil and win free all the holy places, even the sepulcher where Christ slept for two nights and a day, and the hill of Golgotha where he died. I fought long and well with the army. God was with us, but then, as we approached the Holy City, a herald of the enemy came to us, saying that the gates would be opened and the city surrendered if one of our number could defeat one of theirs in single combat atop a nearby mountain. I think it was my pride—and this whole thing a device from on High to show me the folly of that pride—which made me accept the challenge. On the appointed morning I climbed the mountain. I labored all day in the hot sun, burdened by my armor and weapons, inching my way up the nearly sheer stone face. It was nearly evening when I came to the top, a wide plateau, and met my enemy. He had been waiting for me all day, it seemed. I don't know how he could have gotten there. The way I went was the only one possible for an earthly man, unless one could drift to such heights in the heart of a cloud.

"He was a giant. His armor was a shiny black, brilliant in the orange glow of the fading sun. I fought with him, and the struggle was over with painful swiftness. His arm moved faster than the eye could see. I was like an untrained boy with a stick against him. Before I could scarely draw two breaths he had dealt me a wound on the thigh, but he did not follow it with another blow. He left me there, and vanished into the oncoming night. He seemed to walk right off the edge of the cliff.

"The city was finally taken, as you know. Thousands died in the battle, thousands more from heat and foul water, but I saw little of this. At dawn my comrades came in search of me, and there they found me, suffering from a wound which never healed. I hired the most learned men of physick, but they could do nothing. It was beyond the power of leeches to draw the evil out. This work was the Lord's. Priests sang masses for me, and the whole of the army prayed, but it did no good. At last I had myself borne home, where I found my lands in ruin and decay, under a curse of endless rain, as you see them now. I have been waiting here ever since, waiting for sluggard death to come, or a miracle."

"Alas," I said. "I can work no miracles."

"But hold," said he. "Hear the rest: At long last I heard of a holy anchorite who had walled himself up in a cave and gained much wisdom in the dark. I went to him, and spoke through a tiny portal where a stone had fallen out. I saw nothing within, but heard a voice serene with confidence, saying, 'Until the ungodly is

removed from your domain, you shall not be healed.' And thus it is my hope, brave sir, that you can bring about my salvation. I no longer am able to move from my dwelling, but you are strong even yet, and you can go forth and root out whatever evil there is to be found."

I could not bring myself to answer, and he did not press me. The servants fetched a meager meal, which I ate gratefully. The two of us spoke for a while of other things, of poetry and strange dreams, and of impossible tales written in books.

III

That night I was shown to a bed in a room filled with cobwebs. When I slept, I swam backward in time through seas of memory, and saw clearly the tale I had been unable to tell in reply to Gottfried's.

I saw again the morning when the holy Tancred, Bishop of Anjou, Averoigne, and Poictesme, stood before the troops in the dim light of dawn with the walled city at his back. There was complete silence, save for the cawing of expectant crows and the flapping of banners in the brisk wind. He spoke:

"Soldiers of Christ, in yonder city wait ten thousand pagans, idolaters, devil-worshippers, atheists, and Jews, each of them by every breath he breathes an affront to the God who created him and a triumph for the Adversary who corrupted him. This is your task, mighty men of valor and virtue, your task set for you by God on high, to rid the land of this infection, to cleanse with fire and sword the very pavement on which the unclean ones walk. I have prayed for victory this day, and just before I came to you I had a vision. I saw in the sky, above the hills and above the pagan city, the great sign of the Cross, blazing as it did for Constantine when he embraced the Saviour, in this sign we too shall conquer. Jesus looks on. His Holy Mother waits to take any who die today in her own arms into Paradise. *Onward! For Christ and the Cross!*"

"Christ and the Cross!" The cry returned from every throat, and the host surged thunderously forward like an inexorable tide. The first wave broke against the stone walls of the city, and the battle was joined. "Christ and the Cross!" men shouted as they fell screaming beneath curtains of molten iron poured from above. "Christ and the Cross!" resounded once more as mangonels, catapaults, and ballistas filled the air with death. The fighting went on without pause until midday, and then there was a brief respite, scarcely long enough for both sides to wipe sweat from brows, and then the fury was renewed. In the purple evening the huge siege towers rumbled forth, and it was in full darkness that I clambered over the walls with the rest, too filled with wrath and battle lust to even think of waiting for the morrow.

The city was taken. The battlements were cleared of every foe, then the nearer streets, and even before the gates could be opened they were smashed from without by boar-headed battering rams. From above it must have looked like the flood of Noah, inundating the world. On the ground, a nest of hornets, stinging with steel.

When resistance was reduced to small pockets, the slaughter went on like an avalanche which grew and grew with each new falling stone and could not be stopped. Now mounted knights ran down women, old men, and children. Some laughed, thinking it a merry hunt as they speared the fleeing pagans. Anything which could bleed was cut open—men, horses, chickens, dogs. They were insatiable, famished for death. In narrow alleyways soldiers waded ankle-deep in gore. Once a group was found meekly sitting in the middle of a square, waiting for the end. There were priests and scholars present, staring with hopeless resignation, a few of them paging slowly through books. Women sat among them, young and old, with barefoot urchins in their laps. Only a few looked up as the vanguard of the conquerers halted before them. And I and the others, without hesitation, and rejoicing that God had granted us this chance to avenge our fallen comrades, dismounted and ran among them, hewing off heads and splattering brains as methodically as reapers in a field of grain. Bishop Tancred was there too. Forbidden by holy law to shed blood, he used a padded club which did just as well.

Later, as each man went his separate way in search of booty, I came to a holy place in the center of the metropolis, a vast structure of domes and delicate towers. I was at first reluctant to enter, lest I find Mahomet's coffin just inside the door, floating between floor and ceiling, but then I said to myself, "God is with me, and has triumphed this day," and I went in. In a wide, torchlit hall were three maidens, naked and headless. Outside the riot of shouting, occasional screams, doors being smashed, and the roaring of flames, but here it was quiet. I explored other rooms. The soothing darkness swallowed me up. Everything else seemed a remote dream.

Eventually I came to a place filled with books. Someone had been through it before me, and most of the volumes were in heaps on the floor, as if eager hands had sought treasure behind them on the shelves. Bloody fingerprints defaced some of the leaves. In the middle of the room was a coal-filled brazier which provided light.

Miraculously it had not been overturned. At the base of it lay a dead man. His turbaned head was cloven messily in twain. An arm raised in futile defense lay severed at his side. Yet in the other hand he still firmly clutched a thick volume. I pried it from his already stiffening fingers and looked through it. I could not read the script, but the diagrams seemed to suggest a treatise on magic. I knew it for a devilish thing, but was attracted by the sheer forbidden mystery of it. I resolved to keep it, and perhaps have it read to me by a learned prisoner, if there were any.

And then I dropped it with a start, and my heart leaped with sheerest terror as something clamped onto my ankle with the grip of a steel trap. I jumped away and looked down, and it was there still—the hand of the hewn off arm, clinging to me with more than human strength. I kicked and stamped and struck the thing with my sword, nearly chopping my foot off, but it would not let loose. An observer might have thought I was dancing a bizarre jig. I was only free of the thing when I had reduced it to such a pulpy ruin that it was more liquid than solid. I stood gasping, staring down in revulsion, and involuntarily I said aloud, "By the wounds of Christ!"

"Yes, the wounds of Christ and the hand of Christ and the face of Christ shall haunt you forever." A new dark miracle was upon me. The corpse sat up, and the lifeless lips on the ruined face spoke impossibly. "This curse I place upon thee, infidel, man of Europe—the burden of your own conscience. Let your eyes be opened for the first time, and from this day hence you shall find no rest, your pride and your remorse warring endlessly within you. Hated and hating, outcast before your God and your folk, you shall wander over the face of the earth in the face of death and fleeing the iron face of your Christ, and death shall precede you and follow after, bringing ruin to all things you hold to be holy, until you hold them holy no longer—"

"No more! Say nothing!" In a blind, tear-filled fury I struck off the head of the apparition, and hacked and hacked at the body until no part remained joined to any other. I sank my hands into the reddened sea of its breast—if only, if only I could hold the heart in my hands, then I would be sure my will had overcome the other. So I took out the very core of the monstrosity, impaled it on my sword and held it aloft, but there was no comfort in the action. Disgusted I flung it to a far wall, where it splattered like an overripe fruit.

And the voice spoke no more, and panting, ready to faint, I knelt there, leaning on my sword in a parody of prayer, breathing with labored gasps. All the accumulated weariness of the day seemed to fall on me just then. I barely managed to crawl a short

179

space away and sit down, my back against the shelves. I stared dumbly at the ceiling until some traces of reason returned, and then I retrieved the grimoire.

As I did I heard someone coming. I leapt to my feet, sword in hand, ready in case the newcomer should be a foe.

I knew the man. He was Robert of Tharras, a gallant knight who had saved my life in battle once when the enemy had me surrounded and unhorsed. I lowered my weapon at the sound of his familiar voice.

"Ho, Julian! You won't find any gold there. I already looked."

"So I...see...."

"There's nothing worth half a penny in this whole accursed place. No vessels like in our churches. But look—here's a prize."

He held up his spear to my face so I could see in the half light what he had. It was an infant, impaled on the point, covered with blood and trailing guts.

"One less devil-lover to grow up and trouble us, eh? And yet another goodly deed for saintly me." He laughed and rolled his eyes up to heaven in jest. When I said nothing he shrugged and went away, brandishing his trophy aloft.

I was without words. The sorcerer's curse had taken effect even there in the dim silence, revealed on the tip of a spear. It was as if the vast cathedral doors of my mind had opened for the first time, flooding daylight in on my unborn conscience. I asked myself, *What am I doing here? Are these deeds really pleasing to the Living, Loving God and his gentle Mother to whom the courtly heroes pray? And if they are, is He not more rightly to be called Moloch?*

There were no answers there in the room filled with loose papers and the smell of blood, no answers at all as Sir Robert's footsteps faded away and I was left alone, alone as I knew myself doomed forever to be.

The memory faded, but the final image would not. "Take it away!" I screamed, and the spear was still before me. I awoke screaming in the sodden, musty room, and when I had regathered my wits I knew what I had to do. I needed a ritual penance, an exorcism, a laying to rest of unquiet souls. I had to bind what I had loosed, heal what I had wounded, rebuild what I had destroyed.

I went at once to the chamber of Sir Gottfried. He was awake with his books. It seemed he never slept. The pain, he said, was too great for that.

I knelt down before him, presented him my sword for him to touch and bless, and swore to fulfill his quest. At this he took great comfort, and I a little, although I knew I could not be saved as easily as he. My enemy was far, far greater, if closer at hand.

IV

I was unable to see the maimed knight again to exchange blessings before I set off. His servants said he was asleep, truly asleep for the first time since his misfortune had begun. They dared not wake him. Hope had brought him this far, and they would not interfere.

The three of them brought me not my own sword and armor, but more splendid gear.

"These alone of all his treasures our master has been able to save. He bids you take them."

"I shall return them when I am done."

"There is no need! If you are successful, all things shall be awarded to you, and if you are not, alas, Sir Gottfried will have no use for his things of war except to be buried in them."

They helped me on with steel shoes first, then greaves, knee pieces, cuisses, a mailcoat of brightly polished rings, encasing me in steel from toe to head with practiced skill. Fingers knew their tasks, even if faces seemed blank and distracted. I considered these three, and thought it strange that I had never come to know them as persons, just the three, the identical three, like bewitched vegetable men pulled from the root of a single mandrake.

Over the coat of mail they placed a surcoat, covered with intricate designs, like a thing worn by the pagans in the East. Here, lions and elephants ran. There, a castle and a dragon in the sea, and all these things circling about the great sign of the blue lily across my chest. I was given a shield rimmed with rubies, on which the emblem was repeated, and a jeweled sword too, something I had never thought even to touch, too exquisite for a king, fit only for one of the Nine Worthies. I placed a golden helmet on my head, took a long white spear in hand, and mounted my horse, which now wore a saddle rimmed with silver tassels. Thus equipped I set out, while behind me the old men raised their hands aloft to wave me Godspeed. Soon they and the house were swallowed up by the mist and distance.

It continued to rain. Among the clouds overhead, sheets of lightning flared faintly and there were distant hints of thunder. For a while I was comfortable beneath my clothing, but in time the dampness and chill crept in, and then, as if to celebrate this victory, the storm suddenly increased in fury. The light, steady downpour became a torrent, and the wind whipped spray through the opening in my helmet, into my eyes. A veritable river ran under my collar and down my back. Above me, naked branches swayed and huge limbs creaked. I began to look around for shelter from the worst of this squall, but found none. In all directions the leafless forest stretched, barren, wet, and hostile, writhing like a tormented thing beneath the rippling blankets of rain. And as I searched I wondered what it was I hoped to accomplish. What "ungodly" thing was I to find, which was the cause of all Sir Gottfried's woes? If there was any such thing, it would have to find me. I might not recognize it even if I did come upon it. If not, what then? I could not return to the manor house and say I had failed. From the surety of such tidings the knight would certainly die. No, I would continue on, out of the country until I came to some more hospitable part of the world. Perhaps he would think I had been slain by whatever it was I was supposed to fight, and had offered my life up for his. In the soil of this delusion might be planted the very real seed of hope, from which his cure would grow. Under any circumstances, I would continue on my way.

As it happened, my circumstances were these: I rode until nearly nightfall, bent against the rain. I turned in a different direction, but the wind changed to meet me head-on, as if directed by will and intelligence. Beneath my splendid helmet, my teeth chattered. I was as cold and miserable as a grandfather abandoned in an unheated hovel in the dead of winter.

Then suddenly my horse whinnied and reared up, and I found myself staring ahead at two intense green eyes, floating in the mist. And the mist moved toward me, and assumed a shape out of the shadow of the trees—a huge grey dog-like thing as large as a bull, with massive, hunched shoulders and a tail as long as a man's leg. Its paws were a span or more wide, and its fearsome jowls were lined with teeth like dirks of ivory. The monster padded stealthily over the mud and leaves, completely silent.

Yanking hard on the reins, I forced my steed to obey me, lowered my lance, dug spurs into flanks, and raced forward. The hellish face loomed before me, mouth stretched wide in a soundless snarl, and the lance-tip struck something solid. The shaft broke—and this was a war weapon, not something designed for jousting—and there was another shock too quick for me to comprehend, as both I and my mount were flung up into the air, over and backwards into the mud.

Luckily I fell clear of the saddle and was not crushed by the weight of the horse. But still I hit hard, and lay stunned beneath a bush, conscious but unable to move. This was the end. Any second now I would feel one of those massive paws on my chest,

182

and there would be a brief instant of pain and terror as the hot breath enveloped me, the teeth sank into my flesh, and I was torn to pieces. Yet nothing happened. I sat up and looked around, and saw that the creature was gone. A dream? No. My horse was still there, still twitching, its ribs and bowels torn out by a single swipe of a grey limb. And my shattered lance lay nearby. These were concrete proofs of the encounter. I had been deliberately conquered, then spared. But why?

With the jeweled sword I released the dying horse from its agony. I walked on through the underbrush. After a while my spurs became tangled in sticks and vines; I nearly tripped a dozen times; and so I took them off and threw them away. I plodded through the mire for hours, it seemed, with sword drawn and shield ready to ward off any foe. Evening approached. It began to get dark. There was no sound, save for the whisper of the rain, and the splashing and sucking of my footfalls, but this was not to be for long.

The forest cleared into a plain, in the middle of which was a gently rising hillock. Twelve figures stood atop it, and when I went to see who they were, I came upon a group of fantastic beings, shaped like old women from the neck down, but with the heads of hairless, grey dogs. I raised sword and shield, ready to do battle, and the heads came off—they were masks of leather, with glass eyes and carven teeth of wood—to reveal faces I knew.

The twelve witches from the tree, laughing. The answer was clear to me. These were the ungodly things. I was sure, I had released them. Now I would put them to rest. I charged up the slope, sword swinging.

"Ho! Ho! Look, sisters! He threatens us!"

They were too quick for me, faster than earthly things. As before they scattered, but this time they did not flee. They were all around me, behind me, their shrivelled hands clutching, and yet my sword's edge sliced only air.

Then—my senses were confused from this point and I cannot be sure of the details of my history—one of them was on my back. Hands tore away my helmet and grabbed my ears, and one witch, or two, or three rode me as Tom O'Bedlam rides his jackass to death when racing after the moon. Icy, dagger-like fingers clamped into my brain; dirty heels banged against my sides; and we were off, down the far side of the hill and through more woods, into fields, up to my shoulders in a murky stream, with all the other hags flying alongside in the air like predatory birds on the wings of nightmare. How far we went, I can never know. We ran until my legs seemed ready to break, till I was past all pain, over the threshold of delirium, and the blurred landscape seemed to jump and whirl before my weary eyes. We traveled throughout the night, perhaps covering a hundred leagues, perhaps a thousand, or some other impossible distance. At times we seemed to sink under the earth and wriggle like worms, only to escape into darkness and sail through the sky like bats, seeing nothing and yet knowing what invisible things passed before us. And I think for part of the time we were accompanied by wolves and stags and beasts far more fantastical, dragons, hippogriffs, and even the *glimmich*, which plays with dragons as cats do with wounded mice before devouring them. But I am sure that it was nearly dawn when we came to the sea and danced on the sandy beach. The one who was riding me at last let go, and I collapsed in weariness, then fought my way to my feet, feeling around for a sword or dagger. All were gone. A dozen pairs of hands dragged me into a circle, and once more my body was not my own. We formed a circle and whirled around and around, and then we were not on the shore but the ocean, dancing lightly over the waves, until the solid land was a dim line far away. I, numb with terror and exhaustion, could not find the strength of thought to question this new wonder.

At last? At last? At last we came to a place in the sea where a white colossus stood above the waves reaching into the lightening sky, a figure carven from a mountain of salt by demon sculptors. It was not an ugly figure, but majestic, almost beautiful, a superbly formed and muscled man with flowing beard, wild hair, and a crown of seashells on his head. One arm was outstretched, holding a trident. And looking on this giant I understood what it was—not the form of a man at all, but of a god.

We formed our ring around the figure and were still. The water around us was still too, like a plain of glass. Rain splashed onto it.

One of the witches spoke.

"Now may all be revealed to you. Now may you know that we are not truly as we appear, old, yet younger in our first shapes. We were bent thus only by a force more powerful than ourselves, which bound our hands and cast us down. *And yet that force does not touch you!* The stain of baptism is erased from your soul, and we can see, feel, and touch you as a thing real. Behold! There shall be an exchange of burdens, then a new chain forged with living links, then a new life. We take only a worthless thing from you, the weight of your conscience and your offense against your God. To ours this is naught, and onto your shoulders we place what you would call our heathenness, which we call the wholeness of our god's spirit, which has never known the Christ. To one outcast such as you, this likewise is without further injury. By the

184

exchange of sins, both are cancelled out."

All of them cried out, "Let it be so!"

And, astonishing myself as I spoke, I replied, "Let it be so."

And even then I felt a new strength coming into me, my weariness of soul and body draining away. I felt younger, as if dark, painful years were being stripped away. If two men meet on a road, each with a heavy bundle to carry, and each takes the load of the other, the work seems less somehow. It was like that.

All of us, thirteen of us, placed our joined hands against the thighs of the salt giant—I filled with a joy I could not understand—and shouted in a single voice, "Live! Live!"

The giant lived. The whiteness faded into brown, then green, then grey, then the color of living flesh. The hard salt became flexible and soft to the touch. The enormous limbs began to move. The penis rose erect. All of us released our hold and ran back a few paces. Still in a circle, and in the midst of us the thing sank down into the sea, slowly, slowly, like an avalanche without end. When at last the head was submerged the water began to bubble and foam, and rise, as if a whale were about to breach. An enormous tail broke the surface, all covered with glistening silver scales, then sank down again.

In a moment we were alone.

"He is free at last," one of the witches said. "Now a new age begins."

As she spoke, I noticed that all of them had changed. They were no longer crones, but beautiful maidens, each with a face round and glowing like the moon, each with a tiara of stars in her hair, each with a cloak of purple sky about her shoulders.

Surely Sir Gottfried's wound would be healed now, for I had, albeit inadvertently, accomplished my mission. Now there was not one among the company save myself who could be called *ungodly*.

V

The rain stopped. In the east, over the sea, was the glow of the arriving sun behind the clouds. Then the clouds broke overhead, revealing constellations not yet ready to fade.

Out of the sunrise came a white ship with sails of shining silk, gliding swiftly over the water. The twelve stood and waited till it drew near. As it did I could make out its features clearly: on the prow the face of a blindfolded woman, and an arm outstretched to grope the way. On the stern, two faces with wide

185

eyes, and a sword bedecked with flowers.

They left me standing there and went to embark. In my confusion and wonder I realized slowly that this was my chance, my only chance to get free of all I dreaded. Everything was reversed. If I went with what I had feared I would have no fear. If I went with the gods I would escape the one God.

"Wait!" I shouted. "Take me with you! I have served you well, have I not? Take me with you!"

The last of them to climb aboard turned and said sadly, "But you are a man, a mortal man of numbered years. It is not for you to drink the milk of paradise."

And a wind filled the sail, and the ship was carried away with the same rapid grace it had shown in coming.

The sky faded from black to purple to blue. The sun showed its full disc above the horizon. It was going to be a brilliant morning.

Suddenly, standing alone on the water, I felt myself beginning to sink. The reverie was over, and the danger immediate. I turned and ran toward the shore, all the while sinking lower and lower, to my knees, to my waist, to my shoulders, till the weight of the water brought me to a stop. Some stray rational thought saved me. I tore off all my armor, right before the magic which held me up failed completely, and I went under, but surfaced again, and began to swim desperately in the direction of land. Each stroke was an agony, as my weariness returned to me. My arms seemed to encumber me as if they were tied down with steel. Yet somehow I survived, and was rolled onto the beach by the surf, where I slept for a long time.

Later I awoke and wandered, and came upon a fisherman, who was preparing to cast his net. I bade him good day, but he spat and said, "Bah! It is a terrible day. The sea is more bitter with salt than ever before, and the fish elude me. It seems the world has turned its back on Christian men."

13

L'envoi...

So what could I do? I continued questing, and journeyed as a knight errant to the farthest lands. And it happened that on the highway out from the City of Stars, which stands nigh unto the world's rim, I met three knights.

They were coming from the city, and I was going toward it. The sun was down; the stars were out in a windy sky; and by the light of stars and the moon I saw them, resplendent in their polished armor, with elaborate insignia on their shields and long lances in their hands.

I reined in my steed, and sat tarnished and begrimed before them.

"Hail," said one, a broad man with a drooping moustache. "We have not seen a Christian man in many months."

"Nor have I." Such irony. I laughed within, but without mirth. "We are far from home."

"Why have you come so far?" I demanded, before they could put the same question to me. The dolorous history of Julian the wanderer I did not want spread any farther than it already had been.

The first knight fell silent, and another, younger and fair of face, spoke.

"We seek the Holy Grail, from which all peace of the spirit flows."

My astonishment registered.

"You are surprised?" asked the third of them.

"The Holy Grail? I've heard the stories, but I can't think anyone really—"

"Sir, the Lord God On High sent us on this quest, and we cannot sleep two nights in the same place until we have found the Grail."

"How long have you been looking?"

"A long time. We've lost track."

"And what are your names? Are you men of great renown?"

"I am Sir Bedivere. To my right is Sir Gawain, to my left Sir Galahad. We serve the greatest of kings, Arthur of Camelot, of whom you have no doubt heard."

"Yes, I have heard of him." I struggled with words, speech eluding me. "The stories of him are old. I heard them from my father, he from his, he from his...many years, hundreds...it is written in the ancient books of Arthur..."

Worry showed on their faces. Perhaps they took me for a lunatic, but I don't think it was that. For a full minute no one spoke, and then the youngest, Galahad, broke the silence.

"If this be true, and you don't seem to lie—if this be true, tell us, we beg you, what the year is."

"Why—I don't know. I stopped counting long ago."

"Please! Something! The century at least. What century is it?"

"I don't know. I'm sorry, but I don't know."

Together they let out a cry of despair, and they spurred their horses and raced past me, vanishing down the road in a cloud of dust and shadows.

I looked after them and felt the full weight of eternity upon me, then ahead toward the City of Stars and the earth's end, and I think I understood. Not to them, but to me some trace of enlightenment came. I think we have all lost touch with time. History has passed us by, and we are tossed like corks on the tempest of years, unable to touch the shore. Perhaps, like the fabled Merlin I live backwards, growing younger to die in my mother's womb when at last I meet her, but I think even that is taken from me, and from the rest. Men remember us dimly, and glimpse briefly into our faces in the depths of dreams, and do not understand as we spread ourselves upon the centuried wind like smoke and eventually are no more.

We have all become legends, I think.

FINIS

About the Author

Darrell Schweitzer is a well-known figure in the fantasy field. As a critic, he is the author of such distinguished scholarly works as *Conan's World and Robert E. Howard, The Dream Quest of H. P. Lovecraft, Exploring Fantasy Worlds* and *Masters of the Supernatural.* As a fantasist, he has already been nominated by the readers for the prestigious Balrog award for best fantasy of the year, and the SPWAO Award by editors and writers themselves, while his stories have been widely anthologized here and abroad. As an interviewer, his profiles and conversations with science fiction and fantasy greats have appeared in virtually a who's who of the SF magazines, and as an editor, he is widely known for his work with the team at *Isaac Asimov Magazine.*

Starblaze Editions is a continuing series of fine quality science fiction and fantasy books founded under the editorship of Polly and Kelly Freas and continuing under the editorship of Hank Stine. Each Starblaze Edition is carefully chosen for entertaining ideas, imaginative treatment and narrative skill. Each is illustrated by one of the world's most renowned science fiction illustrators. Starblaze Editions provide durable, long-lasting collectors editions at affordable prices. Now available are:

What Happened to Emily Goode After the Great Exhibition by Raylyn Moore
"Highly successful, one of the best novels I've read." *Critical Mass*. Artist: Freas.

Some Will Not Die by Algis Budrys
"A classic post-disaster novel written with a depth of feeling." *Don D'Ammassa*. Artist: Freas.

Confederation by J. F. Bone
"A wealth of detail. Bone's best to date." *Critical Mass*. Artist: Freas.

Apostle by Roger Lovin
"A terrific writer." *Rolling Stone*. Artist: Freas.

Dominant Species by George Warren
"Something new and strange...Stretches the imagination. Entertaining." *SF & F Bookreview*. Artist: Freas.

Takeoff! by Randall Garrett
"A collection of humorous writing and satirical send-ups of popular SF writers. Enchanting fun. Irresistable." *Issaac Asimov's SF Magazine*. Artist: Freas.

Castaways in Time by Robert Adams
"Plunges the reader into the midst of the story and doesn't let up until the end." *Chat*. Artist: Freas.

The Jewels of Elsewhen by Ted White
"A special quality you will care about. Unique." *Analog*. Newly revised by the author. Artist: Doug Beekman.

Forthcoming:

Web of Light by Marion Zimmer Bradley
The second volume of the Atlantean cycle. Artist: C. L. Healy.

Star Seed by D. C. Poyer
"A powerful and evocative new writer..." George Schiters, editor, *Isaac Asimov's SF Magazine*. Artist: Ron Miller.

The Jewels of Elsewhen by Ted White
"A special quality you will care about. Unique." *Analog.*
Newly revised by the author.
The Dawning Light by Robert Randall (Robert Silverberg and Randall Garrett)
"Noteworthy!" *Richard Lupoff.* Artist: Barclay Shaw.
Web of Darkness by Marion Zimmer Bradley
A brilliant new series by the author of the *Darkover* books. Artist: C. Lee Healy.

Subscriptions are available at $10 for any four novels or $10 for any two novels and any one art book; subscribers receive 1/3 off all other Starblaze publications.

Starblaze Specials:

Elfquest
by Wendy and Richard Pini
Fantasy, romance, swords and sorcery in this continuing saga of the Wolf-Riders, a band of elves searching for others of their kind in a savage Earth-like world. Paper $9.95, Limited (Autographed, numbered, specially-bound with a print), $35.00. 8½ x 11, 160 pages, illustrated in color.

Wonderworks
by Michael Whelan
With commentaries by Poul Anderson, C. J. Cherryh, Alan Dean Foster, Anne McCaffrey, Michael Moorcock. Edited by Polly and Kelly Freas. The first collection by a brilliant young illustrator. Paper $7.95, Library $13.95, Limited (Autographed, numbered, specially bound) $30.00. 8½ x 11, 120 pages, 101 illustrations, 58 in color.